I fed Birdy before fifteen. The cold air smelled ever so slightly of spilled beer, but the aromas of muffins and biscuits along with grilled bacon and sausage would get rid of any unpleasant smells soon enough. First things first. I fired up the oven and started a pot of coffee, as much for me as for my customers. I pulled a pan of biscuits out of the freezer, popping them in the oven the minute the beeper said it was preheated.

Wait. Why was it so cold in here? Now I stared at the entrance. The glass in the top half of the antique door was shattered, with thick shards from the gaping hole now littering the floor. I hurried toward the door.

Between the pickle barrel and the shelves of vintage cookware, my gaze landed on a splash of red that didn't belong there. I took a couple of steps toward it and stopped with a gasp. Erica Shermer lay on the floor half behind the barrel. She wasn't moving. She wasn't even breathing, and her eyes stared at nothing . . .

Books by Maddie Day

FLIPPED FOR MURDER

GRILLED FOR MURDER

Published by Kensington Publishing Corporation

Grilled for Murder

Maddie Day

KENSINGTON PUBLISHING CORP.
http://www.kensingtonbooks.com

KENSINGTON BOOKS are published by

Kensington Publishing Corp.
119 West 40th Street
New York, NY 10018

All Kensington titles, imprints, and distributed lines are available at special quantity discounts for bulk purchases for sales promotions, premiums, fund-raising, and educational or institutional use. Special book excerpts or customized printings can also be created to fit specific needs. For details, write or phone the office of the Kensington Special Sales Manager. Kensington Publishing Corp., 119 West 40th Street, New York, NY 10018. Attn: Special Sales Department. Phone: 1-800-221-2647.

Kensington and the K logo Reg. U.S. Pat & TM Off.

ISBN-13: 978-1-61773-927-9
ISBN-10: 1-61773-927-8
First Kensington Mass Market Edition: June 2016

eISBN-13: 978-1-61773-928-6
eISBN-10: 1-61773-928-6
First Kensington Electronic Edition: June 2016

10 9 8 7 6 5 4 3 2 1

Printed in the United States of America

*For my sisters and brother—Barbara Maxwell Bergendorf,
Janet Maxwell, and David Maxwell—
because family matters. I love you.*

Acknowledgments

As always, many thanks to my agent, John Talbot, my editor, John Scognamiglio, and the entire Kensington Publishing crew. I'm delighted to be continuing the adventures of Robbie Jordan in fictional South Lick, Indiana.

Books like this do not get done without the help of fellow authors. Sherry Harris once again ably gave me editorial feedback before I turned in the manuscript and straightened me out on the matter of several gaffes: Thanks, friend (although, at my own peril, I might not have implemented all her suggestions). Sherry, along with the other Wicked Cozy Authors—Jessie Crockett (a.k.a. Jessica Estevao), Julie Hennrikus (a.k.a. Julianne Holmes), Liz Mugavero (a.k.a. Cate Conte), and Barbara Ross—are my lifeboat. I'm also grateful for Sisters in Crime—National, New England Chapter, and Guppies. You're the best. And thanks to friend and Friend Bill Castle for the coleslaw recipe.

For Hoosier color and facts, I again thank Dan Dinnsen for details about Bloomington and the local dialect. Tim Mundorff introduced me to fried biscuits and local scenery, and Jeff Danielson shared local insights and amazing photographs of the natural beauty of the area. My more northern Indiana sister Barbara Bergendorf continues to help with cultural information and support. Mary Falker Howard of Nashville (Indiana, of course) encouraged me to include the Create It with Ginger-bread Log Cabin Competition, so I did, or at least the run-up to the contest. If I've gone overboard in any area of local culture, I take full responsibility.

At the risk of having poison darts aimed my way, I'm grateful for the very severe New England winter of 2015. It enabled me to sit inside in my second-floor office and watch it snow as I belted out the first draft of this book in two months flat. Nowhere to go and nothing to do but write and take breaks for shoveling.

As always, my deep love and grateful thanks to my supportive family: my sisters Barbie and Jannie, my sons Allan and John David, and my main man, Hugh.

Readers, librarians, booksellers: I wouldn't be here without you. Thank you, thank you, thank you! As a reminder, a positive review of a book you read goes a long way to helping the author. Please con-sider posting your opinion on Amazon, Goodreads, Facebook, and elsewhere if you liked my story (and check out my other author names: Edith Maxwell and Tace Baker).

Chapter 1

Was I nuts? I don't know what I was thinking, agreeing to cater and host a welcome-home party in my country store and restaurant tonight. I'd already been working since six this morning serving up breakfast and lunch to wave after wave of hungry customers on the Saturday after Thanksgiving. I sank into a chair as the antique clock chimed. Thankfully, two o'clock was only half an hour until closing time, and just three people remained, lingering over their gourmet hamburgers. A couple played a game of chess on the painted tabletop and the third read a newspaper, exactly the kind of scene I'd envisioned when I'd bought this old country store and opened Pans 'N Pancakes on the edge of South Lick, Indiana.

I gazed at the gleaming counters, the shelves full of vintage cookware, the pickle barrel, proud I'd accomplished nearly all the renovation carpentry myself. My mom had wanted to be sure her daughter would always have a trade, a trade which came in handy when I'd bought the rundown place nestled in the hills of scenic Brown County last winter. Now Turkey Day was over. I needed to get decorated for Christmas, but that could wait until tomorrow. After I got through this darn party. Oh, well. It was income, and my bank account could always use more deposits.

I glanced up when the cowbell on the door jangled. Sue Berry bustled in with her daughter Paula, the hosts of tonight's shindig for Sue's other daughter. I waved them over to my table.

"Everything all set for tonight, Robbie?" Sue asked. She plopped down across from me, her short cap of bottle-blond hair looking more tousled than usual.

"I think so. Have a seat, Paula," I said to the daughter, a woman in her thirties.

"Thanks, but I think I'll stand. My back's kind of bothering me." Paula nestled her other hand in the small of her back, her pregnant belly pushing out a black knit shirt under her open coat. She wore her dark hair pulled back in a messy knot and her face was devoid of makeup, letting the high color of a woman carrying a child shine through, but also showing the dark splotches under her eyes.

"Three months to go. I sure can't wait to be a grandmother," Sue said in a bright voice, beaming up at Paula and then turning back to me. "So the cupcakes are all ordered, and Glen and Max will bring the drinks over a little early. I'm just as thrilled as punch we can do this for our dear Erica."

Sue's other daughter, Erica, had moved back to South Lick a month earlier. I wasn't quite sure why they'd waited a month to welcome her back, but I was happy they'd chosen to have the welcome-back party at Pans 'N Pancakes. Erica's late husband had been my boyfriend's twin brother, so I could hardly say no. Sue and Paula had both been customers over the last month and a half since I'd opened, so they'd had a taste of my cooking.

"I'll have a veggie platter and a couple of dips out," I said. "I've made up a pasta salad and a coleslaw, as we discussed. I have the mini-sliders ready to go, and a couple dozen hand pizzas ready in the freezer. I'll pop those in the oven during the party so they can be served hot."

"Hand pizza?" Paula asked. "Pizza with fingers sounds fun."

I laughed. "They're just small. Like the size of a hand. Maybe I should call them individual pizzas."

"It don't matter what you call them; they are going to be so yummy," Sue said. Her blue eyes sparkled behind a bit too much eye makeup.

"The mini-sliders sound delicious," Paula said.

"Beef, turkey, and black bean. And my friend Phil is going to tend bar." Thank goodness for Phil. My congenial friend was a talented singer and baker, and had helped me out of a jam more than once.

"Good, so the guys can relax and enjoy themselves." Sue beamed her approval. "Hey, Robbie, you ever think about entering the log cabin competition in Nashville?"

Nashville was the county seat five miles away. Nashville, Indiana, not Tennessee. "The what? I'd love to build a house some day, but right now I have my hands full here."

"Mom means gingerbread log cabins, right?"

Sue snapped her fingers. "It's so gol dang cute. Everybody makes log cabins out of gingerbread and other edible stuff. They judge it over at the Brown County Inn."

"You could make a cabin of a country store and enter it," Paula said. She gestured around the store. "You know, with the front door standing open. You could have little shelves of cookware showing, and a few tables and chairs. Put a couple of rocking chairs on the front porch like you have and I bet you'd win a prize."

"It sounds fun, if I could find the time." When could I fit baking and decorating a log cabin into my schedule, though? Monday, my day off, was the only possibility. On the other hand, it would be good publicity for the store.

The door jangled again and a frowning, broad-shouldered man strode in. "There you are," he said, spying Paula.

Paula twisted her wedding band around and around. "Max, I told you I was going out with Mom."

"Max, honey, come meet Robbie." Sue gestured to him.

After Max approached the table, Sue said, "Robbie Jordan, this is Paula's husband, Max Holzhauser. Max, Robbie."

He extended a big, meaty hand. "Nice to meet you, Robbie." He barely got the glower off his face, which featured a jutting Neanderthal brow and heavy eyebrows now pulled together in the middle. His thick hair, tucked behind his ears, brushed his collar.

I shook his hand. "Likewise. Sit down?" *What was he so mad about?*

"Can't. Let's go, Paula." He took hold of Paula's upper arm. She wasn't much taller than my own five foot four. He was not only a little over six feet tall, he was also stocky and heavy boned.

Paula pried his hand off, twisting out of his grasp. "I'm doing errands with my mother, Max. I'll be home in time to get ready for the party." Her jaw worked.

"Have it your own way, then." He cracked his knuckles. "You always do."

One of my chess-playing customers looked up and frowned at the disturbance. I watched Max leave, hearing the door close with more force than necessary, and glanced at Paula. Sue had taken one of her daughter's hands in both of hers and was stroking it.

"Things will work out, sugar," Sue murmured as the bell on the door continued to jangle. "He'll get a hold on that temper of his, bless his heart. You'll see."

The timer on the oven dinged right after the wall clock chimed eight. We were an hour into the party, and it was in full swing. I hurried over to draw out the last pan of pizzas. I slid them onto a tray, the cheese bubbling in tan spots, the aroma of fresh crust almost too alluring. I sliced each pizza into quarters and carried them to the food table. I wiped my hands down my blue-and-white store apron, which featured our logo of a cast-iron griddle held by a grinning stack of pancakes, and surveyed the now-packed room. Late this afternoon Phil and I had pushed the tables to the sides and stacked half the chairs in a corner to leave room for mingling.

Near the WELCOME BACK TO SOUTH LICK, ERICA! banner, a small group of men, including Max, Sue's husband Glen, and green-eyed Jim Shermer clustered with beers in hand. Paula, now made up and in a green dress that didn't try to disguise her baby bump, sat talking with Tiffany Porter, an attractive local jewelry maker who owned a gift shop in town. Phil stood behind the bar table chatting with Sue. His dark face was aglow and he beamed his wide smile that always reminded me of Denzel Washington's.

Other townspeople, some of whom I'd met, many I hadn't, chatted in small groups, with a few women browsing the shelves of cookware. Country music played from a couple of small speakers someone had set up next to an iPad, and the buzz of conversation over the tunes was loud.

The only person missing was the guest of honor, Erica. She was more than an hour late. People were starting to talk, and Sue had pasted on a smile so fake it looked like it came from a photo-editing app. It had to have upset the family to have Erica's husband take his own life, and I wondered why she'd taken so long to move back home. Or if Sue was now worried something had happened to Erica.

I picked up an empty slider platter and headed back to the open kitchen area, smothering a yawn before drawing another pan of sliders out of the warmer. I'd made little rolls for buns, precooked the patties, and assembled the tiny burgers shortly before the party started. All I had to do now was serve them. Then maybe I could sit down for a few minutes.

As I set the platter of sliders on the food table, Tiffany walked up to me.

"I really like all your cookware, Robbie." Her full lips curved into a smile, lighting up her face, and her almond-shaped eyes crinkled at the edges.

"Thanks. Half of it was already here when I bought the store, and I've acquired the rest."

"Don't you just love thinking about who cooked with it when it was new?" she asked, gazing at the far wall.

"Exactly."

"I'd like to ask you a quick question about one piece."

"Sure." We moved across the room together. Tiffany, four or five inches taller than me, especially in heels, walked with a fluid motion like an athlete might. Her light-brown hair fell in graceful waves below her shoulders,

She pointed with an elegant finger that ended in the perfect white tip of a French manicure. "What's that round thing with the two long handles?"

"That's a sandwich press." It featured two slightly convex cast-iron disks joined by a hinge, and two long handles extending out. "After you insert a cheese sandwich between the disks, you clamp the press shut and then hold it over a gas flame or even a campfire to toast the sandwich. It makes the best grilled cheese in the world. You can grill other kinds of sandwiches, too, of course."

"And it's beautiful, too."

"Sure is. Browse as much as you want. The pieces for sale have tags on them."

"Thanks." She moved on down to the shelf area.

I turned back to the party and made my rounds, picking up empty dishes, tidying the food display. I paused when I passed a smiling Jim, my new boyfriend and my former real-estate lawyer. I knew he wanted more than the occasional date, but I was so busy with the store and restaurant, and he with his practice, we usually only managed Sunday nights together, since Pans 'N Pancakes was closed on Mondays.

"Everything looks great. And tastes even better," he said, smoothing an errant black curl off my forehead.

He looked more delicious than any food I could make, with those emerald eyes, that curly red hair he wore a bit long and shaggy, and his trim body. Tonight he wore a deep blue shirt with well-cut black pants, but he could look smoking-hot even in an old T-shirt and ragged jeans.

"Thanks. It seems to be going pretty well, doesn't it?" I smiled back at him.

"Except Erica isn't here." His forehead furrowed. "I wonder what's keeping her."

"It's not a surprise party, is it? Sue never said anything about that."

"No, I don't think it's supposed to be a surprise. Oh, well. Erica has always been a bit, shall we say, dramatic." He pulled his mouth. "She probably wants to make a grand entrance."

I saw Sue glance at the phone in her hand and touch it a few times with her index finger.

"Gol dang, she's almost here!" Sue announced with a big smile. "Get ready, y'all."

Sure enough, it wasn't two minutes later when the cowbell jangled and a woman pushed in, shedding a puffy, white, thigh-length coat as she walked. She wore a snug red dress that crossed over in the front and nowhere near covered her cleavage. This had to be Erica. She was closer in height to her tiny mother than to Paula, and her spiky blond hair and light coloring was more like Sue's, too. Through the door behind her emerged Abe O'Neill, a cute guy I'd met earlier in the fall who worked for the local electric company. He set a banjo case on the floor as the talking fell to a hush.

Erica left Abe at the door and swanned over to her mother on four-inch red heels. She gave Sue a hug and then waved to the room.

"Hi, everybody," she called out. "Thanks so much for all this."

Her father, a man in his sixties whose dark hair was shot through with silver, raised his beer. "Welcome back, sweetheart."

A chorus of "welcome back" echoed throughout the room. Next to me, Jim raised his bottle of Cutters Half Court IPA. "Welcome back, Rickie."

Erica turned her head sharply, then tilted her head in a seductive pose when she saw who'd said it. She clicked on her heels over to where we stood and slid her arm through Jim's.

"Oh, Jim. You're the only person besides Jon who can call me that." She pursed her lips in a pout.

"And he's gone." She stroked his arm with her other hand and cast luminous blue eyes up at him.

A shadow passed over Jim's face as he carefully detached from Erica's arm and pushed his glasses back up the bridge of his nose. Jon, his twin, had killed himself in Chicago a year ago. Jim had told me how hard it'd been for him, and still was, to lose his twin, and to suicide, too. "I'm sorry. I wasn't thinking. I'll call you Erica from now on."

"No, I want you to call me Rickie. Please?"

Jim cleared his throat. "Have you met my girl-friend, Robbie Jordan? This is her restaurant and country store." He slung his arm along my shoulders, giving my arm a squeeze.

Erica narrowed her eyes and studied me before flashing a big smile. She held out her hand. "His girlfriend? Well, isn't this a surprise?"

"Nice to meet you, Erica. Welcome back." I forced a smile and shook her hand. I snuck a glance at Jim, who straightened his collar and was looking any-where but at Erica. I gazed around the store. Almost everyone had stopped what they were doing, food halfway to their mouths, bottles halfway raised, to watch Erica.

"Isn't this a cute place you've got here," Erica said. "It was a real dump last time I lived in town."

"Robbie did all the renovation work herself, too." Jim's smile at me was genuine.

"Imagine that. You're so talented," she said in a voice oozing insincerity.

"I'll be bringing out some hot sliders in a minute, and the pizzas over there are probably still warm, if you're hungry. Now if you'll excuse me, I'll let you two have some time to catch up." I cast another quick look at Jim before heading to the kitchen area, and if that wasn't a panicked expression on his face, I don't know what was. Well, he was a big boy. He could handle his former sister-in-law. Or not. I sure wasn't going to get in the middle.

Chapter 2

It was nine o'clock before I finally got a chance to take off my apron and sit down near my desk in the far corner. When Sue had made the arrangements for the party, she'd also made it clear she hoped I would join them when I could. She'd said I should consider myself part of the family and not only the caterer. So I'd worn my black swingy dress with the cap sleeves and my turquoise cowboy boots. A multicolored chunky necklace brightened up the dress. And even though I had to wear my thick, curly, Italian hair pulled back when I was working, I'd added a sparkly pin for a party touch.

A group of guys over near the door, including Abe, laughed at some joke, and several couples danced in the middle of the space. Erica flitted from group to group, a bottle of beer in her hand. By the smiles and hugs, people seemed genuinely glad to have her back in town. I let the party flow around me, glad to hold a plastic cup of white wine and get off my feet. It'd been a long day, but I loved seeing the place full. Part of my dream in restoring the store and adding the restaurant had been to make it a community gathering place. Just like this.

A tune sounding like West Coast swing came on and Jim strolled up, his eyes sparkling. "May I have the pleasure of this dance?"

We'd gone dancing at a local roadhouse on our very first date, the one that unfortunately ended in news of a murder in town. We shared a love of dance, although my experience was mostly freestyle, while he knew steps to all different kinds of dances, from swing to contra to international folk dancing. He'd told me that was how he stayed fit, by going dancing every chance he got.

I grabbed one more sip of wine, then said, "Why not?"

I extended my hand and let him pull me up and lead me to where others were dancing. He was a good half-foot taller than me, and it felt perfect to lay my hand on his shoulder and have him take my other hand in his. He waited until the song started a new phrase, then led me through the steps. I tried to stay loose and follow, not my strong suit, but we'd gone dancing several more times in recent weeks and I was starting to get the hang of it. He'd told me about staying in the box, about imagining a rectangle defining our moves. It helped. Next to us, Phil twirled the woman he was dancing with, and then bent her down in a dip. He caught my eye and grinned, then straightened and waltzed away.

The music changed to a slower tune. Jim pulled me in close, and the feel of his warm, smooth shirt under my cheek, his head bent down over mine, was heavenly. But after only a minute in paradise, a woman's shouts broke our bubble. I pulled away from Jim. Erica and Tiffany stood a couple of yards away facing each other.

"You're lying." Erica pointed a red-lacquered fingernail at Tiffany's face. "I didn't do any such thing."

The room quieted, with only the music continuing. Glen Berry rushed to his daughter's side. "What's going on here?" He looked from one woman to the other, the silver at the temples of his close-shorn dark hair catching the light.

Tiffany set her hands on her hips, nostrils flaring in her golden-skinned face, earrings mixing gold and silver that flashed in the light. "She's been stealing from me. She said she wanted to learn how to make jewelry. But all she wanted to do was own it."

"It's not true and you can't prove it." Erica glared at Tiffany. "Why'd you come here, anyway? So you could party with a thief? Get some free food and drink?"

"I was giving you the benefit of the doubt. But that bracelet?" Tiffany pointed to an intricate hoop of silver twisted with other metals on Erica's wrist. "It's missing from the store."

Erica snorted. "My late husband gave it to me. I wouldn't steal your precious stock. It's not very well made, anyway."

Tiffany took a step toward Erica. Glen stepped between them and pushed out both hands. "Now wait a chicken-picking minute, girls. Y'all don't need to fight about this."

"You're right," Tiffany spit out. "Larceny is a matter for the police." She grabbed her bag from the table and rushed toward the door. She tore her coat from the coat tree and, with a fierce jangle of the bell, was gone at the same time as the coat tree swayed and crashed to the ground.

I glanced at Jim and shook my head, then hurried to the coat tree, arriving at the same time as Abe. He set it back to standing, while I gathered up a couple of coats from the floor. I dusted them off, one by one, and handed them to him.

"Thanks," I said. "That was quite a scene."

"I'll say. Erica has never held back from drama, that's for sure." He hung up the last coat.

"Did you bring her here?" Earlier in the fall Abe had asked me out to dinner. It'd ended up being the day a murderer had run me off the road on my bicycle and I'd broken my clavicle, so we'd never gotten to the dinner. Anyway, I was seeing Jim. And it looked like maybe Abe was going out with Erica.

He laughed the delightful rolling laugh I remembered. "No way. I just happened to arrive at the same time she did. But we used to go out. Long time ago."

"How have you been lately?"

"I'm good. Keeping busy." He stuck his hands in the pockets of his jeans, which he wore with a white Oxford shirt and a gray blazer. The look suited him.

"Still playing banjo?" I gestured at the case, which he'd set behind the coat tree.

"You bet. Might still drag it out tonight if inspiration strikes." He flashed me his big smile, that same dimple creasing his right cheek, his brown eyes smiling, too.

"I'd love to hear you play."

"Could happen. Hey, sorry we never got our dinner in. I know you're, um, hanging out with Shermer, but if an evening ever frees up, you give me a call, okay?"

"Okay. Right now I think I'd better get back to cleaning up the food table." I headed for the decimated dinner array, but paused at the drinks table.

"How's it going, Phil?" I asked. A couple of bottles of bourbon had made an appearance on the table, and neither was full, by the looks of it.

"Not bad, not bad at all. I'm keeping an eye on a couple of folks, though. Might need a little backup from the owner at some point." He raised his eyebrows and pointed his gaze toward Max.

"He's overindulging?" *Gah.* Acting as a bouncer wasn't what I'd signed up for.

"Getting a little sloppy." He gestured at the bottles of whiskey. "With this stuff, we could have quite a few overindulgers"

"Sue said it's okay to have the whiskey?"

He shrugged, and winked one of his startlingly blue eyes. "It was her husband who brought it. So I guess it is."

"Now," a man's voice said from a few tables away.

I looked in that direction. Max stood in front of where Paula sat talking to a couple of women.

"It's time to go." His deep voice carried to Phil and me.

Paula shook her head. "I'm having fun, Max. I'm staying."

"You need to come home with me. I'm concerned about our baby." He reached down and grabbed her wrist, pulling upward.

Not this again. Probably not a good idea to try to intervene, but I hated seeing him rough with her.

"Max." Now Paula raised her voice. She swatted at his hand with her free one. "Let go. It's my sister's party and I'm not leaving. The baby is fine."

Max drew his mouth down and looked like he might erupt. "Get your own ride home, then." He let go of her wrist and stalked toward the door.

Erica waylaid him halfway there. "Hey, big guy." She set one hand on her hip and laid the other hand flat on his chest. She gazed up at him, a little smile curving her lips. "You be nice to my big sister now, hear? She just wants to have a little fun before she becomes a mama."

"You, too, huh?" Max's face hardened. "Get out of my way, Erica." He lifted her hand off his chest. "I'm simply thinking about her health, but I guess I'm the only one who is."

"Now, now, big Max. We all love Paulie, you know that." Erica still smiled but her voice turned as steely as my best knife. "And we love you, too. I don't want to be seeing you guys argue."

Max glared down at her. Without speaking he turned and left the store.

Whew. Erica sashayed back to the fold while I tried to remember what I'd been doing before the eruption.

"Oh, Robbie, hon," Sue called from the table where she sat, waving her hand. "Can you bring out them cupcakes?"

Shoot, of course. The dessert. I never should have removed my apron.

"Coming right up," I said. I hurried to tie on a

clean apron, and rushed through consolidating the rest of the food at one end of the table. I spread a clean cloth on the other half, retrieved the cupcakes from the walk-in cooler, and carried out the big box from the local bakery. After I opened the box and slid the foil-topped cardboard tray onto the table, I set a stack of small plates and napkins next to the dessert. The cupcakes were decorated with tiny versions of the town's landmark Jupiter gazebo, once the site of a famous sulfur spring and spa, thus the town's name. When I'd moved here from Santa Barbara, I'd found a name with the word *lick* in it slightly vulgar, but I'd learned it was like a salt lick, a naturally occurring place where animals went to lick salt and other essential minerals. So the Lick in the name only meant salts had been part of the mineral springs.

"Dessert, anyone?" I called out in my best outdoor voice. I stood back and watched people flock to the table. What was dinner without some sugar to top it off, especially when people were drinking?

Erica and Jim approached together. She picked up a cupcake and peeled back the paper with those red fingernails in four slow, seductive movements, watching Jim as she did. She took a bite, then ran her tongue around her lips. Jim glanced at me and rolled his eyes before grabbing a cupcake and turning away from her. I turned away, too. I had pans to wash.

The crowd had thinned to a half dozen or so by eleven o'clock. The elder Berrys had thanked me profusely, and Sue had pressed a check for fifty dollars over our agreed amount into my hand before

they'd left an hour earlier. Erica had shed her heels
and sat on the sofa, which I'd arranged with a
couple of chairs in a nook for a small informal
sitting area. She had her feet tucked up under her
and a half-inch of whiskey in the cup she held. Paula
sprawled next to her with her feet up on a chair.
Abe sat picking out tunes on his banjo, accompanied by a guy who had pulled out a harmonica,
while Phil, the aspiring opera star, sang along to
blues, gospel, bluegrass, whatever kind of music
they played. They were in the middle of "Suwanee
River" when Jim leaned toward me.

"I've got a migraine brewing."

"Oh, too bad."

"I'm going to head home." He massaged the back
of his head above his neck. "Sorry I can't stay to
help clean up."

"Yes, go. Don't worry, cleanup's nearly done,
anyway, and I'll get these guys to set up the tables
and chairs again for tomorrow morning." Which
was going to come along way too early. At least I
didn't open until eight on Sundays, a small blessing.

I walked Jim to the door. After he slid into his
coat, Erica called out.

"Goodnight, Jimmy. See you later." She waved a
lazy hand.

"G'night, Erica. Bye, everybody." Jim raised a
hand in return, then turned back to me and leaned
in for a kiss.

It was a delicious one. "Talk to you tomorrow," I
said as he opened the door.

"Sounds good." He disappeared, then stuck his
head back in. "It's snowing."

I followed him out and stood on the wide covered porch, wrapping my arms around myself. It was indeed snowing, the first storm of the season, with fat white puffs of snow floating gently down in the streetlight. I watched Jim drive off in his Prius, then hurried back inside.

Another storm appeared to be brewing inside, too. The music had stopped and Phil stood, mouth agape, facing Erica.

"What century are you living in?" he asked, his voice shaking.

Erica didn't meet his eyes, instead leaning down to slip on first one shoe, then the other. She turned to Paula and extended her hand. "Come on, let's get out of here. Guy can't take a joke. You're going to sleep over at my place, anyway, aren't you?"

"That was no joke," Phil said in a now steady voice, with a low and serious tone.

Erica headed for where I stood near the door without looking back.

Paula looked at Phil, a distressed look on her face. "I'm sorry, Phil. What she said was totally uncalled for."

He shook his head with lips pressed flat. Erica grabbed her coat and shrugged it on, then handed Paula hers when she arrived at the door.

"Thanks so much, Robbie," Erica said with a smile that didn't include her eyes. "It was a great party."

"Yes, thanks, Robbie." Paula barely suppressed a yawn.

"Are you okay to drive, Erica?" I asked. She'd been drinking all evening, but her speech wasn't slurred.

She batted at the air. "Don't worry about it. I have a designated driver, right, Paulie?"

Paula pointed a finger gun. "At least pregnancy is good for something."

"And we're going to have a sister slumber party at my house," Erica added.

Paula rolled her eyes, but smiled. "If you insist."

"I need to protect you from that husband of yours. Give him a night to cool off."

"Careful, it's snowing out there." I held the door open for them and made sure they both made it down the stairs and into a small red sporty-looking car before I went back in. Abe and the harmonica guy had started playing again, but Phil wasn't singing. I walked up to where he stood with arms folded near the kitchen area, staring at the door.

"What happened?" I asked.

"Erica's a racist. She said . . . well, I'm not even going to repeat it." His voice shook again. "Can you believe it, in this day and age?"

I stroked his arm. "Unfortunately I can believe it, but I'm sorry it had to happen." A yawn overtook me. "Oops. It's been a really long day."

Phil looked at me. "Hey, go to bed. We'll clean up and get the place set up for tomorrow. I have a key, remember. I'll lock up." He glanced at the remaining guests. "Right, guys? We'll set this place right again and let Robbie get some sleep?"

"Absolutely," Abe called over, and the harmonica guy raised his hand.

"Thanks, my friend." I pulled Phil in for a hug. "What would I do without you?" His hair, cut in a kind of high flattop, brushed my forehead. It looked wiry, but it was extra soft.

He laughed, the tension sliding off his face. "Well, don't get too used to me. When I land my big opera role, I'll be out of here faster than—" he watched me with a grin.

"I know, than green grass through a goose." I laughed, too, and made my way toward my apartment door at the back of the store. "'Night, everyone. Thanks so much for the help." I unlocked the door, then locked it again behind me.

My black-and-white foundling kitty, Birdy, watched from his perch on the back of the easy chair. I gave him a scritch on the head and listened to his chirping purr, the reason I'd named him Birdy.

"Birdy, what do you think Erica said to Phil?" He didn't answer. Most of the time I didn't even think about Phil being African-American. He was just a talented, generous friend. Besides having an amazing voice that'd gotten him plush roles in the Indiana University music department, he baked all the brownies and cookies for the restaurant, he'd designed the logo for the store, and he helped out when his schedule permitted. Plus he was fun, and a good friend I was grateful to have. But I was sure he ran into racism on a regular basis. Our country hadn't really made all that much progress in moving beyond prejudice, despite having elected a black president. That Erica would insult Phil to his face, though, surprised me. Then again, I didn't really know her. And from what I'd seen tonight, including her attempts to honey up to Jim, her fight with Tiffany, and her run-in with Max, I wasn't very eager to.

Chapter 3

Yawning, I rolled out of bed and stretched. I'd known six o'clock was going to come way, way too early this morning. Overall the party had gone well, although it'd been a little tense at times. I was glad it was behind me. Even with all that, it was good publicity for my restaurant and I hoped it would snag me more catering opportunities in the future.

Now I needed to prep for today's breakfast: whole-wheat banana-walnut pancakes, apple muffins, omelets to order, and cheesy biscuits with my special gravy. Customers went nuts over biscuits drowning in gravy. One more day before I could rest on Monday. At least I had a short commute to work.

After crunching through my hundred sit-ups, I showered and threw on black skinny jeans and a long-sleeved blue store shirt displaying a small store logo on the front and a large one on the back. I fed Birdy before heading into the store by six fifteen. The cold air smelled ever so slightly of spilled beer, but the aromas of muffins and biscuits along with grilled bacon and sausage would get rid of any unpleasant smells soon enough. First things first. I fired up the oven and started a pot of coffee, as much for me as for customers. I pulled a pan of biscuits out of the freezer, popping them in the oven the minute the beeper said it was preheated.

Wait. Why was it so cold in here? Now I stared at the entrance. The glass in the top half of the antique door was shattered, with thick shards from the gaping hole now littering the floor. I hurried toward the door.

Between the pickle barrel and the shelves of vintage cookware, my gaze landed on a splash of red that didn't belong there. I took a couple of steps toward it and stopped with a gasp. Erica lay on the floor half behind the barrel, her purple-tinged arms splayed stiffly out to the sides, her red dress hiked up a little. She wasn't moving. She wasn't even breathing, and her eyes stared at nothing.

My feet felt like they'd landed in wet concrete and my heart thudded faster than the Wabash Cannonball. My thoughts raced, too. How'd she get here? Phil had promised to lock up last night, and Erica had gone home with Paula. Erica had come back here with a killer? My skin tightened as I stared at her, my brain aroil. *The poor thing.* Someone had broken in and left her dead on my floor. It couldn't be suicide, could it?

All right. I needed to move, concrete or no concrete. I grabbed my cell phone out of my back pocket and pressed nine-one-one.

After the dispatcher asked me to identify myself and what my emergency was, I said, "Robbie Jordan.

Nineteen Main Street. Someone broke into my store overnight, and there's a dead person on the floor." Which had to be the most awful sentence I'd ever uttered in all my twenty-seven years. I took a deep breath to try to calm the panicky feeling threatening to close up my throat.

"What store is that, ma'am?"

"Pans 'N Pancakes. It's a country store and restaurant." My voice came out quavery.

"Do you feel safe, ma'am?" she asked.

"I guess. The glass in my front door is broken." *Was I safe?* Erica must have thought she was safe, too.

"Do you recognize the victim?"

"Yes. It's Erica Shermer." My legs started to shake.

She instructed me not to touch anything and to stay on the line until an officer arrived. I gazed at Erica. Her feet, purple all the way up past the ankles, were bare, and her red-painted toenails stood out starkly garish in the darkened skin. My stomach lurched at the sight of her blue eyes staring into infinity, the light gone from them. Her face was stiff and bore dark purplish patches on her forehead and nose, with a darker mark on her cheek, but the rest of her skin showed a yellowish tinge. How could someone have broken the glass without my hearing it? I was terrified to think of this happening while I slept only yards and a couple of walls away.

The coffee machine gurgled and hissed to a finish. I set the phone on a table and walked like a zombie into the kitchen area. I really needed some caffeine, and hoped it didn't seem disrespectful to Erica. I poured half a cup, splashed some milk in to cool it, and drank it down. A siren keened in the distance, getting louder by the second. I wished Jim had stayed the night so I wouldn't have to face this all alone.

Within minutes Sergeant Wanda Bird stood on the wide covered porch peering in the front windows. She leaned down and looked through the broken glass. "Got another door I can come through?" she called.

"Yes. Come around the left side of the building. I'll open the service door." I saw another officer start to string wide yellow tape across the steps before I hurried to the side door, unlocked it, and flipped on the outside light. Pushing the door open, I inhaled the sharp cold air. The snow had stopped in the night, leaving a blanket of lovely pure white sparkling in the light, a scene at odds with the ugly reality of death. I wanted to go to Erica's side, feeling like someone should keep her company. But that didn't make sense. Nobody was ever going to keep her company again.

Wanda strode in a minute later holding an iPad, her strawberry blond hair slicked back into a severe bun. Her uniform strained on her stocky figure, her well-padded hips reluctantly conscripted into pants cut for a man.

"She's over there," I gestured.

She clasped the digital tablet in her hands behind her back and approached Erica, leaning over to peer at her.

"This Erica Berry, Sue and Glen's girl?"

I nodded. "Her married name was Shermer, though."

"Oh, yeah." She gazed at the corpse and then glanced at the front door. "I'm assuming that glass wasn't broke last time you saw it?"

"No. I catered a party here last night, and it was fine when I went to bed."

She came back to where I stood. "I'm going to need you to vacate the premises. This place is a crime scene now." She set her hands on her hips.

Vacate the premises? "Where am I supposed to go? I live here." I pointed to my apartment in the back.

"Head on in there, then. I got a couple-few questions for you. I'll come and find you." Even though she looked very different from her tall, lanky cousin, Buck, the second-in-command on the force, they shared the same southern Hoosier way of talking, as did pretty much everybody else in town.

"I have biscuits in the oven! I can't just—"

She let out a big sigh. "All righty. Stand next to the oven. Don't touch anything. I'll start questioning you in here. When the biscuits are done, take them out and then get out of here. Understand?"

I bobbed my head, moved into the kitchen area, and dutifully took up position next to the oven as two other officers came in through the service door. Wanda could have told me to take the biscuits out now, but she probably thought it was a shame to waste perfectly good baking.

"Photographs, Kenny," Wanda called to one of the officers.

"Got it," he said, pulling out a small camera. He

approached the body with the tentative moves of someone who'd never been near a murder victim before.

"George," she said to the other officer, a fresh-faced kid now looking slightly green. "You guard the door. Don't let anyone in without my say-so. And don't touch anything."

George seemed glad to back away. He assumed his station facing the service door, elbows out, hands behind his back.

"So, Ms. Jordan, any idea how the victim came to be deceased on your floor?" Wanda tapped on her tablet. We might live in a country village, but we have a well-equipped public-safety team.

I'd had dinner with Wanda at Buck's house a couple of months earlier. Was she calling me Ms. Jordan because I was a suspect? "I don't know how Erica got here. She was at the party here last night. Well, she was the guest of honor. But she left at about eleven with her sister Paula."

"Do you know where they went?"

"They said something about a sleepover." I thought. "'A sister slumber party,' is how Erica put it. At her house."

"Who else was at the party here?"

"Let's see. Her parents, Sue and Glen Berry. They were the ones who hosted it. As I said, her sister Paula was here, too, and her husband."

"Max Holzhauser?" Wanda asked.

"That's right." I sniffed. The tantalizing odor of the biscuits failed to counter the fact that a body lay on the floor. The timer on the oven dinged. Wanda rolled her hand, waving permission. I slid out the pan, set it on a cooling rack, and turned off the oven. The warmth barely penetrated the numb feeling in my hands.

"Back you go, then." Wanda pointed at my apartment. "We'll talk in there."

I unlocked the door to my apartment and showed her into my living room. "Want to sit down?" I left the door open to the restaurant.

"No, thanks. Go on about who else was here last night."

I stayed standing, too, despite rubbery legs, as I listed the other guests, at least the ones whose names I knew. Jim, Abe. I stopped, remembering the flare-up with Tiffany.

"That's all the ones you can remember?"

"No. Tiffany Porter was here."

"She's got herself a jewelry shop in town."

"And there were maybe a dozen or two who I didn't meet." I leaned against the wall. "Oh, and Phil MacDonald was bartending. You can get a guest list from Sue Berry, I'm sure."

"Who could have wanted the victim dead?" Wanda watched me.

"So you think it wasn't suicide or an accident?"

"'Spose it coulda been. But I doubt it."

"I don't really know who would want to kill Erica. Except . . ." Birdy rubbed against my leg, so I reached down and stroked him until he started chirping his purr of happiness. At least his life was safe and innocent. Unlike Erica's. Or mine, it seemed.

"Except what?"

I straightened. "Well, Tiffany accused Erica of

stealing from her. Erica denied it, and Tiffany left. But theft isn't a reason to kill someone."

"You let us do the investigation. People have some pretty odd reasons for committing acts of violence, I'll tell you. Anybody else not get on with the victim last night?"

"Max was upset with her when he was leaving. He wanted his wife, Paula, to go home with him and she didn't want to. Erica stuck up for Paula."

Wanda nodded, tapping words into the iPad.

"And then Erica said something racist to Phil."

She glanced up.

"She claimed she was only joking, but it upset him." I looked at Wanda, suddenly wishing I hadn't mentioned the incident with Phil. "But he wouldn't hurt a flea. You know Phil, right?"

"Yup. That's it?" she asked. "Anybody else unhappy with Erica last night?"

"That's it, as far as I know." I didn't really want to tell her about Erica making Jim uncomfortable with her seductive moves.

"And where were you all night?" Wanda drummed her fingers on the table.

"I was asleep in my bed. I didn't hear anything."

"Alone?"

"Yes." I still couldn't believe I'd slept through a break-in and a murder. "What happens now?"

"We check out where everybody was at last night. Follow up leads. County homicide task force will probably want to get involved." A vein throbbed in her forehead. "Don't much like working with those guys. They come swaggering in, thinking we're small-town hicks. But we have to let them help."

I'd overheard a couple of local guys, talking at the post office last month, who made it sound like pretty near every crime case in town ended up cold. Unsolved, that is. I knew their accusation wasn't true, because the authorities had solved Stella's murder only last month. The difficult aide to the mayor had been found dead in her home with one of my cheesy biscuits in her mouth on the evening of my store's grand reopening. Not what I had hoped for as the culmination of months of work. But the local force, with a little help from me, had eventually nailed the killer. Anyway, I was sure the county ultimately had more experience with murder than South Lick's finest.

"Sergeant?" a voice called from the store.

I followed Wanda to the door but stopped when she turned and gave me a look. She hurried over to where Erica lay.

The officer she'd called Kenny gestured with his chin. "Blood on the ground under her head." With nostrils flared, he pointed.

"Right," Wanda said. "Make sure you get a shot of that."

Kenny leaned over and snapped a picture of the floor. Erica's legs lay flaccid and her head didn't move on the stiff neck and torso. Her arms still stuck out to the sides and forward like a grotesque mannequin coming in for a hug.

Chapter 4

I hurried to shut Birdy in my bedroom, then returned to the open door and watched. Kenny now was going around spreading black powder on surfaces, while Wanda typed into her tablet. George still guarded the door.

I glanced at the now cooling biscuits. I was guessing I wasn't going to be able to open this morning. There went a day's profits, or worse. A murder in my store could turn the entire town's stomach. My business could easily tank. I felt bad worrying about money when a woman lay dead on the floor, but I had my life savings and my dreams invested in this place. I hugged myself as another shiver ran through me. I glanced over at the sad sight of Erica's body and quickly looked away again.

Danna hurried into the side door and glanced at me in the doorway to my apartment. "Robbie, what's going on? Police cars, and yellow tape across the porch?" My only employee, nineteen-year-old Danna Beedle, put on the brakes when George extended his arms to the side.

"Crime scene, miss." His voice was unexpectedly deep for one who looked so young.

Danna's hand flew to her mouth and her pale green eyes flecked with brown widened in horror as she spied Erica. She turned her head in slow motion to look at me.

"I found her next to the pickle barrel," I told her. "I'm sorry, I didn't get a chance to call you." A teenager shouldn't have to see a dead body, even a smart, competent teen like Danna.

"That's terrible. The poor thing. Do you know . . ." She glanced at the body again. "Wait, that's Erica Berry, isn't it? When I was little, like eight or nine, she used to lead our church choir. She has, I mean she had, a gorgeous voice. She could sing anything. Then she got married and moved to Chicago."

Wanda hurried over. "I'm sorry, miss. This is a crime scene. You're going to have to leave."

I had no idea why Wanda was acting like she'd never met Danna, when I knew for a fact they'd had several conversations right here in the restaurant.

"Hey, Wanda." Tall, talented Danna had been a godsend when she'd applied to work as cook, waitperson, dishwasher, and everything else in Pans 'N Pancakes right after its grand opening in early October. We'd made it through Stella's very unfortunate murder, followed by sabotage at the store, and my shoulder was pretty much healed from the accident I'd experienced in my encounter with the murderer. We'd really found our rhythm, me and Danna, and I hoped we could keep it up through the holiday season.

Danna glanced around, but she avoided the spot

where Erica's body lay. "But we're not going to be cooking today, are we?" She rubbed the strap of a well-worn messenger bag slung bandolier style across her chest and kept her hand on her left shoulder. Her long, reddish-blond dreadlocks were neatly tied back with a wide green and turquoise band matching the stripes in an oversized bowling shirt she wore belted as a tunic.

"No, you're not." Wanda pointed to the door. "Now, if you'd—"

Buck strode in the side door, followed by a thick-set man with thinning red hair. Buck almost bumped into Danna. "Excuse me, Danna," Buck said. "Getting yourself all messed up in a murder again, are you, Robbie?" he called over to me. He patted George on the shoulder and ambled over to where I stood. He looked down from a foot above me and shook his head with a baleful look.

"Morning, Buck," I said. "I wouldn't say I was getting myself messed up in it, exactly. Somebody else did, though."

The other man took a step forward. He wore a green sweater and a shirt with one point of the collar over the sweater and one under. His thin hair looked like he'd gotten dressed in a hurry, too.

"That there's Carl Mayers, George," Buck said. "County coroner. Let him on in. Carl, this is Robbie Jordan." Buck gestured to me. "She owns the place. And that's Danna Beedle, her employee. You know Wanda, right?"

"Pleased to meet you, Ms. Jordan, Ms. Beedle," a slightly breathless Carl said. "Hey there, Wanda." He wiped beads of sweat from his forehead.

"Should I go home?" Danna asked.

Buck waved toward the door. "Yes, go on home," he said. "Don't talk about what you seen here, though."

"I won't. Robbie, text me when you know about reopening."

"Of course," I said, and watched Danna head out.

"So what do we got here?" The coroner puffed over to the body and squatted.

Wanda followed him and recited what I'd told her about finding Erica.

"Did you touch her, Ms. Jordan?" Carl asked.

"No, not at all. I didn't even go very near her." My knees were feeling shaky again so I leaned against the doorjamb for support. "She was dead when I found her. I mean, she wasn't moving at all and . . ."

The coroner lost interest in me. "Looks like bruising on the right cheek." Carl pointed to Erica's face. "Turn her over for me, will you?"

"She's got upper body rigor," Kenny drawled. "You want I should break it in the shoulders? 'Cause otherwise she ain't gonna lie flat."

My own shoulders clenched in a shudder at the thought of them breaking her shoulders, whatever that meant.

"Nah, that's okay. Just hoist her up so I can see her back."

Kenny lifted Erica's upper body off the floor. Carl leaned in and examined the back of her head then oofed back to standing.

"Contusion. Get a picture of it, will you?" Carl directed.

Kenny looked around with a bewildered look

until Wanda grabbed the camera from him and took the picture.

"Go ahead and lay her on down again," Carl said. "We got some shifting lividity and some fixed," Carl rubbed the top of his head, leaving a few strands of hair puffed up like a disheveled pompadour. "She's a little bit of a thing, not much body fat, so I'm not surprised at the rigor even though it seems early. You said she left here at eleven?" he asked, walking over to me.

"Right around then. Her sister Paula drove her," I said. "What's *shifting lividity*?"

"Huh," Carl grunted, not answering me. He glanced at the wall clock and then at me. "And you found her at six thirty?"

"That's right."

"You didn't hear nothing in the night?" Buck asked, hands in his pockets. "No glass breaking or nothing?"

I shook my head. "You'd think I would have. But my bedroom is way at the back of the building, and it's too cold now to have any windows open. Plus, I use silicone earplugs, because I sleep so lightly. I didn't hear a thing." *And if I had?* Would it have made a difference in Erica's life?

Buck shook his head. "That's a crying shame, for sure."

"Do you think she was killed here?" Wanda asked the coroner. She stood with feet apart, her hands clasped behind her back.

"Can't say at this time." Carl wiped one hand off on the other, back and forth, a few times. "All righty. I'm done," he said to Buck and Wanda. "You send her on over to the county morgue in Nashville when you're finished. I'm all kinda backed up for autopsies, but I'll see if I can't shove her to the head of the line." He headed for the door, but paused by the rack of biscuits. "Okay if I grab one of these?" he called back to me.

"Help yourself. And come on back whenever we get to reopen. The biscuits are great with gravy."

"And her pancakes are to die for," Buck added. "Uh, so to speak."

"I'm sure they are." With a wistful look, Carl grabbed a biscuit. "I'm sure they are." He disappeared through the service door.

"When do you think I'll be able to reopen?" I asked Buck. I wrapped my arms around myself, still feeling the chill of spotting Erica on the floor, still numb from the shock.

"Dunno. Right now, I'm waiting on the county detective to show. Can't take Erica away till after he says we can." He ruffled his already flyaway sandy hair until it stood straight up. "Going to have to confiscate your pickle barrel, I'm afraid."

"Why?" I heard my voice rising.

"Might could have evidence on it. Maybe that's where she hit her head at."

"That's awful. Take it if you have to, but you'll have to empty it first." There went one of my country store dreams, a big pickle barrel full of crisp fat dills. I wrapped my arms around myself, for comfort more than warmth.

A trim woman in dark slacks and a tan blazer over

a turtleneck appeared in the service doorway. She paused, taking in the scene as she wiped her feet on the mat, then fixed her gaze on Buck.

He ambled toward her. "I'm sorry, ma'am. Restaurant is closed. Crime scene."

She pulled a card out of her blazer pocket and handed it to him, then opened the side of the jacket. I caught a glimpse of something silver pinned inside.

"Octavia Slade, state police homicide detective for Brown County. You're Lieutenant Buck Bird, correct?" Her dark hair fell just below her ears and framed a barely lined face. Brown eyes behind black-rimmed glasses looked like they didn't miss a thing.

"My reputation precedes me, ma'am, and heck, call me Buck, would you? But I thought we was waiting on Oscar."

"Lieutenant Thompson is on leave at present. I recently transferred down here from Tippecanoe County, and I'm the detective on this case." She moved toward Erica's body. "Fill me in."

"Wanda?" Buck gestured. "This here's Sergeant Wanda Bird, Detective Slade. She was the responding officer."

Wanda shook the detective's proffered hand. "Ma'am. I'll let Ms. Jordan tell you what transpired."

"You want me to come in now?" I asked.

Wanda waved me in, so I skirted along the back wall, staying as far from poor Erica's body as I could.

"You can stay back there." The detective motioned for me to stop in the kitchen area and moved toward me.

"I'm Robbie Jordan, Detective. This is my store and restaurant." I extended my hand.

The detective shook hands, her skin cool and smooth. "Now, Ms. Jordan, please tell me what happened, start to finish." Her gaze was focused and friendly at the same time. She drew a small notepad and an elegant silver pen out of her pocket.

"I found Erica dead on the floor next to the pickle barrel after I came in this morning." I heard a shake in my voice and swallowed hard to master it.

"You knew her?"

"I met her only last night. Her parents threw her a welcome-home party here in the restaurant. I told Wanda all about it."

Her gaze shifted to Erica's body. "I'll get it from her, then. You gave her the list of people at this party?"

"I told her the ones whose names I knew."

"I'm sure I'll have more questions for you after I review it. Did the victim have problems with anyone at this party?"

"I told Wanda all about it," I said. "Erica seemed to rub several people the wrong way. Her own brother-in-law, my friend who was bartending, a local jeweler."

"That's all? Nobody else?" She narrowed her eyes like she could peer into my brain.

I squirmed mentally and made a snap decision. "She was flirting pretty heavily with a local lawyer, too, her former brother-in-law. Her late husband's brother. Her husband died last year."

"Wanda has his name?" The detective jotted something in her notebook in small, neat letters.

"No. I forgot to tell her that part. It was Jim Shermer, Erica's husband's brother."

She lifted her face slowly until she looked at me. "Did you say *Jim* Shermer?" She stressed Jim's first name.

"That's right." Did she know Jim, or know of him?

She blinked a couple of times. "So the victim's last name is Shermer."

"Right. Her parents are Sue and Glen Berry, who live here in South Lick."

Detective Slade turned away. "Buck, has Carl already been by? I heard he'd been summoned."

"Yes, ma'am. He said he'd try to push poor old Erica to the front of the autopsy line tomorrow."

"Good." The detective walked around Erica and the pickle barrel, then strolled to the front door.

"I assume this happened in the night?" She pointed to the broken glass but gestured for me to stay where I was.

"Yes. I don't know exactly when, though. Sometime between 11 p.m. and 6:30 this morning. I live in the apartment in the back." I pointed toward the door into my personal space. "But as I told Wanda, my bedroom is way at the rear, and I wear earplugs when I sleep. I didn't hear a thing."

"How convenient." She arched a single eyebrow. Why had she said that? Did she think I was lying? My palms began to sweat. "I wish I'd heard something, at least."

"Yes, well, then you would have had to deal with a murderer and you might be dead, too." She leaned over and looked through the jagged hole and at the simple bolt mechanism on the inside. She used her pen to poke around in the shards on the floor. She motioned Kenny over.

"Did you get pictures of the glass and the door?"

He shook his head. "Not yet, ma'am."

"Well, make sure you do. I think there's some blood on it. Dust the lock for prints, too, and bag up the shards. Might have DNA on them if whoever broke in cut himself. Or herself." She straightened.

"Ms. Slade—" I began.

"Call me Octavia. I don't stand on ceremony."

"Octavia, this place is my livelihood. I know you have to do your job, but how long am I going to have to stay closed?"

"What are your usual hours?"

"Sundays eight to three. I'm normally closed on Mondays."

"It's going to take some hours to process this place, I'm afraid. I don't see why you can't open up again on Tuesday, though, depending."

"Thanks," I said. "I'd better put a sign up out front, then."

Octavia held up a hand. "Wait a sec." She looked at Wanda. "I don't suppose you took care to pre-serve footprints out front?"

Wanda cleared her throat. "No, ma'am. That, uh, did not occur to us. Although I'm the only one of us who went up the steps and approached the door."

"Waste of fresh snow," Octavia grumbled. "Go ahead, put up your sign," she told me.

And none too soon. By the time I walked around the side to the front with tacks and a sign I'd hastily printed out in my apartment, a couple stood at the bottom of the steps staring at the yellow tape.

They'd been here for breakfast at eight sharp every Sunday since I'd opened.

"I'm so sorry," I told them. "There was an, uh, accident in the store this morning. We're closed for today. But I'll be open Tuesday as normal." I smiled as brightly as I could manage.

"What happened? All these police cars and such?" the man asked.

"Did somebody die?" the woman chimed in, her eyes wide.

"I'm not at liberty to say." *Damn.* The news would be out soon enough.

The man shook his head and took his wife's arm. "We'll have to drive into Nashville for breakfast, honey pie."

I tacked the sign to the post at the bottom of the steps: Pans 'N Pancakes closed for today due to circumstances beyond our control. See you on Tuesday! The couple climbed into their car and drove off, adding two more sets of footprints and tire tracks to the trampled-down mess of snow at the base of the porch. Octavia was right. If Wanda and the men had kept a wide berth around the front of the steps, maybe the footprints of the murderer could have been identified, since it had probably kept snowing long after Phil and the others left last night. I peered at the steps. Or maybe it wasn't a waste of fresh snow, after all.

Making my way back around the side, I paused to gaze across the road at the woods, the snow coating the bare branches of the trees like a giant had shaken powdered sugar over them. The hills rose up in the distance, today looking a grayish-blue. The colorful riot of the changing leaves of October was long gone.

"I saw some footprints in snow on the front steps," I said to Octavia when I came back inside. "Maybe two different sets."

Wanda gave me the stink eye from across the room. One set of prints had to be hers. But wasn't it her job to have checked for footprints before she went up the steps for the first time?

Octavia nodded. "We'll check it out. Good eye, Robbie. My evidence team will be here soon. You can head back to your apartment now." She glanced upward. "Or wait. This is a two-story building. What's upstairs?"

"It's empty. Like a big loft, really. I plan to develop it into guest rooms someday." My real dream was to expand into offering bed-and-breakfast rooms. I already made breakfast every day, and I could manage to turn over linens and clean rooms in the afternoons after the restaurant closed. But that was a future dream. I pointed to a door in the far corner of the cookware area. "That leads to the upstairs."

She pulled out a phone and turned away. As I walked away, I heard her tell someone to make sure they had the footprint kit, and to come around the side.

I stood in the doorway to my apartment, observing the action. Everybody seemed to have a job except Buck, who sat watching the officers work. I knew from getting to know him after the murder in October he projected a real country hick image, but inside he was smarter than most of the county residents. I'd bet that mind of his was even now cranking out ideas, although Octavia might not think so from the exasperated look she cast him.

A rush of cold air ushered in several officers, dressed in the state police uniform of navy blue long-sleeved shirts, with light blue neckties that matched their pants. All three carried equipment cases in various shapes. After Octavia spoke to them, a stocky man went back outside. She directed a tall female officer to check out the upstairs first.

"Careful," I called out. "The floorboards are a little iffy."

"We already done the dusting, Octavia," Buck said to her with a slow smile.

George and Kenny paused from emptying the pickle barrel into a couple of big pots I'd given them, and watched Octavia take a seat at Buck's table.

"It's okay, guys. Proceed," she called. "We're all on the same team here. Dave, why don't you check for bloodstains?"

The man she'd addressed gave a mock salute and knelt to open his case.

Buck raised a finger in the air and looked in my direction. "Any chance of some breakfast for the team, Robbie?" He stressed the word *team.*

"I can do that, since I'm not getting any actual customers. That okay, Octavia?"

She looked up from where she and Wanda were conferring over Wanda's tablet. "No. Not until we're finished with the crime scene."

Chapter 5

I watched the team wheel Erica out as I oversaw sizzling bacon and sausages and a growing stack of pancakes. My legs were starting to feel more solid than shaky. Octavia had finally given me the go-ahead to cook more than two hours later, at which Buck had looked hugely relieved. The footprint guy had been busy outside and the staties had examined all kinds of things inside after the tall officer cleared the upstairs.

George and Kenny had zipped Erica into a body bag while I cooked. Her legs and feet had stiffened while she'd lain there, and the guys had had a hard time getting her into the bag. I'd felt my stomach roil, watching, and I kept my eyes pretty much on the griddle after that.

"Food's about ready," I called before they reached the door.

The guys paused.

"Put her in the wagon and lock up, then come eat," Buck said. "She'll stay plenty cold, God rest her young soul."

It took a couple of full trays to bring the loaded plates to the three tables where people had chosen to sit. I'd decided not to short-order cook but to give everybody the same food, since I doubted I was getting paid for these meals. The last plate was for me, and I sat with Buck, Octavia, and Wanda. Buck's legs stretched so far under the table I could barely scoot my chair in. Octavia had pushed her bacon to the side.

"I don't eat meat," she said when she saw me looking.

"Sorry about that," I said.

Buck looked longingly at the forlorn bacon until Octavia laughed.

"Take it." She pushed her plate toward Buck.

"Thank you, ma'am. Hey, Robbie, any of them biscuits left?"

The man was a bottomless pit when it came to eating, but then again, he had a lot to fill, as tall as he was. I rose and grabbed the platter of biscuits, which still held a half dozen. The officers at the other tables had split along local/statie lines, and conversed quietly among themselves. I'd just shoveled in a too-big bite of pancake when my aunt Adele burst through the service door.

George, who'd been stationed at the door again, held up his hand.

"What in tarnation is going on here?" The edges of Adele's no-nonsense steel-gray hair peeked out from under a multicolored knit hat, with long, brilliant green cloisonné earrings dangling below her hair. Her faded blue eyes flashed. "Are you okay, Roberta?"

"Ma'am," George said.

"Let her in, George." Buck waved a hand even as Octavia shook her head.

Adele hurried to my side.

"I'm fine, Adele." My mom's sister was the only person I allowed to call me by my full name.

Adele looked at the officers, who, to a one, looked back. "Well, something's up on God's green earth, that's certain. What are all them cherry toppers doing out there? I ain't seen so many panda cars together in a long time. Howdy, Buck, Wanda." She waved.

"Pull up a chair and sit down," I said. There were definitely lots of police cars out there, and the state police colors were blue and white but knowing Adele, they were all panda cars to her.

Octavia's eyebrows pulled together. "The restaurant is closed until future notice, ma'am."

Adele grabbed a chair and squeezed in between Buck and me. "I'm no ma'am, ma'am. I'm family."

I stretched my arm around Adele's shoulders. "She's my aunt. And former mayor of South Lick as well as former fire chief. Adele, this is State Police Detective Octavia Slade. Octavia, Adele Jordan. The reason I'm in Indiana."

"Nice to meet you, Octavia." Adele reached her hand across the table. Octavia shook hands with a look of reluctance. "Sure smells good in here," Adele said.

I sniffed. The scents of meat and pancakes had

finally taken over for pickle brine and death. "Breakfast?" I stuffed in one more bite and grabbed my last bacon as I stood. I knew what Adele's answer would be and I had enough batter left for one more plate.

"You bet," Adele said. "Now, who's going to fill me in on all this commotion?"

The last of the officers cleared out of the store, leaving only Octavia donning her coat. Adele was washing dishes, and I held a rag in my hand, ready to set the place to rights again. I'd duct-taped a big piece of cardboard over the broken glass when the police gave me the all-clear, just to keep the cold out, but I was going to have to get the glass replaced as soon as possible.

"I'll need to speak with you again, I'm sure," Octavia said to me. "And you need to keep the store closed until further notice."

"All right. But I thought you said I could reopen on Tuesday."

"I expect you'll be able to, but I can't guarantee it." She handed me a credit card. "Go ahead and put all the breakfasts on this."

"Really? I was offering them on the house."

Octavia shook her head. "State regs. We can't accept freebies."

"Got it." I took the card and swiped it through card reader on the store iPad, which I'd mounted on a stand at the counter next to the antique cash register. I pressed the total for the meals and swiveled it around to face her.

"Sign with the stylus," I said. "Or with your finger, either one." I would have fed everyone for free, but it was great to be paid, too. My profit margins were pretty slim, and I'd only been open a month and a half. I was already worrying about the food in the walk-in going bad if they were going to make me stay closed for a while, and if anybody would even want to eat here again after hearing about the murder. I imagined talk already going around about how surely I would have heard something in the night, or gossip about how I had a grudge against Erica for flirting with Jim. Small towns are a blessing and a curse. People's love for you can turn to suspicion or even hate in a matter of hours.

Octavia scribbled a signature.

"Thanks. And good luck with the investigation."

"If you think of anything that might help us, overhear anything, please let me know." She handed me one of her business cards.

"I will."

"We'll be parking ourselves at the South Lick police station for the duration of the investigation—too far to go back and forth to the state police post in Bloomington all the time." She turned toward the door.

"I definitely know where the town's police station is," I said, remembering my grilling there last month when I was briefly under suspicion of murder myself.

"Bye, Detective," Adele called.

Octavia waved before closing the door behind

her. I wandered over to the desk and set the card on it.

"Bet you didn't expect any of that this morning," Adele said, her hands deep in sudsy water. The wall clock chimed once, marking the half hour into the now quiet air.

"You can say that again."

"Are you doing all right?" she asked.

"I guess I am. I was shaky and kind of numb for a while." I pushed a stray curl off my forehead, then started wiping down the tables. "I wish none of it'd happened, especially not seeing Erica dead. And then having to close the store." I'd seen plenty of folks stop by while the teams were at work. They peered at my sign out front and then walked away, shaking their heads.

"Any idea who killed her?" Adele glanced at me.

I shook my head. "She seemed to rub everybody the wrong way last night except her parents and maybe her sister. She was heavy into flirting with both Jim and Max. She made Jim uncomfortable and Max mad. Although he was already pretty mad."

"He's a veteran, you know. Could be he has PTSD issues."

"Interesting. He seemed to really want to control Paula," I said. "What does he do for a living?"

"He's a locksmith, I believe."

"And Tiffany who owns the jewelry shop—"

"Tiffany Porter?" Adele asked. "She's very talented."

"That's her. She accused Erica of stealing from her. And then Erica delivered some kind of racist insult to Phil. To Phil!" I shook my head. "The sweetest guy in the universe. She claimed she'd only been joking. He wouldn't tell me exactly what she said, it was that bad."

"But none of that is exactly cause to take and kill someone."

"Of course not." I rubbed my chin. That *take and* phrasing was common around here, and to my ears was completely superfluous, since *take and bring* simply meant *bring*, just like *take and kill* really only meant *kill.*

"Last night Paula, Erica's sister, went home with her," I went on. "Erica said they were going to have a sister slumber party. But she must have gone out again, or been abducted from her own house. I wonder if Paula heard her leave." I picked up a feather duster and swiped at the powder that was everywhere. Dark powder on light surfaces and light powder on dark. Had they gotten any useful fingerprints? Mine would be on nearly every surface, of course. Plus, hundreds of customers had come through here in the last month and a half, picking up a vintage chopper here, examining an antique whisk there, checking out cookware from sifters to salt boxes, checkered crocks to cast-steel cleavers. The feather duster barely dented the powder, so I grabbed a rag instead and headed over to the shelves of cookware, which were always in need of dusting, anyway.

Wait a minute. On the wall where I hung my collection of not-for-sale favorite kitchen implements, I saw a blank spot. I racked my brain, trying to remember what had hung there. The wall where the empty spot was showed a lighter circle, maybe six inches across. I peered at it. Was there also a long narrow light stripe? I snapped my fingers. The vintage sandwich press was missing.

But why? Had some light-fingered partygoer made off with the press when I wasn't looking? Tiffany had been interested in it last night, but I knew she hadn't walked out with it. It wasn't exactly the easiest tool to steal, anyway, with those two-foot long handles. *Or* . . . a tremor rippled through me. Had the murderer whacked Erica on the head with it?

Chapter 6

"It's just that I noticed it was missing off the wall," I said to Octavia after I'd reached her by phone.

"How big is it again?"

I described the press. "So it's long, and it's kind of heavy because of the cast-iron disks. With the right leverage, I guess. Wait a minute." I looked at Adele, who waved at me.

"She can look at mine if she wants," Adele said.

I raised my eyebrows. "Octavia, my aunt Adele has one exactly like it at home. She says you can look at it."

Octavia blew out a breath. "All right. Give me her number, and I'll send someone out to pick it up."

"She's still here. I'll have her call you when she gets home, okay?"

She agreed and I disconnected the call, staring at Adele.

"Could someone have used the press to kill Erica? The police did find what they called a contusion on the back of her head. It's totally horrible even thinking about it." My voice shook, and I swallowed.

"If the killer used the press on Erica, he took it away with him, or else the police would have found it."

Adele dried her hands on a blue-and-white-striped towel. "Guess you're lucky they didn't use the chopper." She pointed to the two-handled curved blade, which fit exactly in a shallow wooden bowl.

"*Ack*. You're right. I don't even want to think about that."

"I'm heading back to the farm now, hon. Left Sloopy out."

"How's he doing?" I liked her energetic border collie.

"Good. Loves his job, rounding up the flock. And Samuel's coming over a little later on." A blush tinted Adele's deeply lined cheeks.

Phil's grandfather was Adele's main squeeze, and good for them, finding full-blown romance in their seventies.

"Sounds like a nice afternoon." I remembered something I'd been meaning to ask her. "Adele, I want to add some new gift items for the holidays. You know, local crafts and such. You've got yarn from your sheep that you sell. Could you bring some over? We can set up a special display, maybe bring in more shoppers before Christmas."

"That's a great idea, hon. I have a decent supply, and in the most gorgeous colors. I'll bring it by next time I come to town."

"Thanks. Now go home to your dog and your man. I'll be fine." I held out my arms for a hug from the only relative I'd ever known besides my mom. Mom had died suddenly last January at only fifty-three, and the taste of missing her was still bitter.

She'd taught me cabinet making and how to love life, and she'd left me enough money so that, combined with my savings, I could buy this country store and make it over into a restaurant.

She hugged me. "Any word from Roberto?"

"His foot is healing up well. I Skyped with him on Friday, and we're planning my trip." Last month I'd discovered my absent father was a professor in Italy who'd never even known of my existence. Mom had never told him about me, or me about him. After I contacted him, he'd welcomed me into his heart and invited me to come to Tuscany for Christmas to meet him and the half-siblings I wasn't even aware I had.

"That's just ducky, hon," Adele said. "All righty, I'm out of here. Now don't you worry about having to be closed. Folks are going to come on back as soon as you reopen, you'll see. People around here have gotten used to your tasty meals."

"I hope so." I mustered a smile as I saw her out the side door. I closed the door and thought for a moment, and opened it again. I needed to board up the top part of my door. Cardboard wasn't secure at all, and with a murderer out there, being secure was high on my list. I knew I had some plywood left over from the store renovation out in the old barn that'd come with the property.

Half an hour later, I shot in the last screw with my power drill and stepped back to examine it. I hated to have to put screws into an antique door, and it wasn't pretty, but the door was as secure as it was going to get for today. I'd order replacement glass tomorrow. It was too bad, because the antique glass had made lovely wavy patterns on the floor when late-day sunlight streamed through it. I thought they made unbreakable glass for doors now, so perhaps having it broken was a blessing, as long as it didn't set me back too far financially.

Now that that chore was finished, I didn't know what to do with myself on a Sunday morning at eleven thirty. I hadn't had a Sunday off since before I opened in early October. I puttered around, returning the uncooked bacon and sausage to the walk-in, stashing the clean dishes, sweeping up. At least I hadn't made a big batch of pancake batter I'd have to throw out. A batter made with baking powder wouldn't freeze well or keep in the cooler, either. The coleslaw I'd made yesterday for today's lunch would probably keep, although by Tuesday it might be too wilted to serve. I might as well chip away at it for my own lunches. I drew out the bowl full of the colorful salad—a cheerful mix of green and red cabbages and carrots—from the walk-in and headed for my apartment.

At the door, I turned back to look at the cookware wall. That empty space where the press had been bugged me. I wanted to hang something over it, move a frying pan or a popcorn popper into its place. But the detective would certainly want to check out the wall for prints or DNA or something. I turned into my apartment and locked up tight behind me.

After I let Birdy out of the bedroom, he sauntered after me into the kitchen and rubbed against my leg.

"Hey, kittycat." I rubbed his head and picked him

up, putting my face close to his until I got one little scratchy lick on the nose, then he squirmed out of my hands and jumped into the sink. A dutiful cat mom, I turned the faucet on low and watched him lap up the running water, an H_2O source apparently much preferable to fresh water in a bowl on the floor.

But I kept picturing Erica. Wondering who'd killed her, who'd broken into my store. I'd never seen a dead body before. It'd been an upsetting, terrible sight. I knew some funerals included an open casket, but I'd never been to one. And in that case I was sure they prettied up the dead.

It was Sunday, so maybe the puzzle would distract me. I downloaded and printed out the *New York Times* Sunday puzzle from my subscription, clamped it onto my puzzle clipboard, and found my special pen, which Buck had returned to me after it was found at the scene of the crime in October. It was one of the pens my mom had had printed with the logo for her cabinetry business, a long table inscribed with JEANINE'S CABINETS. I put my feet up on the futon sofa and got to work.

After I'd filled in the top left corner, though, my mind drifted back to the Who Killed Erica puzzle. Even though she wasn't well liked, she didn't deserve to die at the hands of another. And I sure didn't deserve to have a dead woman dumped on the floor of my store. I couldn't figure out the connection. Why kill Erica? Why leave her here?

I watched Birdy perform feats even the best yogi couldn't master as he bathed his lithe black-and-white self in a spot of sunlight on the floor. Solving this murder wasn't my job, of course. But it might require the same kinds of contortions, except of the mental variety.

After I finished the puzzle, it wasn't even noon. I stretched my arms as I wandered through the kitchen to the back door, pushing it open. The sunshine was already melting the couple of inches of white stuff. Early snows this far south never lasted long.

I still wanted to distract myself from the deeply disturbing events of the morning. But there was too much snow on the ground for me to want to take my nice road cycle out for a long ride. Good thing I'd ordered a bike trainer I could click my cycle into. I set it up in the living room, changed into biking shorts and a tank top, and put on a collection of arias sung by Luciano Pavarotti. I was the only twenty-something I knew who liked opera. It was one more thing I'd picked up from Mom, and after I learned my father Roberto was Italian, I realized why the Italian baritones were her favorites.

I'd been pedaling for about half an hour, getting into the zone of exercise where my mind switched off and the endorphins flowed, exactly where I wanted to be, when my phone rang. I squeezed my eyes shut, not wanting to interrupt the Zen. But with a dead woman found in my store this morning, I needed to reset my priorities. I hopped off the bike and grabbed the phone from the sleek maple coffee table my mother had crafted, then resumed riding at a slower pace.

"Robbie, I heard what happened," Jim said without preamble. "Poor Erica. The family is devastated. I was just over there."

"I'm sure they are." Unease twinged through me. I hadn't even thought of calling Jim and talking about the murder. Shouldn't he have been the first person I'd want to share the news with, and my confusion and distress about it? At some point I'd need to ponder why calling him hadn't occurred to me.

"And poor you," he continued. "They said you found her body. How are you?"

"I'm okay, but it was awful to see her dead right there on my floor." I rocked in my seat, twisting my silver pinky ring, the phone tucked between my ear and my shoulder.

"I can imagine. It's terrible you had to go through that."

"And the store's closed. Until Tuesday, if not longer, according to the detective assigned to the case."

"Well, that's no good," he said. "I'm sure they're only doing what they have to, though."

"I guess."

"I'll have to let my parents know," he said. "Erica was their daughter-in-law, even though they didn't get along so well with her."

I stopped pedaling. "I wonder what else the police think they're going to find in my store. It was swarming with both the local police and the staties for several hours, although they're all gone now."

"Not sure," Jim said. "Who is the detective on the case?"

"Her name is Octavia Slade."

"Really?" His voice rose higher than usual at the end of the question.

"Why, do you know her?" I asked. He was a lawyer, after all, but he practiced real estate law, not criminal. His reaction to hearing Octavia's name was oddly similar to hers hearing his.

He didn't speak for a minute, then he said, "I do. Or I did."

I didn't ask what he meant. He'd tell me when he was ready to. Maybe it didn't mean anything.

He cleared his throat. "Listen, I also called to see if you wanted to go dancing with me tonight."

"That sounds like a perfect way to get my mind off finding Erica. But you just lost your sister-in-law. Are you up for dancing?"

"We were never close, although I wouldn't mind getting my thoughts off her death, either."

"So I guess your migraine didn't happen last night?"

"I caught it just in time."

"Okay, then. Dancing it is," I said.

"We could go back to the roadhouse where we went line dancing. Or, if you want, there's a special contra dance in Bloomington tonight, and we could get dinner beforehand."

"I've never been to a contra dance. It's like square dancing, right?"

Jim laughed. "Square dancing is different. Contra is usually done in lines with people facing each other."

"Will I be able to figure out what to do? And do I need an outfit?" I knew for sure I didn't have a full skirt and a matching Western shirt in my closet.

"I think you'll be able to pick it up. There's a caller who tells you what to do. And I'll help. It's really a lot of fun."

"What about the outfit?" I asked.

"You can wear anything, but mostly women wear skirts. Actually, there are a couple of guys who wear skirts, too."

I could hear the smile in his voice. "Do you?" I asked.

"Definitely not," he said. "But don't wear a heavy sweater—it gets pretty warm in there. Layers are good."

"It's a date, then."

"I'll pick you up at five, so we have plenty of time to eat and get to the newcomer instruction starting at seven thirty." He said goodbye and disconnected.

I loved dancing, but Jim preferred dances with steps and moves, dances that actually needed instruction. I, on the other hand, liked to work it out, move to the music however my body wanted to. *What was I getting myself into?*

Chapter 7

I headed over to Shamrock Hardware, a few blocks away, after my exercise, a shower, and a sandwich. By one o'clock I was back at the store unloading a couple of big bags bursting with Christmas decorations and new extension cords from my old Dodge mini-van. Might as well take the opportunity of the store being closed to make it look cheery for the holidays. And Shamrock had had everything I needed except fresh greens. For that I'd drive out to one of the local Christmas tree farms tomorrow. I set the bags on the floor and looked around, eyes narrowed, planning it all out. Strings of tiny white lights over the door and around the windows. Garlands here and there. Twenty silver balls. A dozen red bows and . . . my gaze fell on the empty spot on the wall again. Shoot.

Digging my phone out of my back pocket, I strode to the desk where I'd left Octavia's card and pressed her number.

"Slade," she said in a crisp voice right when I thought the call was about to go to voice mail.

"Octavia, it's Robbie Jordan. I wondered when you'd be done with my store. I mean, I wanted to decorate it for the holidays. Is that all right? I don't want to impede the investigation or anything."

She sighed audibly. "I suppose you can go ahead. We've already printed the place and checked for other evidence. But leave the area alone around where you said the item was missing. Can you do that?"

"Of course." I wandered over and studied the wall.

"I'll get evidence techs out there today. You'll be in the store?"

"I'm leaving at five, but I'll be here until then."

"Hang on a sec, Robbie."

I heard a voice in the background and Octavia's muffled voice. I waited.

"Sorry," Octavia said when she came back on. "I'll get someone over there before five, then." She cleared her throat. "Lieutenant Bird wants me to let you know we have Philostrate MacDonald here for questioning. I'm telling you against my better judgment, as a favor to the local force." The tension in her voice was as taut as a new blade on a coping saw.

"Phil? Why in the world? He wouldn't hurt a fly."

"He was seen leaving the store late last night." She clipped her words, pronouncing each word separately, articulating every final *T*.

"I told Wanda he'd offered to clean up after I went to bed, didn't I?" This was outrageous.

"I'm not sure that was in Officer Bird's report, no. But you did tell her Phil was upset by a racist remark the victim made to him."

"Sure. Wouldn't you be? He wouldn't kill her for

that, though. And besides, he has a key. Why would he break the glass in the door to get in?"

"To throw us off his trail could be a reason. Anyway, I have to go." She disconnected the call.

I stared at the phone. Not Phil. Never Phil. What could I do to help him? I was suddenly not much in the mood for cheerful holiday decorations. I pressed Adele's number, and after several rings she answered in a breathless voice.

"Sorry, I was outside," she said. "What's up?"

"Phil is at the police station being questioned by the detective. About the murder." I paced to the boarded-up door and back to my pile of decorations.

"That's just plumb wrong." She made a *tsking* sound. "I'll tell Samuel. He's right here."

"Think Phil needs a lawyer?"

"He might could. Don't you worry a whit, hon. We'll take care of him, Samuel and me."

"Okay." I thanked her and disconnected. I paced some more, the length of the store and back. I hated feeling helpless, but I'd done all I could, so I might as well decorate. Having busy hands sometimes let puzzle-solving thoughts into my brain, too. And if ever there was a puzzle that needed to be solved, it was the question of who really killed Erica Berry Shermer. Because I knew as sure as I was a Californian that Phil didn't. I called and left him a message on his cell, asked him to call me back. I almost said more, but disconnected. We'd talk later.

Wincing at the sight of the plywood, I dragged over the stepladder and looped the first string of lights over the front door. I'd asked at the store if I could order new glass today, but they'd said Don, the owner, had to do the ordering and he didn't come in on Sundays.

I plugged another string into the first one and stretched it between the windows and on top of the window frames, adding more strings as I went, until I reached the end of the front wall. I knew Phil hadn't killed Erica—didn't I? I was as sure as I could be. He was a gentle, generous, fun-loving soul. So who was the real murderer? Erica and Tiffany had argued, but it wouldn't make sense for Tiffany to kill someone she'd accused of stealing, not if she wanted to get her jewelry back.

I started stringing lights on the other side of the door until I got to the cookware area. That part would have to wait to be decorated until the evidence people were done with it. Max had seemed angry with Erica for taking Paula's side. Surely not mad enough to kill her, though. Maybe the murderer was somebody in Erica's past. Or someone who'd followed her here from Chicago. I'd ask Jim tonight if he knew anyone in Erica and Jon's group of friends or business associates. I couldn't remember what Jim had said his brother did for work, if he even had. Jim had spoken only once to me about his brother's suicide. He'd said losing his twin was like losing a chunk of himself, and that he'd had no idea Jon was that despondent. Or why he would be.

I inserted the last plug for the lights into a wireless device and plugged the device into the wall. I stepped back and flipped on the switch. The sight of all the little white lights did, in fact, cheer me. I turned to the kitchen area and hung green garlands under the counter and over the door to the walk-in, adding a red bow here and there to brighten them. All I needed was a model train set running around an oval in the front window, with tiny snow-covered houses and a miniature Pans 'N Pancakes in the center of town.

I wasn't particularly religious, but I loved the Christmas season, especially here in the Midwest where the days were short and the temperatures chilly. Christmas in Santa Barbara, where I'd grown up, was a different experience altogether. Mom and I had usually taken a Christmas brunch picnic to the beach and soaked up some cool sunshine while we celebrated. Once, when I was eight, we'd come to Indiana to spend Christmas with Adele. It had snowed on Christmas Eve, and I couldn't believe I was seeing the winter wonderland I'd only read about in books. At home the winter air smelled of orange blossoms and sea breezes. Out here? The crisp taste of apples and the sharp smell of snow were more the order of the day.

After I finished decorating, it was still only two o'clock. I looked around the store. Normally at this time of day on a Sunday the restaurant would be full of hungry folks taking a late lunch or even brunch, since I served breakfast all day. I always tried to include something brunchy like Santa Barbara-Style Eggs Benedict or Herbed Waffles with Cheese Sauce on the Sunday Specials chalkboard. But now, with no customers and with yellow police tape keeping them away, I was too antsy thinking of

Phil down at the station to simply sit and read. I'd been meaning to clean the walk-in cooler, though, and there was no time like the present.

I turned the temperature to *Off* and propped open the heavy door. The cold air flowing out from the cooler was going to chill the store, so I also turned the store thermostat down to fifty-five, and then grabbed a heavy sweater from my apartment. Who was going to care if it was cold? The evidence team were the only people I expected, and they probably worked in all kinds of conditions. I ran a bucket of warm water, dissolved baking soda in it, grabbed a big sponge, and headed in.

The metal shelves were wire racks, not solid, so they were easy to swab off. I worked vertically, shifting boxes and containers to the side so I could clean the racks from top to bottom. Poor Phil, I thought as I worked. Hadn't I told Wanda about him offering to clean up and getting the guys to help him, Abe and the harmonica dude? I thought I had. And who would have reported seeing Phil leave the store at midnight? South Lick wasn't exactly known for being a hotbed of nightlife, having only one establishment that stayed open past ten at night, and that was a bar across town. Cars going by my store at midnight were as rare as a decent tomato in November.

Frustrated, I shifted a box with a little too much force and it fell onto the floor, spilling the green and red peppers I used for omelets onto the concrete floor. I cursed as I knelt to pick them up. The non-melodious doorbell at the service door made its two-toned sound before I was finished. I hurried to it and then paused. I knew the team was supposed to be coming. But there wasn't a window or even a peephole to look out at whoever pressed the bell. And a killer was out there somewhere. I hurried to the front window to see a state police car parked outside. I laughed and shook my head. Like a murderer was going to ring a doorbell. I pulled open the service door to see two of the blue-uniformed guys who had been here this morning.

"State police evidence team, ma'am."

"Come on in," I said. "I'll show you where I found the tool missing." I led them to the wall and pointed. "That's where the sandwich press was. You can see the mark on the wall."

"You haven't touched the wall or the shelving?" the taller one asked.

"Not since I hung the press up there last summer. I ran a duster over it a few times since I opened in early October, but I didn't touch any of it today."

"When's the last time you saw the object?"

"Actually, last evening. I know because someone asked me what it was."

"Name?"

"My name? I'm Robbie Jordan. I thought you knew—"

"No, ma'am. The name of the person who asked you about the press." He drew out a notebook and a pen.

"It was Tiffany Porter. She loves antique cookware as much as I do."

He looked down his nose at me, and then jotted her name in his book. "She a local?"

"She owns a gift shop in town. I don't know if she lives right in South Lick or not, though."

"Got it. We'll get to work now. I understand you have to leave in two hours, at seventeen hundred?"

"No, at . . ." I cocked my head. *Oh. Military time.* I did the math. "Yes, that's right."

"We'll be done by then." He turned away.

I thanked him and got back to my job in the cooler. I finished at about the same time the officers did, and managed not to groan at all the new fingerprint powder they'd left. I locked the service door after them, put away my bucket, and headed into my apartment to figure out what I owned to wear that was suitable for contra dancing. As I stared into my closet, my cell rang from the other room. I dashed in and connected.

"Robbie, hon," Adele said. "Phil's home again. Samuel got him the best lawyer in town. They didn't arrest him or anything."

"What a relief. Thanks for letting me know. So they didn't have any real evidence against him, right?"

"Not that they told us. Now, what are you doing tonight? Want to come by for a bite of dinner?" she asked.

"I actually have a date for dinner and contra dancing."

"With your Jim, I assume?" Adele's voice held the sound of a smile.

"You got it. He said contra is fun, that I'll be able to learn how to do it, and that I don't need a special outfit."

"I've been plenty of times. You'll love it." She blew me an audible kiss and hung up.

It would take a lot of fun to get my brain off the

puzzle of an unsolved murder, but if anybody could do it, it would be the green-eyed dancer. Jim and I were still figuring out our relationship. I liked him, and he was cute to the point of hot. But I'd been so burned by my rotten ex-husband in California, I still wasn't quite sure how entwined I wanted my life and Jim's to be. Luckily, he wasn't pushing me to commit to anything.

Now for my closet. I dug around, finally locating a knit dress in a bright flowered print, with short sleeves and a flared skirt that flattered both my slender waist and my ample hips. I could pair it with leggings and a light sweater I could always shed if, indeed, I grew hot contra-ing. Dancing with Jim usually heated me up, anyway, so his caution about wearing layers hadn't really been necessary.

Chapter 8

I studied the menu at the Uptown Cafe. After Jim had picked me up, he'd admired my swingy dress. Guess I nailed that one.

"Ever eaten here?" Jim asked. We were there early before the dinner rush, and it was Sunday, but all the barstools behind us were full and other customers clustered standing around it, holding drinks, talking, laughing. I'd never been to Bloomington on a Sunday at happy hour.

"No. What do you recommend?" I tucked my hair behind my ear. I'd chosen to wear it down, since I never got to at work, and I loved the feeling of my full-bodied curls hanging loose and bouncy. It was kind of a pain to keep it long, what with how much time it took to shampoo and comb it out. I gladly spent the time for evenings like this, letting my hair do as it willed and being able to savor the sensation.

"Check out the section called *Cajun-Creole Cuisine.*" He pointed to my menu. "That's my favorite. In fact, I already know I'm going to have the gumbo."

"Ooh, shrimp and grits sounds yummy." I read from the menu, "Jumbo shrimp and andouille sausage, atop cheddar cheese jalapeño grits. That's what I'm having."

"The grits are pretty spicy." Jim closed his menu and smiled. His pale green long-sleeved shirt matched his eyes, which also smiled.

"I can do spicy. I'm a California girl, remember? I grew up on chilies."

The waiter wandered over looking very much like a college student, with a pierced eyebrow and bleached-blond hair slicked to a kind of Mohawk peak atop his head.

"What can I get you tonight?" he asked.

I told him I wanted the shrimp and grits.

"I'll have the gumbo," Jim said, handing him his menu.

"Want that Hoosier style?" the waiter asked.

"What does that mean?" I asked.

Jim laughed. "It means with mashed potatoes instead of rice. No," he said to the waiter. "I'll take it Louisiana style. And can we get some bread to start?"

The waiter gave a thumbs-up as he collected my menu, then turned away.

I leaned in toward Jim. "Who ever heard of mashed potatoes and gumbo?" I asked him.

He grinned. "People from Indiana, that's who." He tasted the beer in a full pint glass. "Man, this is good. Want a taste?"

"No, thanks. Beer doesn't go so well with Pinot Noir." I sipped my wine. "I'm surprised I've never been to this restaurant before. Although I think I might have met one of the chefs when I cooked at the Nashville Inn." I'd been chef at the inn for three years, cooking and saving as much money as I could to open my own place. I gazed at him. "I heard some bad news this afternoon. The police took Phil in for questioning about the murder."

"Phil?" His eyebrows went halfway up to his red hair.

"My reaction, exactly." I shook my head. "They totally have it wrong. Luckily, Adele called later on and told me Samuel had hired a really good lawyer. The police let Phil go. Or Octavia did, more likely."

Jim looked away as if studying the bar running the length of the room behind me. He rubbed his thumb over his fingernails as he always did when he was thinking.

I watched him, my radar activated. "So how do you know Octavia?"

He looked at me. "We dated for a while. In our twenties, so ten years ago or so."

Aha. "Nothing wrong with that. But you seem kind of, I don't know, like there's more to the story."

"There is." He sipped his beer, looking anywhere but at me. "But I don't want to talk about it now, if it's okay with you."

The waiter returned with a basket holding a sliced baguette and a little dish of butter. I buttered a piece and took a bite, savoring the crusty, chewy loaf. What had gone on with him and Octavia he didn't want to talk about?

"So who do you think would have killed Erica?"

I asked after a couple of minutes of neither of us speaking, only chewing and sipping in silence.

Jim finally glanced at me with a look of relief like he'd been rescued from circling sharks. "Good question. There was the flare-up with Tiffany Porter, but I don't know why she would have killed Erica for stealing from her."

"What about somebody from Chicago? I was thinking about Jon," I said, reaching across the table for his hand. "Maybe somebody from their life up there had a grudge against Erica."

He gazed across the room and then back at me. He squeezed my hand before letting it go. "Interesting idea. I'm not sure how to find out. I was at their wedding, of course, but so were two hundred other people. They held it at the Story Inn, four years ago." He smiled as if at the memory. "What a day that was. Perfect June weather. Her family rented the whole place for the weekend. Have you ever been there?"

"I've eaten in the restaurant a couple of times but never stayed in one of the rooms." The Story General Store, now an inn, was in the little town of Story, south of Nashville, and the business had bought up all the buildings in the town center.

"They also rent out the cottages on the property, not only the ones above the dining room," Jim said. "I heard it was a couple of dropped-out grad students who originally bought the store and fixed it up, and then gradually turned it into an inn serving gourmet dinners."

"That's right. The decor inside gave me some

ideas for my store and restaurant. I'm actually hoping to renovate the upstairs rooms in my building for my own bed-and-breakfast. If I ever find the time."

"That's a good idea. I remember you said that when you made the offer on the property. Anyway, some of Jon and Erica's Chicago friends came down and stayed in a couple of the cottages. Erica was high on being a bride, of course. I didn't see anybody not getting along. I suppose someone with a grudge against Erica might not have been invited, though."

"You must have visited Erica and Jon in Chicago."

"A couple of times. Not enough. That reminds me. I spoke with my folks. They wanted to come down for whatever services the family holds, but my mom isn't well enough. She's still healing from breaking her hip last month." He drank from his beer, then set it down. "I'll have to think back on who I met at the wedding. There was one guy, kind of pale and nervous, but I can't remember his name. He and Jon were friends. I can ask Paula, too, what she knows about their acquaintances."

"How about a work conflict? What did Jon do for a living, by the way?"

Gloom settled on his face. "We both went to law school. I chose real-estate law, but he was a criminal lawyer."

"Being a criminal lawyer must be a hard occupation, whether prosecuting a criminal or defending one." It suddenly occurred to me that maybe someone from one of Jon's cases had killed Erica to get revenge on Jon, even though he'd been dead for a year.

"He was just getting established when . . ." Jim fell silent.

"I'm so sorry, Jim."

He gave me a wan smile. "It still seems so fresh. And so confusing. He had a great life, loved his work, doted on Erica even though she could be a handful, as you saw last night." He shook his head. "And then he shot himself. I didn't get it then and I don't get it now."

"I know the fresh part. I still automatically reach for the phone to call my mom and tell her something. Then I remember I can't."

The waiter appeared with our dinners and set them in front of us. "Can I get you anything else?"

"I think we're good, thanks." I smiled at him.

"No more talk of death tonight, all right?" Jim asked after the waiter turned away, then let out a long breath, staring at his plate.

"Absolutely not."

We sat in silence for a moment. I picked up my fork but he hadn't started eating yet, so I waited. I glanced at the big TV over the bar, where it looked like a football game was about to begin, with close-ups of eager fans wearing painted faces and big grins. "So how about them Colts?"

We parked outside an old two-story limestone building, a block from the sprawling Indiana University campus. By the parking lot lights I could see a tall arched entrance that came to a gentle point, with ELM HEIGHTS SCHOOL carved in stone above the door.

"You can lock your bag in the car if you want," Jim said.

"Good idea." I set my purse on the floor before getting out. "What is this place?" I asked, coming around the front of the Prius once it gave off the little mini-beeps indicating it was locked.

"It's the Harmony School now, a private pre-K through high school. It's where they hold the dance. But it was the Elm Heights Elementary School before that. Elm Heights is this neighborhood."

"Do you know how old the building is?"

"It was built in 1926. The style is called *collegiate Gothic*, appropriately enough." Jim led me toward an open door. Strains of fiddle and piano music grew louder as we approached. Jim took my hand and quickened his step.

"You love this, don't you?" I asked.

He smiled down at me and squeezed my hand. "You got that right. Doesn't hearing the music make you want to hurry in there and start dancing?"

Not really, but I wasn't going to pop his bubble. A minute later we were shedding our coats onto chairs forming a row around the edge of a high-ceilinged school gymnasium. On a stage at the end of the room, a fiddler and a man at a piano were playing next to a bass player. In front of them a woman in a pink dress spoke into a mike directing two lines of people.

"Shall we?" Jim gestured with his arm toward the end of the lines and grabbed my hand again.

"No time like the present." I took a deep breath and let myself be led onto the dance floor.

Forty-five minutes later the caller took a break, saying the instructional period was over. A white-haired man holding a banjo climbed the steps onto the stage.

"You did great," Jim said. He beamed at me, his forehead glistening, his eyes bright.

"I was starting to get the hang of it. And you're right. You get hot," I said, shedding my sweater. The newcomer session hadn't been half bad. The caller was patient and funny, and Jim had rescued me a couple of times, steering me in the right direction.

"Told you. You like the group?" he asked as he wiped his forehead with his right arm, and then un-buttoned his cuffs and started rolling up the sleeves.

"I love the music. Who are they?"

"They're called the Oldies But Goodies."

"They're great. Be right back." I left Jim chatting with two gray-haired women to go put my sweater with my coat. I turned back toward the floor and had taken a couple of steps when Tiffany Porter hurried toward the row of chairs. *Who knew so many people liked contra dancing?*

"Hi, Robbie," she said, slipping out of a green jacket. She wore her hair tied back in a band at the nape of her neck. From under the jacket emerged a blue sleeveless dress revealing slender and toned arms. Her muscular legs were bare above blue ankle socks and low-heeled shoes with a strap across the instep. "Haven't seen you here before. You like to contra?" She gazed at the floor, exuding the same restless eager feeling I'd picked up from Jim.

"It's my first time. I came with Jim Shermer."

"You're sure going to love it." Her eyes sparkled.

"I hope so. Hey, too bad about what Erica did to you," I said. "And too bad about Erica."

She stared at me, her nostrils flaring. "I never should have hired her. The woman is unscrupulous and manipulative."

I tilted my head. "You mean, was."

"What?" She looked puzzled.

"You didn't hear? Erica was killed sometime between when she left the party last night and this morning, when I found her on the floor of my store." I watched her.

Tiffany brought her hand to her mouth as her eyes widened. "You're kidding." She dropped her hand. "No, why would you be? That's awful."

"It is. I'm surprised you didn't hear it around town." If I wasn't mistaken, her surprise looked genuine.

She shook her head. "I spent all day with my dad here in Bloomington. He has dementia, and I try to spend Sundays with him. I'm all he has. Gee, poor Erica. I wonder who killed her?"

I lifted a shoulder and let it drop. "There's a state police detective on the case. Plus the local force, of course. I hope they figure it out soon."

"Erica was a jerk, but she didn't deserve to die. Do they know how she was killed?"

I shook my head to the plaintive notes of the

fiddle tuning up. As a tune started up, Tiffany turned her head toward the stage and smiled, then looked at me.

"Have a fun dance," she said. "I'm sorry, but us not dancing isn't going to bring Erica back." She sashayed into the center of the gym.

She didn't act like a murderer, not that I knew what acting like a killer was. I'd had contact with only one in my life, and it'd been only last month. I sincerely hoped it was the last time, too.

Chapter 9

I savored the last of my coffee at the desk in my living room the next morning. Jim had dropped me off after the dance. After I'd invited him in, he left, pleading an early morning meeting. Birdy purred from the corner of the desk and sunshine streamed in. Monday was my only day to sleep in and I took full advantage of the chance. Even though my internal clock tried really hard to wake me up at five thirty as always, I'd put a pillow over my head and managed two more hours. Now it was eight thirty and almost time for me to head down to Shamrock Hardware and order new glass for the door, and pick up a Christmas tree somewhere, too. I checked my email first. Nothing new from Roberto, and nothing else I needed to attend to. There wasn't anything I could do about Erica's death, and I hoped I could keep from brooding on it today. The online weather report was for an unseasonably warm day with temps that might even reach sixty. Warm air would get rid of the last of Saturday's light snow, and maybe I could get out for a long bike ride later.

I threw a jacket over my jeans and sweater, grabbed a tape measure, and headed into the store to measure the opening in the door. I stared at the plywood. I'd have to measure from the outside, so I let myself out the service door, making sure it locked behind me. When I came around the front, a green-and-white South Lick police car pulled up. Buck unfolded himself from the driver's seat and greeted me.

"How's the investigation going?" I asked.

He spread his hands. "Welp, it's underway. Octavia sent me over to tell you she's all done here. You can go ahead and reopen whenever you'd like." He removed the yellow tape.

"That's good news. Thanks for letting me know." Good thing the sign on the door already said I'd be open Tuesday.

"Not serving breakfast today, are you?" He cocked his head in a hopeful look. "I'm just a teensy bit hungry."

"You're always hungry, Buck." I laughed. "Sorry, not today. I'm never open on Mondays, remember? Anyway, I'm headed over to order replacement glass for the door."

"Good idea."

"Octavia said she brought Phil in for questioning yesterday." I set my hands on my hips. "You know Phil. He wouldn't hurt anybody."

"It was Octavia there who wanted to talk to him. You know we got to talk to everybody who might could've had a problem with Erica." A car drove by and Buck raised one finger in a wave.

"Who else are you questioning? Or rather, is Octavia questioning?"

"Of course the family. Paula and Max, and Mr. and Mrs. Berry," Buck said. "Octavia was looking for that Porter woman yesterday but couldn't find her."

"I saw Tiffany last night in Bloomington. She didn't even know Erica had been killed."

Buck studied me. "Or that's what she said, anywho." He took off his hat and rubbed the top of his head.

"She seemed completely surprised when I told her the news," I told him. "Said she hadn't heard because she'd been with her father in Bloomington all day."

"One thing you learn purt' darn quick in this here business, Robbie, is there's a whole slew of folks out there with gosh-awful-good acting skills."

"I suppose."

"Say, you going to make a gingerbread log cabin for the contest? We need a couple few more entries from South Lick."

"We?"

"Ah, shoot, they went and put me on the judging committee over there to Nashville. I guess my appetite's sort of legendary in the county, and judges get a special bag of gingerbread treats as a reward. We don't get to eat the houses themselves, of course."

"I don't know. I've never made a gingerbread house before. Sue and Paula were suggesting the same thing to me on Saturday."

"Deadline's next Saturday. You got all week, you know." He gave me a lopsided smile.

As if I didn't have anything else to do with my

week, and as if I hadn't recently found a body in my store. "I'll think about it."

"Okay, then." He put his hat back on. "It's back to the salt mines for me. You take care now, hear?"

"I'll do my best." I watched him drive away, did my measuring, then started to walk the few blocks to the hardware store. Was Buck right about Tiffany lying? If so, she was pretty good at it. She was athletic and, being taller than me, was definitely taller than the petite Erica, who couldn't have been more than five foot one and a hundred ten pounds dripping wet. Tiffany was certainly capable physically of whacking Erica on the head and moving her into my store. But why would she?

I greeted Don O'Neill where he stood behind the wide counter at the back of Shamrock Hardware. He was the owner of the traditional store, with its narrow rows packed with every imaginable item you might need to fix, maintain, or improve a building, inside and out. From screws to brooms to copper wire to paint to bird feeders, he stocked it all. The air smelled of old wood, grease, and turpentine, with a faint overlay of pesticide.

"How've you been, Don?"

"I'm well, thank you. Glad the business with Stella is gone by, God rest her soul," he said, his brown eyes looking a little worried, as always, his comb-over neatly in place today.

He must be glad, having been a suspect in the murder himself for a while.

"So what can I do for you today, Robbie? Abe

told me you had a problem over to your restaurant yesterday." The only things Don had in common with his handsome younger brother were those brown eyes and a kind heart.

Small-town news network again. I wasn't really surprised Abe knew what had gone on. "I sure did. Poor Erica is dead, and whoever did it broke the glass in my front door. Do you sell, I don't know, glass that doesn't break, or something thicker than the antique stuff I had?"

He shook his head. "Such a tragedy. But sure, we can order glass any thickness you want. Of course, any glass will break with enough force."

"I guess."

He peered at his computer screen, then turned it to show me the options. "This would be a good choice," he said, pointing. "You got the measurements?"

I looked at the description of the glass, then handed him the slip of paper where I'd written the size of the opening. He tapped in the numbers and showed me the price.

"Let's do it." I choked a little at the price, but that was the cost of owning a business. And I was doing well, at least so far. The stream of customers was steady, my expenses didn't outrun my income, and I was able to pay Danna a fair wage.

"It oughta be in about Wednesday. Thursday at the latest." He wrote out a slip. "You can pay Barb at the register."

"Thanks." I moved to the cash register and waited until the man in front of me walked toward the door. I said hello to Barb, a trim woman with spiky salt-and-pepper hair who always wore red lipstick and a big smile.

"Hey, there, Robbie. Too bad about Erica, ain't it?" She shook her head as she took the slip I handed her.

"I'll say." I handed her the credit card I used for all store purchases.

"I stopped by the Berry house last night with a green-bean covered dish, you know, with your cream of mushroom soup and your deep-fried onions," she said. "Took and brought them a sack of cookies, too. They seemed real appreciative."

"How sweet, Barb. I'll make something for them this afternoon. What do you think they'd want?"

"Well, bless your heart. I'm sure they'll be most grateful. I'd say comfort food, like. Maybe a meatloaf'd be good?" She extended the credit card slip for me to sign, creasing it down the middle so it wouldn't curl up. "Or one of them lasagnas."

"Sue and Glen must be wrecks losing Erica so soon after her coming home," I said. "And Paula? It has to be awful for her to lose her sister when she's pregnant."

"They're all shook up. Just setting around crying, mostly. Writing Erica's obit. Planning the funeral." She shook her head as she handed me my receipt, then studied me. "Say, you going to make up a gingerbread version of Pans 'N Pancakes?"

Geez. The whole town wanted me to enter the contest. "Everybody's been suggesting the same thing. I don't think I have time, though."

"At the least you should oughta go over and see them all set out next week. They're awful dang cute. I made one last year of this store and won second prize."

"So you're good with icing?"

"One of the best, if I do say so myself." She glanced behind me.

I twisted my head. A woman held a toddler's hand and juggled an armful of curtain rods.

"Sorry, I'll get out of your way." I stepped beyond the register. "Thanks, Barb. See you soon," I said.

"Sure thing," Barb answered. She peered over the counter, smiling. "Hey there, cute stuff."

The little boy hid behind his mom's legs. He was indeed a very cute thing. I stepped out into the sunshine and paused. I was starting to feel the itch to have kids myself, regardless of my uncommitted status. I didn't want to go through life single and without a couple of mini-Robbies to tell stories to, do puzzles with, guide along life's path. I'd been so close with my mom I couldn't imagine not being mom to at least one child. It'd be better to have a sweet reliable man in my life to share the parenting with, though. And maybe, just maybe, Jim was going to turn out to be the one.

I smiled to myself and headed off to the small grocery around the corner. Spending an hour making meatloaf and scalloped potatoes to give away seemed like a worthwhile use of my day off, after I cut a tree, of course. Maybe I'd pick up gingerbread house ingredients, too.

* * *

An hour later, I turned onto Greasy Creek Road and parked my van at Wise Hollow Christmas Tree Farm. Too bad I couldn't combine a bike ride with picking up greenery, but unless I got a wheeled cart to lug behind my cycle, there was no way I could strap a tree to the back of my bike. I giggled picturing the sight.

The store wasn't much more than a lean-to in front of rows of Christmas trees stretching down a gentle slope as far as I could see, with a band of woods on the left edge. Wreaths and garlands were set up on stands and also lay in stacks on the covered porch. The tang of fresh-cut pine plopped me directly into the Christmas spirit. A tree was really going to make the store look festive, especially if I put it in the front window. And maybe it would take customers' minds off murder.

A woman emerged from the store holding a wreath. "Howdy, there. Was you wanting a tree?" She laid the wreath on the pile with thick, weathered hands. Her cheeks looked reddened from working outdoors and her blue canvas jacket had been mended with duct tape.

"Yes, I would. And some greens and a couple of wreaths, too."

"We got all that, as you can see. And you can cut your own tree." She pointed at several two-foot bow saws leaning against the porch and then gestured out at the trees. "Pick any old tree, don't matter which." She looked me up and down. "You look purt' strong, but give me a holler if you need help hauling the tree on up here."

"Thanks, I will." I didn't own a stand, but I was sure Shamrock would have more than one model in stock. I could always leave the tree in a bucket of water for a few days until I got a stand. I grabbed the curved handle of the saw, which did look like a hunter's bow, with the blade being the string, and headed down the path between two rows of trees. The trees seemed to be different types, some with almost blue needles, some greener, some bushy and thick, some more sparse. I didn't have any experience with kinds of Christmas trees. In Santa Barbara, we decorated the giant ficus in the living room instead of buying a cut tree. My mom's choice, not mine, but I got used to it. I looked for tags identifying the tree varieties but didn't see any. I didn't spy any workers or even other folks browsing the trees, either. Cotton-ball clouds floated lazily above in the sunny sky, and from the woods came the loud rapping of a pileated woodpecker.

I could use a tall tree, since the stamped tin ceiling of the store was pretty high. But I also didn't want to crowd out any of the tables. Even a medium-sized tree would look festive. I wandered down one row, cut through to another, and kept going. After reaching out and stroking branches as I walked, I decided I wanted a variety with softer needles, and searched for the perfect shape.

"Perfect tree, where are you?" I called out, since I was pretty sure nobody else was around to hear me. As I ran my hand over a branch of the tree next to me, something rustled nearby. *Uh-oh*. Maybe there was another tree customer out here who'd heard me talking to inanimate objects. I glanced behind me but saw only trees. I stepped into the next row. Same result. Then I heard the rustling again.

I froze, my heart thudding. Despite this pretty weather, there was a murderer out here somewhere, a killer who'd broken into my store. What if they'd followed me? What if they thought I knew something? Kill once, kill twice, what's the difference? At least I held a big lethal weapon in my now-sweaty hand. Would I be able to use it? At five feet four I was shorter than most other adults, although I was strong from all my carpentry work and my cycling.

The heck with finding the perfect tree. I turned in the direction of the store and safety, trying to walk without making any noise, avoiding stray branches on the ground. I was hurrying as fast as I could without actually breaking into a run when there was another rustle the next row over. I brought the saw up in front of me with extended arms, trying without success to keep them from trembling. A branch cracked.

Abe stepped out a yard in front of me. I let out a yell.

"Boo!" he said with a big grin, his dimple creasing his cheek.

I swore. I dropped my arms and the saw, too. "Geez, Abe. You scared the life out of me." I let out a big breath and patted my chest with one hand. "I thought Erica's killer was out here stalking me. You're lucky I didn't swing the saw at you."

He held up both palms. "Sorry to scare you, Robbie. I sure didn't mean to. I saw your van here and thought I'd see if you needed any help with your tree. Which I guess you haven't cut yet."

"You scared me, all right, but I'm glad it's you and not someone with worse intentions. There is an unsolved murder in town, you realize."

His expression sobered. "True. I should have thought of that."

"Don't worry about it." I picked up the saw. "You're looking for a tree, too?"

"Yep. I always get one for my grandma. Just a small little bitty one, that's all she has room for. She's in assisted living."

"Aw, how sweet." I gazed at him. What a nice guy. I glanced around. "Hey, there it is." I pointed.

"There what is?"

"My perfect tree." And it was. About eight feet tall, of the variety I liked, with a classic cone shape. I strode over and knelt, bringing the saw to the trunk.

"Want me to cut it for you?" Abe asked.

I laughed. "Thanks, but I'm good. I'm a carpenter, remember?"

"*Doh.* Of course."

"But you can hang onto the top, if you would, to make sure the trunk doesn't bind." The saw went through like butter. Abe kept the tree upright so the blade didn't get stuck in the last inch, and a moment later I was standing next to my brand-new Christmas tree.

"Let me help you walk it back, at least," he said.

"Cool. You take the trunk, I'll keep the rest of it off the ground." We headed toward the store side by side, with me gripping the slender trunk near the top. "You don't work today, then?"

"Nope. I was on yesterday. You know, there's always weekend work with an electric company." He cast me a sideways look. "Terrible news about Erica."

"It is. For her, for the whole family."

"And for you, having to find her," Abe said in a sympathetic voice.

"Thank you."

"Do they have any leads?"

"No. Buck told me the detective is talking to anyone who might have had a problem with Erica."

"Hope they reserved an auditorium." Abe whistled. "I went to high school with Erica. She was always picking up a boy and then dropping him, and she backstabbed any girl who came near her. Who didn't have a problem with Erica?"

make it seem homey? I grabbed one of the store's blue-and-white-striped dishtowels and spread it over the box, setting an antique cookbook on top. There. It definitely no longer looked like a murder scene.

I took a minute to clean and rearrange the cook-ware wall, too, covering the spot where the sandwich press had hung and wiping off all the new finger-print powder. As I did, I noticed something on the floor glinting in the light. I reached for the object, which was nearly hidden behind an old metal bread box, and straightened, examining it in my palm. The thing was a small brass-colored metal stick about as long as my pinky, with a little bump at the end. I picked it up with my other hand and saw it was really two things joined by a kind of hinge at their broad, flat ends so you could fold them together or extend one or the other. It looked like a tool, but I'd never seen anything like it. And I sure didn't have the slightest idea where it'd come from, or how it got on my floor. It could be anybody's. I wasn't the only person who'd walked around this area.

Or maybe the killer had dropped it. I stared at it and shook my head. This little thing couldn't have made a wound on Erica's head. My imagination was getting away from me. But I needed to let the police know about it, regardless. They could figure out if it was important. I slid the object into my front pocket and retrieved my phone from the back pocket.

First, I called Octavia's number but she didn't pick up. Rather than leave a vague message, I called the South Lick police, instead. After I was con-nected with the department and identified myself, I said, "I found an object not far from where a body was discovered here yesterday." I heard rustling and voices in the background.

"Excuse me, what's that you said?" the dispatcher asked. "You found a body?" The connection made her voice both tinny and rasping, and she wasn't one of the dispatchers I'd talked to before.

"Yes, but that was yesterday. I said I found an unfamiliar object." I found myself slowing and raising my voice like certain people did when they addressed someone not fluent in English. "I just wanted to let the detective know."

"Is it the murder weapon?"

"I don't think so. Please let her know I have it, will you?"

I was answered with more voices in the background, a beeping, a different tinny sound, and more rustling.

"Sure, sure. Will do. Thank you, Ms. Jordan." The dispatcher hung up abruptly.

My responsibility discharged for reporting something that probably wasn't even related to the murder, now it was time to get cooking for the Berrys. Normally I did personal cooking in my own kitchen, but today I decided to use the commercial kitchen. My own space was too small to really spread out in. After I switched on the oven, I minced an onion. I took out a bowl and used one hand to mush together the ground beef and ground lamb with some oatmeal, an egg, half a jar of salsa, and the onions. Easy peasy. I pressed it into a disposable aluminum loaf pan so the Berrys wouldn't have to worry about returning it, covered the top with ketchup, and slid it into the oven to bake.

As I scrubbed potatoes, I thought about what Abe had said about Erica. He'd made it sound like she was disliked by everyone in the high school. Jim hadn't said anything about going to school with Erica. Maybe his family had already moved to Chicago by then. I knew his parents lived there now. All I had to do was call him. But cheese-scalloped potatoes came first.

I sliced the potatoes thinly and buttered another aluminum pan, this one flat and rectangular. I layered in half the slices. I minced another half onion and sautéed it in butter, then stirred in flour. I was adding the milk bit by bit to make a cream sauce when the front door opened, the cowbell jangling like an alarm. I must not have locked it again after I came in from hanging the wreaths. I whipped my head over to see Phil holding two flat, covered pans. *Whew.* But it was stupid of me not to have locked the door.

"Phil, I'm glad to see you. And the brownies. Come on in. I'm making a cream sauce so I have to keep stirring." Phil baked all the desserts for the restaurant lunches, including a killer brownie. *Oops. Bad choice of words.*

Phil didn't look his usual bright self. He set the pans down on a table and leaned his arms on the counter facing me.

"Are you all right?" I asked.

"Sometimes the world just gets me down. First Erica slurs me, and then they suspect me of killing her."

"Adele told me the detective had you in for questioning."

"The esteemed Detective Slade. Same questions,

over and over. Did anybody see you leave? No. Can anyone vouch for your whereabouts between midnight and five a.m.? No. Did you kill Erica Shermer and leave her body in the store? No. And on and on."

"I'm so sorry you had to go through that." I stirred grated sharp cheddar into the sauce, then poured half of it over the first layer of potatoes, smoothing it with a spatula. "They must not have any evidence against you or they wouldn't have let you go, right?"

"Right."

I sprinkled chopped green onions on top, then layered on the rest of the potatoes, topped it with the rest of the sauce, and sprinkled some more cheese on top. I slid it in the oven, set the timer, and glanced up at Phil, who gazed at the oven with longing written all over his face.

"Are you drooling?" I asked with a laugh.

"That looked so, so good."

"Unfortunately, I'm making it to take to the Berry family. Got a meatloaf in there, too. But I can make us sandwiches."

Phil whistled, his usual enthusiasm for life returning. "I haven't eaten since yesterday morning, I think. But seeing you put the dish together suddenly made me ravenous." He pulled up a chair and straddled it, facing me while I worked.

"I'm hungry, too, and it's noon, after all." I fired up the griddle. As I sliced cheese, I said, "So everybody is urging me to enter the Nashville Gingerbread Log Cabin Competition. What do you think? Should I?"

"Make a gingerbread Pans 'N Pancakes? What a totally awesome idea. Want me to help?"

"Would you? I can bake the walls tonight, but I'll need some help assembling it. All the parts have to be edible."

Phil rubbed his hands together. "We can make the rocking chairs on the front porch out of black licorice."

"And a pickle barrel out of something, with green mini jelly beans in it."

"You could have a person in the doorway holding a take-out sack of biscuits. Made of real tiny biscuits." His eyes gleamed. "We'll have to make a template for the walls and roof. Got some paper?"

"Of course. Over in the desk drawer. The base can be no bigger than eighteen inches square, but the house should be smaller, of course." I watched as he brought paper, ruler, scissors, and a pencil to a table and bent over it. "The cabins are due Saturday. Think it will be too late to assemble it on Friday night?" I flipped the sandwiches.

"Should be okay. Gives us time to get stuff together, candy and whatnot. I went to the display of all the entries last year. I have some ideas."

A few minutes later I set two plates of grilled ham and cheese on the table, with a pickle next to each sandwich. Pickles from a jar in the walk-in, not ones from the confiscated barrel. Octavia had insisted those be trashed, since they might have been contaminated. Which had made my stomach roil again.

Phil pushed the patterns toward me. "See? I've

got the front porch overhang and everything." He pointed to a set of shapes he'd cut out.

I leaned over and checked them out. "I love it. Exactly the right size, too." I sank into a chair.

Phil bit into his sandwich. "*Mmmm*," he murmured as he chewed.

I picked up mine and then laid it down again.

"What's wrong?" Phil asked.

"Grilled sandwiches. Yesterday morning I realized my sandwich press was missing from the wall over there." I pointed.

Phil swiped a thread of cheese off his cheek. "So?"

"It's heavy. It has long handles. I'm afraid it was used to bash in Erica's head. And these sandwiches reminded me of it."

"Ick." He made a face.

"Agree." I took a deep breath and let it out. "This whole mess is like trying to work a crossword and having only half the clues. And it's not even my puzzle to work."

By one o'clock the food was cooling in the walk-in and I wore my medium-cold-weather riding clothes: long-sleeved jersey in hot pink with a wicking shirt under it, good gloves, and calf-length riding pants. It was about fifty-five degrees and the sun still shone, but cycling created its own wind chill. I promised Birdy I'd play with him when I got back. He'd probably be snoozing in a patch of sunlight outside the whole time I was gone, or doing whatever kitties do.

After I popped my phone into the back pocket of

the shirt, and added a twenty-dollar bill and my house key, I clicked my helmet onto my head and my shoes into the pedals, and headed out on the road to Beanblossom, a small town north of Nashville. I could pop in at Adele's farm and touch base, then do a loop out to Gnaw Bone and back through Nashville.

I wanted a good couple of hours of hard cycling. Lucky for me, it was hilly around here, and half the trip would be pumping uphill. This was not the Midwest most people imagined, with its flat plains of grain. Northern Indiana was certainly mostly flat. But lore had it the glacier had stopped moving southward at Martinsville, a small city south of Indianapolis, so the weight of the massive ice river hadn't flattened out the hills in the bottom third of the state. Which was fine with me. My Santa Barbara upbringing always had the backdrop of the Santa Ynez mountain range rising up to the east behind the city, and the world wouldn't seem right without contrast on the horizon.

It took me about thirty minutes to arrive at the gravel road leading to Adele's sheep farm. I bumped slowly along the edge of the road so my wheels wouldn't catch in a rut. Listening to the drone of a small plane in the distance, I inhaled fresh clean air. The woods opened up to an iconic vista of a gentle sloping pasture dotted by rocks in the foreground and sheep in the distance. As I neared the cottage and modest barn behind, I spied Adele in the kitchen garden next to the house.

"Yoo-hoo," I called out, climbing off my cycle. I

leaned it against her old Nissan pickup, unclipped my water bottle, and clomped over to the garden.

Adele straightened, a length of white material in her hand, a Colts cap shading her eyes. "Hey howdy, favorite niece."

"I thought I was your only niece." I kissed her soft cheek before stretching my arms to the sky, my muscles warmed and energized by the ride.

"Yep." She stretched the word out into two syllables, one going down and the next going up. "And you are. Out for a ride on the last nice day of fall?"

Sloopy trotted up and gave me a friendly bark.

"I hope it's not the last one." I leaned down and petted his head. "Hey, Sloops."

"Might could be. And it's why I'm covering up my greens." She gestured to a row of plants with half hoops of wire stuck in above them every foot or so. "I put this row cover over and it keeps them a tad warmer. Like tucking them into bed. Won't do anything once it gets real cold, but I'll have eaten them all by then."

"Good idea." I took a swig of water.

"What are you up to this fine day?" she asked.

"I just thought I'd ride over and say hi. And tell you the detective said I can go ahead and reopen tomorrow."

Adele pursed her lips. "I don't like this business at all. It was plain wrong of that Octavia to haul poor Phil in there yesterday. Good thing Samuel's on the ball. He called up a lawyer who got the boy out in a flash."

"Samuel's not here?"

"No. I don't know where he's at today. Probably

off with those Bible buddies of his. He sure takes studying scripture serious." She spread her hands. "Not my personal idea of a fun retirement, but he likes it. And if there's one thing you learn about falling in love with somebody at our age, you gotta accept the other person, warts, weird hobbies, and all."

I nodded. "Probably wise advice for any age."

"You bet. Now, can I get you a snack or anything?"

"No, but I'd take a refill on my water." I followed her into the kitchen, which—as it often did—smelled alluringly like a bakery.

"Got fresh bread." Adele pointed to a loaf sitting on a board on the table.

"Apparently. I can't turn down a slice of your bread, can I?" I filled my water bottle and sat at the table as Adele sliced and buttered a thick slab for me.

"Did the detective say anything else about finding the murderer?" she asked.

I held my hand in front of my mouth. "I didn't talk to her," I mumbled around a mouthful of chewy, crunchy, yeasty bread, my favorite kind. I swallowed. "Buck came over to take down the yellow police tape and told me I could reopen. I only hope I don't lose customers tomorrow because a body was found in the store. I can see how that might freak people out."

"Don't worry your head. We'll fix it if the time comes."

"I heard Erica had plenty of enemies. Or at least people she rubbed the wrong way."

Adele tapped the table with a gnarled finger. "I might have heard tell about that, myself."

"Jim and I were wondering if someone from her life in Chicago might have snuck into town and killed her. You haven't seen any strangers around South Lick, have you? It's not tourist season anymore." The fall leaf-peeping season was huge around here, but all the leaves had lost their color and hit the ground by now.

"Can't say I have."

"I don't know why they'd leave her in my store, though." I shook my head. "Well, I don't know why anybody left her there, no matter where they came from."

"Trying to remove suspicion from themselves, I'd wager."

I finished the last bite of bread. "I'd better go work off these calories. Thanks, Adele." I stood.

She stood too, handing me my water bottle and then pulling me in for a hug. "Love you, honey."

"Love you, too." I clomped out and mounted my wheeled steed. I rode off not seeing the pasture, the fence, or the fat, furry sheep now crowding behind it next to the road. All I saw was my broken door, Erica's body, and the blank spot on my wall of cookware.

Chapter 11

Holding my covered aluminum pans full of food, I rang the doorbell of the Berry home at a few minutes past four thirty. I'd had exactly the long ride I'd wanted, and taken a quick shower before driving over here.

The couple lived on the other side of town, on Beanblossom Road, and I realized I'd ridden past it this afternoon. The house was a well-maintained single-story house with a sun-room between the house and the attached garage at the left side. I knew Glen owned a couple of liquor stores in the county, and it appeared he was doing pretty well, judging by the fresh paint and what looked like a professionally landscaped yard. The front door sported a huge fresh wreath. Pinecones and gold ribbons wove through it, with orangey-red bunches of bittersweet berries popping out here and there. The day was still mild, but with only an hour until sunset, the sun had already sunk behind a band of tall trees across the road.

A pale, slight man with thin, reddish hair opened

the door. "Can I help you?" His right hand tapped his leg with a fast flutter.

"I'm Robbie Jordan, a friend of the family, and I brought food."

"Okay." He held out his arms.

"Um, I'd like to come in and pay my respects." I tried to peer past him. Maybe the family was too upset by Erica's death and had asked him to play gatekeeper.

Max loomed behind the man. "Who is it, Vince? Oh, Robbie. Come on the heck in."

"But I thought . . ." The man's voice trailed off.

"It's fine, Vince." Max, who towered over the man, put his hand on the door above Vince's head and pulled it open wide.

Vince backed up until he bumped into Max. "Sorry." He scurried out of the way.

"Robbie, this is Erica and Jon's friend, Vincent Pytzynska, down from Chicago. Vince, Robbie." Max moved to the side.

"Nice to meet you, Vince. I'm sorry it's under such sad circumstances." I stepped into the front hall. *From Chicago*. When had he arrived?

Vince stuck out his hand and I extended my right hand under the pans to shake it. He had a remarkably strong grip for someone so thin and nervous. "Likewise," he said. "When I heard about poor Erica, I just had to come down. Jon and I were good friends, and now they're both gone." His voice shook a little as he talked.

"I won't stay long, but I wanted to deliver some food, and my sympathies to Sue and Glen," I said, gazing up at Max. "And to Paula, of course. To all of you."

"Good of you," Max said in a somber tone.

"How's Paula doing?" I asked. "Being pregnant and all."

His eyes softened. "My wife is beside herself with grief, but the baby seems fine. She hasn't gone into early labor or anything like that."

"Paula slept over at Erica's house, right? Did she say if she heard Erica leave the night of . . ." What was I doing, bringing up the murder? I inwardly scolded myself.

Max shook his head, fast. "Paula's a very sound sleeper. She doesn't hear a thing all night." He turned. "Follow me."

Vince stood back. "After you."

The three of us walked single file down a hall wallpapered in a floral print. Max paused at a door open to a room with a neatly made double bed and a crib in the corner.

"Look," Max said softly, pointing. "The guest room here is all ready for our baby."

I wasn't sure what to say, and Vince cleared his throat behind me.

"Sorry." Max laughed. "I can't wait to be a daddy." He turned back to the hall.

This side of Max was very different from the irate husband and brother-in-law I'd seen on Saturday. Good for him for wanting to be a father. I hoped he'd be able to keep a handle on his temper once the baby arrived.

In a minute we emerged into a big kitchen with a family room beyond. The kitchen island was full of dishes covered with plastic wrap and two half-demolished platters of cold cuts and breads. Three walls of windows showed leafless trees at the back border of a neat lawn, with a rectangular fenced-in vegetable garden to one side. Sue sat in the middle of a long sofa with an arm over Paula's shoulder, and Glen paced back and forth in front of the back wall holding a small glass of something amber-colored. He whirled when I walked in, then hurried toward me.

"Robbie. Thank you for coming by." Glen patted my shoulder.

"I brought meatloaf and scalloped potatoes." I glanced around until Max shoved something over to make room for the pans on the island. I set the pans down and took Glen's hand in both of mine. "I'm so sorry, Glen."

He squeezed my hand. "You found our Erica, didn't you?" His mouth turned down under haunted eyes.

"Yes, I did." Sue and Paula gazed at me, too. I swallowed. Several fat, lit candles sat on a hutch in the dining room. Their scent was cloying and threatened to close up my throat. I couldn't stand scented candles, and these exuded a thick, fruity aroma mixed with sandalwood. "I did find her, and wish I hadn't. I mean, I wish she were still alive."

"She was my baby." Glen dropped his hand, his eyes welling.

Max took Glen gently by the shoulders and led him to an overstuffed easy chair.

"Come on and sit down, hon," Sue called to me from the sofa, patting the seat on the other side of her. "And bless your heart for bringing us some comfort."

"I don't want to bother you all."

"I insist," Sue said with a wan smile.

I obliged. As the one who'd first seen Erica dead, it wasn't exactly comfortable to be in the company of her family, but I'd brought it on myself by coming over. I hadn't planned on staying longer than it took to extend my sympathies.

"Can we get you something to drink? A can of pop, or a glass of wine?" Sue asked, patting my knee.

"No, thanks." *Pop* was another localism, what we'd called *soda* in California.

Paula didn't smile at all. She glared at me with red-rimmed eyes. Vince remained standing in the kitchen, rearranging the things on the island with quick little moves.

"Now," Sue said, "please tell me our Erica didn't look like she'd suffered." She tilted her head with pleading eyes.

I took a deep breath. "No, she looked peaceful." What was I supposed to say? That she'd appeared anything but? That her eyes were open, her body grotesque, her expression one of terror?

Paula held a hand out toward Max. "Help me up, babe, would you?"

In three steps he was in front of her, holding out his hand to her. After she stood, he put a protective arm around her waist and stroked her belly with his other hand, a tender look on his face.

She flung off his hand. She glowered at me. "For all we know, you killed her yourself."

Chapter 12

Sue gasped. I opened my mouth, then shut it, having no idea what to do or say. I blinked and stood. It seemed Paula and Max had exchanged roles.

"Now, hon, don't you be talking nonsense," Sue said, tugging at Paula's hand. "Robbie here wouldn't hurt our Erica. Sit on down, now."

"No, Mama. I mean it. All this stuff about somebody breaking in. It was Robbie's store. She could have broken the glass herself."

I shook my head. "I should go."

"Hang on a sec, Robbie," Glen said, standing and holding up his hand. "Paulie, she wouldn't have any reason to do away with Erica. She didn't even know her."

"Well, who would?" Paula's voice turned into a wail. "Who'd kill my little sister?" After she turned, sobbing, into Max's chest, he led her out of the room.

Sue and Glen exchanged a glance at the sound of a door clicking shut down the hall. "Robbie, we're so sorry. We ain't holding up too well, none of us," Sue said.

"But that's the question, isn't it?" Vince spoke up. "Who would have wanted Erica dead?"

Glen sank down on a stool at the island and set his forehead in his hand. He glanced up, rubbing his hand all the way over his head, landing it on his neck. "Fact is, our girl made a lot of waves in this world, and they weren't nice smooth ones, either. She sure had a knack of rubbing folks the wrong way. Right, Sue?"

"Right." Sue's eyes were drawn down at their outer edges. "I don't know what I done wrong raising her up. Paulie ain't that way. Even as a little girl, Erica would say things to hurt people's feelings, bless her heart. She'd manipulate situations so it was always somebody else's fault, and she didn't hold back none getting the news out. You must have seen her in action, Vince, being friends with her and Jon up there in Chicago."

"I did." Vince took one of the stools, too. He jiggled his knee up and down with a fast movement.

"And then in high school, whoo boy. That girl made trouble like nobody's business." Sue shook her head. "We thought, once she met Jon and married him, she'd smooth out, like. He was such a calm, sweet man." She glanced at me. "Like his brother, Jim."

"She didn't seem so smooth to me," Vince said. "I was friends with Jon, you know. We worked in the same firm. But I'd go out with them sometimes. Erica was so smart, and so pretty. Jon was her slave, really. He adored her."

"We were so proud of her getting her master's degree in design up there," Glen said, a wistful note in his voice.

"She worked hard at it. But, well . . . I don't want to speak ill of the dead." Vince gazed at the floor.

But you're going to anyway, I thought. The phrase invariably led to a negative comment about the deceased.

"Go ahead," Glen urged.

"I'm afraid she flirted with me. All the time," Vince said. "I could see it hurt Jon, so I pretty much stopped seeing them as a couple. I'd get a beer with Jon once in a while after work, but I didn't want to go near Erica."

I watched Vince as he fidgeted. Why had he come down here after her death, then, if he didn't even like Erica? It was a five-hour drive and he must have had to take time off from work.

"We're awful glad you came down to pay your respects, anyway, Vince," Sue said. "You're the only person we're aware of who knew her up there."

"Jim told me his parents wanted to come down, but his mom isn't well enough," I said.

Sue pushed her lips out. "I meant besides the Shermers. They called us, Robbie, and expressed their sympathies. She was their daughter-in-law, after all."

"Do you think someone from her past, like from high school, still held a grudge against Erica?" I asked.

Glen spread his hands. "It's possible. South Lick is a pretty small town. I guess I'd better let the lady detective know about Erica's ways."

* * *

I flipped on the Christmas lights in the store once I got home, a little past sunset. Their twinkling spots of cheer lightened my mood after my very unsettling visit. Paula accusing me of killing Erica. The odd, jittery Vince. Erica's own parents saying how difficult she was.

Shaking it off, I got busy prepping for tomorrow. First up, assemble the gingerbread dough, so it could chill for a couple of hours before I baked it. After I scrubbed my hands and pulled on an apron, I mixed up the stiff dough, marveling at the small quantities necessary to make only a single recipe. I wasn't used to cooking regular portions anymore. I set it in the cooler, then measured out the flour for the biscuits, half whole wheat and half unbleached white, into my big stainless bowl, mixing in baking powder and salt. I sliced butter into the mix with the oversized vintage pastry cutter, pressing the U-shaped wires down again and again until the flour was the texture of coarse meal. Why would Paula have thought I might have murdered Erica? I didn't have a reason in the world to kill her. To kill anybody, for that matter.

Making a well in the flour, I cracked in eggs and stirred them with a fork before adding milk and grated cheddar. And then there was Vince. He said himself he didn't care for Erica and had stopped spending time with her. So why drive all the way from Chicago after she was killed? It didn't seem like he knew Sue and Glen previously. *Wait.* Jim had described someone like Vince from Jon and Erica's wedding, so he'd at least met the family.

I floured the big marble pastry slab and kneaded the dough only enough to bring it all together, then slid it into a clean plastic bag, sealed it, and set it in the walk-in cooler. I carried out two heads of cabbage, one green and one purple, and a bag of carrots to make a fresh batch of coleslaw for tomorrow's lunch crowd. As I trimmed the carrots and peeled them one by one, I wondered if Octavia would check out Erica's history back to her high school days. Abe's story about how Erica treated people absolutely jibed with Sue and Glen's.

I chopped the cabbage into chunks and fitted the grater attachment onto the industrial-sized food processor. I fed the carrots in, switched to the slicing plate, and stuffed in the cabbage, watching the satisfying process of a machine shredding it all in seconds instead of me chopping it for half an hour. After scooping the mix out into a wide bowl, I assembled the dressing, adding the dollop of prepared horseradish key to the flavor of the dish. Hands were the best way to combine it all, so I scrubbed my hands again, then pushed up my sleeves, poured the dressing on, and dug both hands into the cool, mayonnaisey mix of slaw bits.

My cell rang in my bag where I'd dropped it on the desk. Naturally, someone chose this very minute to call me. I debated for only a moment whether I should rush to wipe my hands off and answer it. *Nah.* If it was important, whoever it was would leave a message. Or better, text me. I scooped and tossed the salad until it was evenly coated, wishing the puzzle of who killed Erica was so easily dealt with.

After I covered the slaw and carried it into the walk-in, I checked the wire shelves. Bacon and sausage for the morning? Check. Gallons of orange juice? Yes. I knew I had plenty of syrup, and the gravy I'd made for yesterday would still be good, both the meat gravy and the version I offered with a base of miso for vegetarians like Jim. I had fruit for the fruit salad Danna would prepare as soon as she got in tomorrow. I shivered from the cold, but kept visualizing the menu. I'd grate potatoes for hash browns in the morning. What about lunch? I had lettuce, pre-sliced cheese, veggie burger patties. . . . My eyes widened. I'd forgotten to order more meat for the burgers. And it had to be at least six o'clock by now, so I couldn't call the supplier.

I hurried out and clicked the heavy door shut after me. My stomach complained bitterly of emptiness. I'd had only a quick protein bar after my ride, and it'd been a while since my sandwich with Phil, but I made myself turn on the digital tablet and bring up the restaurant inventory app before I let myself find dinner. With such short notice, I decided to order both pre-formed beef and turkey patties as well as the five-pound amounts I usually bought, and prayed the supplier would be able to deliver tomorrow. I preferred to form the patties myself, adding my special herb mix to the meat, which came from a local farm. Was there anything else I needed to order? I tapped in an order for a few dozen buns, just to be sure, and added a half-dozen avocados. They always arrived rock hard and needed time to ripen for next weekend's brunch offerings. I added a rush request for delivery by eleven the next morning, even though they'd charge me extra for it. One of these days I'd get more organized.

The ordering done, I wiped down the counters and cleaned everything I'd used, then I grabbed my bag and headed into my apartment. I decided to keep the holiday lights on all night. They looked so pretty and festive, and they might signal to the town things were back to normal at Pans 'N Pancakes.

"Hey, Birdy," I said to my little, uncomplicated friend. He ran to his empty food dish, and then wove through my legs, mewing his request: *Please give me my dinner, already.* I scooped his food into his dish and made sure he had clean water.

But what was I going to have for dinner? I pulled open the fridge to see pretty slim pickings. The older coleslaw. A carton of eggs. The dregs of a jar of pesto. Half a container of goat cheese. And a loaf of sourdough bread. The chef didn't seem to be taking very good care of herself on the home front. I rubbed my forehead. It was hard to manage a restaurant and a half-decent personal life, too. I pulled it all out and resolved to go to the grocery store tomorrow afternoon.

One pesto-goat-cheese-omelet with toast and coleslaw later, I sipped a glass of Pinot Grigio and played with Birdy. I swung a toy mouse I'd hung on a string from a dowel, like a fishing rod. Birdy watched it, then sprang up over and over trying to catch the mouse, which I kept just out of reach. When he grew tired of the game, I pulled out my phone. The image of Vince kept jumping into my brain just like Birdy's leaps, and I wanted to know more about him. Max had told me his last name, and as I recalled it was something like *Pitsinski*. I started searching, but it definitely wasn't that spelling, so I started subbing in other likely vowels and consonants. I'd entered Vincent Pytzynski Chicago when Google asked me if I meant Pytzynska. *Aha.*

I peered at the results. There was the law firm. There was him announced as Jon's best man at the wedding. There was . . . *what?* I tapped the link. Vince had attended Brown County High School, only five miles from here, and had been president of the math club. So he wasn't from Chicago, after all. And might well have known Erica, since South Lick High and Brown County played each other in sports and often combined other activities like dances and projects. *Now wasn't that interesting?* Ms. Detective Octavia Slade might want to know this particular piece of information.

I headed back into the restaurant to bake the gingerbread walls. I'd read they needed to dry out for a couple of days before being assembled and decorated. I preheated the oven and rolled out the dough, then placed Phil's templates on top, carefully cutting around them. After setting the timer for eight minutes, I wandered around the store tidying up the shelves, humming "The First Noel," doing my best to simply be present in the moment.

Twenty minutes later, the gingerbread sat cooling on a rack under a light dishtowel, and I sat curled up on the couch in my apartment with a book of Sudoku puzzles, Birdy purring at my feet. I usually whizzed through Sudoku, except right now my focus was shot. I'd called Octavia and left a message, telling her what I knew about Vince. I told her I didn't know if he was staying with the Berrys or not, and I spelled his name in the message. He was an odd dude. I didn't know why he would have murdered Erica, but anything was possible.

The little light in the corner of the phone pulsed at me: the call that had come in while I was making coleslaw. After I checked and saw it'd been Jim, I called him back.

"Hey," I said.

"Hey, yourself. Called you earlier."

"I know, I'm sorry. I was literally up to my elbows mixing up coleslaw, and then I forgot to check my phone until right now. What's up?"

"I was going to ask you over for a fancy omelet dinner. But I got too hungry and ate alone."

I laughed. "I had exactly the same dinner. Also alone."

"How was your day?"

"Pretty interesting." I yawned. "And full." I told him what I'd learned about Erica. "But you must have known all those details already. That she was difficult?"

"Some of it. I didn't know about when she was a teenager, though. I always say I grew up here, but we moved to Chicago before I started high school. As I told you, I didn't make the trip up to spend much time with Jon and Erica after I moved back here five years ago. I was too busy getting my practice going."

His voice grew soft. "Now I can't spend time with either of them."

"I know what you mean. After my mom died with no warning while I was already living in Indiana, I wished I'd gone back to visit more often. But we can't change the past."

He fell silent. Finally he said, "What's the rest of your week look like?"

"The usual. Breakfast and lunch for the town. At least I hope customers will show up and not stay away because they're freaked out I found a dead body on the floor."

"I'll see what I can do to talk it up. I'll be in Nashville all day tomorrow, though, and I have a closing at six. Hey, did the Berrys say anything about a service for Erica?"

"No, they didn't. Jim, remember you mentioned meeting a friend of Jon's at the wedding, the pale nervous one? Was his name Vincent?"

"Right. How did you know?"

"He came down today to pay his respects, or at least that's what Sue said. He was there at the house this afternoon."

"Good of him," Jim said.

"I keep thinking about him. He acts really odd. Anyway, I Googled him. One article said he went to Brown County High School. He might have known Erica here."

"He never mentioned it at the wedding. But I didn't spend much time talking with him."

"I left a message about him for Octavia. In case she wants to check him out." There, an opening for him to tell me the rest of the story of how he knew Octavia.

"You're thinking this Vincent might have killed Erica?" Jim asked.

Opening ignored. "I don't know. What if Erica wronged him and he held a grudge all these years? Who knows if he arrived today like he said—"

"Or came down Saturday? It seems a little far-fetched, Robbie."

"Not as far-fetched as Paula accusing me of murdering Erica."

"That's crazy. She did, really?" he asked.

"Yep." I yawned again. "Listen, I have an early day tomorrow. Let's have dinner later in the week, okay?"

"I'd like that." His voice lowered to a sexy rasp. "I think about you all the time, you know."

"Same here, Jim. Same here." I laughed. But did I think about him all the time? Not really.

"Good night, then."

I said good night and disconnected. Jim was a really great guy. He was smart, fun to be with, sexy. And he cared about me. A lot. I liked him, too, also a lot. But I didn't think about him all the time. Sometimes, sure. Was that going to be enough? I frowned and blew out a breath. Was I getting cold feet? I supposed I was still protecting myself from being dropped. When my mistake of a husband, Will, had abruptly left me for a hot California fighter pilot, I'd felt burned by more than jet fuel. My heart had a big sear mark on it and the scar was still tender. And yet I yearned for love, and Jim was a perfect candidate. Intelligent, attractive, healthy, successful—and interested in me.

Why did life have to be so complicated?

Chapter 13

I glanced at Danna at eight the next morning. "This is not good," I whispered. Despite the air smelling delectably of bacon and maple syrup, despite the festive lights and decorations adding sparkling cheer to the place, only two tables were occupied. Business in the hour since we'd opened had been lighter than it ever had since the restaurant's grand opening in early October. A couple of the regulars had come in for coffee and breakfast, but we hadn't experienced the usual bustle of a weekday morning. The two women who stopped in almost every day for biscuits and a game of chess hadn't even shown up.

"For sure. It's totally too dead." Danna stared at the big bowl of fruit salad. Today her head was wrapped in a brilliant turquoise scarf, keeping her reddish-gold dreadlocks off her face and out of the food. "I shouldn't have made so much."

"I've only baked one pan of biscuits, and half of those are still in the warmer." My bottom line was really going to suffer if this kept up. I walked over and peered out the front window at a dark sky that had let loose a deluge in the last half hour, then rejoined her. "It might be the rain, or because we're just past Thanksgiving, but I bet it's the murder."

"And I cut up all those mangoes for omelets. Hope they don't go to waste." She pointed at the pile of minced green bits.

I always did a double take when she referred to green peppers as mangoes, like so many others did in this area. We sure didn't call them that in California, but when in Rome. . . . A man sitting with a friend waved at me, holding up his coffee cup and smiling. I hurried over with the full pot and refilled the mug.

"Can I get you gentlemen anything else this morning?" I asked. I wasn't sure I'd seen them here before, and was grateful for their coming in today, of all days.

"We're all set, thank you, Miz Jordan."

I handed him their check.

"Pretty quiet in here, isn't it?" he said.

I smiled. "Sure is."

His companion pursed his lips. "We got a few friends said they weren't coming in here where a dead body was found. Said it might be bad luck. I told them that was crazy talk, but they were set on it."

"I hope that's not a widely held view," I said.

The first man batted away the thought. "We'll go back and tell 'em we survived just fine."

"I'd appreciate it." After they thanked me and left, I cleared their table and counted the money they'd left. "Wait," I called out, but they were gone. There was an extra twenty in the pile of bills.

I carried it over to Danna. "Think this was a mistake or simply a whopping big tip?"

She lifted a shoulder. "Take it as a tip. Why not?"

I'd just slid the bill into the Tips jar on the counter when the door jangled. In walked Adele and five women, all carrying puffy cloth bags stuffed with bulky shapes. Long knitting needles stuck out of Adele's. Right behind the women came Samuel MacDonald and a collection of men. I smiled and walked toward Adele and her ladies, who were shaking rain off their jackets and furling umbrellas.

"Good morning and welcome," I said. "Sit anywhere you'd like, please."

"Told Purl Jam we should oughta come on over here for our meeting," Adele said.

"Pearl Jam? Isn't that an oldies rock band?" I asked.

"P-U-R-L," Adele spelled out. "Like in *knit and purl.* We're a knitting club, and most everybody uses the yarn from my own sheep."

"Aha. I love the name." I distributed my two-sided laminated menus to the six of them, who'd taken the biggest table in the room, the one which seated eight. One woman had already pulled a half-finished something or other out of her bag. Her needles clicked quietly, industriously.

I called over to Samuel's group. "Aren't you part of the men's Bible breakfast group? But you usually come on Fridays, don't you?" I grabbed another stack of menus and took them to the table where the men had settled in, four Bibles in front of them.

"Little extra study doesn't harm anybody. Especially when we can get such a tasty breakfast." Samuel, dressed as usual in a button-down shirt with a colorful silk tie, glanced at the other men, two of whom nodded, but one frowned.

"Where'd the Berry girl die?" he asked, craning his neck to look all around.

"Billy, you don't need to be asking a question like that," Samuel said. He rubbed his wiry, grizzled hair, which he wore cut short all over, and his hooded eyes studied his friend.

"It's okay," I said, taking a deep breath and blowing it out. "I found her across the room over there. Don't worry; it's all been scrubbed down. Now, can I start you gentlemen off with some coffee this morning? And are you ready to order?"

And that opened the floodgates. Townspeople streamed in, despite the weather, despite having just come off a big holiday. Despite the murder. By nine o'clock all the tables were full and a party of three women browsed the cookware shelves while they waited for seats to open up. Danna worked the griddle and I bustled around taking orders, clearing tables, refilling mugs, and answering the ever-present question: I had no idea who'd killed Erica. In my spare moments I rolled out, cut, and baked two more batches of biscuits, grateful I'd prepped the dough the day before.

Samuel waved me over. "Do you want us to vacate this table?" he asked.

"Are you kidding?" I asked. "You and Adele are the magic that drew everybody else in. You stay put."

He laughed, and returned to reading aloud to his friends from his well-thumbed Bible. "'For behold, the Lord is coming forth out of his place to punish the inhabitants of the earth for their iniquity, and the earth will disclose the blood shed upon her, and will no more cover her slain.'"

By ten thirty the rush had ebbed enough for me to sit down with Adele for a minute with a mug of coffee and a plate holding a couple of sausages and a broken biscuit. The rest of the knitters had left, but Adele had stayed on and helped bus dishes. In between loading up the dishwasher and wiping down tables, she made sure to tell every single customer they were welcome and to bring in a friend tomorrow. Samuel's gang had ended their session with a hand-holding prayer before they'd left. They also left a generous tip. My heart was swelling up with all this support.

"You can't believe how much it meant to me this morning, Adele." I took a sip of coffee. "For you and Samuel both to bring in a big group, well, it was magic. Or magnetic or something. Look how busy we've been." I chewed a sausage, savoring the peppery, salty, juicy meat. I'd be hopeless as a vegetarian.

"It wasn't anything. We all want you to succeed, and you can't help it if somebody unloaded a dead woman in here."

"True. Did your knitting ladies enjoy themselves?" I slathered butter on the biscuit. It didn't matter it wasn't warm. I'd earned my breakfast today.

"We always enjoy ourselves." Adele let out her signature deep, rolling laugh. "Criminy, all we do is gossip. It's just a bonus we can produce something while we do it. And say, I took and brought you those skeins you wanted. Let me get them out of the car." She hoisted herself up and headed for the door.

I stood, too. "Danna, sit down for a while, why don't you?" I smoothed down my apron. As I did, I felt a shape in my pocket, the object I'd picked up from the floor near the cookware. I'd worn the same jeans this morning as I'd put on yesterday after my shower. Funny that Octavia hadn't gotten back to me about it. I pulled it out and flattened my palm when Danna approached. "Any idea what this is?"

"No, not really." She lowered herself into a chair. "Where'd you find it?"

"Near the cookware yesterday. What do you think it is?"

Danna shook her head. "No clue. You could ask Don over at Shamrock."

"Good idea."

"Ask Don what?" Adele walked up, both hands holding a couple of big paper bags with handles.

I showed her the device. "I found this under the cookware shelves yesterday. I'm trying to figure out what it is, and who left it there."

Adele pursed her lips. "Maybe somebody at the party? Or one of your customers. You got lots of folks coming through here, hon." She joined Danna at the table.

The bell at the service door sounded. At last—the delivery guy.

"Man, just in time." When both Adele and Danna looked confused, I went on. "I forgot to order more meat after I used it all up for the party sliders. Last night I asked for a rush delivery, and we got so busy this morning I forgot all about it."

"Wait, Robbie." Danna laid her hand on my arm. "How do you know who it is?" Her light eyebrows were drawn into a furrow. "You don't have a window in the door, or a camera out there, right?"

I stared at her. "What do you mean?" It wasn't like Danna to be frightened of anything.

"Well, what if it's Erica's killer at the door with a gun or something?" she whispered.

I set both hands on the table and leaned down. "Danna. It's mid-morning on a Tuesday. The restaurant is open, there are lots of people around. I'm pretty sure we're safe."

She relaxed her forehead and gazed at me, blinking a few times. "Maybe I'm extra worried because I'm staying by myself."

When I widened my eyes, she added, "Mom's up in Indy at a meeting with all the other mayors in the state. Last night I heard a noise outside and totally freaked out. I hauled the dog under the covers with me. Later I realized it was probably only the wind, but . . ."

"Hey, hon." Adele slid her arm around Danna's shoulders. "You don't have to worry. Everything's going to be just ducky. I never heard of a killer ringing a doorbell."

"Yeah, I guess."

The bell rang again. "We're safe, Danna," I said. She was only nineteen, after all. I headed for the door and pulled it open with only a hint of nervousness. When I saw our regular delivery guy, I could have hugged him, but I restrained myself. He handed me the slip to sign, and then unloaded a big, cold, waxed cardboard box into my arms.

"Thanks. Hang on a minute, would you?" I asked him. I set the box down, then showed him the object. "Did you drop this last time you were here?"

He looked at me like I was nuts. "No, ma'am, I did not. I got to get to my deliveries, now." As the door clicked shut behind him, I slid the thing back into my pocket. Really, anyone could have dropped it.

I stashed the meat in the walk-in and headed back to the table. "Let's see the yarn, Adele." I watched as she drew out skein after skein of soft wool dyed in gorgeous shades of the rainbow. Some were purples and pinks combined, others greens and blues.

"Makes me want to take up knitting," Danna said, fingering them. "Would you teach me sometime, Adele?"

Adele grinned. "Why, surely. Always like to pass along crafts to the young."

"I could make an awesome Rasta hat with this yarn, and a scarf and socks to match."

Danna always dressed with a creative and unconventional touch. Today, besides the turquoise scarf, she was wearing hot pink overall shorts over turquoise tights and black polka-dotted hi-tops, with a black knit shirt under the overalls. I could totally picture her in a rainbow-hued floppy beret.

I stood. "Let's figure out where to display the yarn, and then I've got to start lunch prep."

Adele handed me a big envelope and a couple of clear acrylic sign holders. "I printed up signs and prices." She slid the yarn back into the bags and stood, as well.

"Great. How about over there?" I strode to a set of sparsely populated shelves. I consolidated the cookware and cleared a space for her. "Maybe I should bring in some other local products for sale, especially now for the holidays. I'm sure I could find honey and maple syrup. What else?"

"There's an Amish farmer around here makes real nice soaps," Adele said, laying out the yarn. "I'll text you his info when I get home."

"Thanks." I stroked one of the soft skeins.

"I'm heading out now, hon. You set up the signs as you like them."

"Will do."

"You both have a good day, you hear?"

Danna waved from the griddle, where she'd resumed scrubbing. I hugged Adele and watched her go.

"Yoo-hoo." One of the last two customers waved her hand. "Can we get the check, please?"

"Of course." I hurried over and pulled it out of my apron pocket, handing it to her. "Was everything all right?"

"De-super delicious," the man at the table said, beaming. "You think you might ever put fried biscuits on the menu? They're real tasty, especially with some of your apple butter."

I smiled back. "It's possible. I know they're a popular item around here."

"Now, hon, we want you to know we don't care at all about that murder business." The woman looked at me with serious eyes. "Don't you be worrying about it."

"I appreciate it, ma'am." I accepted the bills the man handed me.

"Y'all keep the change," he said.

I thanked him, headed for the cash register, and rang up the meal, adding even more generosity to the Tips jar. Ten minutes later, I was busy slicing tomatoes next to Danna, who was assembling a potato salad, when the cowbell on the door jangled again. Would today ever calm down? Not that I really meant it, but we'd been going strong for nearly three hours. I turned to see Octavia walking briskly toward me.

"I got your message. What's this about someone we should check out?" She was again dressed in neat slacks, turtleneck, and blazer, but the lines in her face were deeper and her eyes looked tired.

"I need to keep working, if it's okay." At her nod, I continued. "A friend of the Berry family, a guy who lives in Chicago, was visiting the Berrys yesterday when I brought by some food for them. His name is Vincent Pytzynska and he was a friend of Erica's husband."

"Jon Shermer."

I kept slicing. "They'd gone to law school together up there." I told her what Vince had said about Erica making him uncomfortable. "He said he'd stopped going out with them as a couple. But he seemed odd to me. I Googled him when I got home, and it turns out he's from around here, went to Brown County High School."

"And?" She tapped her fingers on the counter and then folded her arms.

"Well, Erica went to South Lick High, and she and Vince must be about the same age. Being from away, you probably don't know the two high schools do lots of activities together. Sue and Glen Berry told me Erica had plenty of conflicts with people, even in high school. And I thought . . ." My thought sounded pretty lame, even to me. I glanced over at Octavia.

"You thought this Vincent might have come down from Chicago, found Erica the night of the party, killed her, and left her in your store." She raised a surprisingly thick eyebrow.

I selected another tomato to slice. "He was acting very nervous, and I thought you might want to check him out. That's all."

"I will. And you might not believe this, but we do appreciate alert citizens giving us ideas. As long as that's as far as it goes."

"I'm not trying to interfere in your job."

"I didn't say that, but Buck did let me know about your trying to assist with solving the murder last month. Let's be clear that's not going to happen this time."

"It's not." I pushed the slices to the side with the knife.

"Good. The South Lick police might have their

own way of doing things, but the state police have very clear guidelines on the involvement of civilians in investigations."

"How's the investigation going, anyway?"

"Nice talking with you, Robbie." Octavia headed for the door.

"Likewise," I called after her. *Huh. As if.*

Buck wandered into the store at about eleven thirty. He hung his raincoat on the coat rack and shook drops off his hat before adding it to the hook. He slid down into a chair near the kitchen area, his long legs stretched out to the next county.

"Let me guess," I called to him. "A double cheese-burger with everything, plus coleslaw and chips."

"And a bottle of co-cola, if you don't mind."

"I'm on it." I threw two beef patties on the griddle and slid the halves of a bun into the warmer. After I set up his plate and scooped out a generous portion of coleslaw, I called over. "What kind of soda do you want?" I knew by now Buck called all soda pop *co-cola.*

"Give me one of them root beers, will you?"

I brought him the bottle from the drinks cooler and a straw. He never wanted a glass for it.

He glanced around. "Danna not working today?"

"She is. She just had to run down the street to the bank. So how's it going?" I asked.

"All right, I guess," he said, stretching out the first two words into about five syllables.

"I was surprised you didn't come by for some breakfast this morning."

"Robbie, now I can't be stopping by every whip-stitch." He grinned and shoveled in a bit of slaw.

I could tell he was trying to fool me with the local expression. "You haven't been here since yesterday. I wouldn't call that too often."

"Yeah, anywho. Octavia called a meeting lasted half the morning. Least she had the decency to order in some donuts. But they don't stick to your ribs much, know what I mean?"

"I do. They're delicious, though. How can you lose with what is essentially deep-fried cake?" I went over and flipped the meat, laying a slice of cheddar cheese on each. I refused to stock American cheese even though customers occasionally asked for it. It wasn't a real food, more plastic than cheese.

A moment later he had his lunch and since the place was empty, I plopped down across from him. "Any news on the investigation?"

"You know Octavia don't want us talking to the general populace about it."

"It's been almost three days, though. You guys need to solve this thing."

"It needs solved, all right." He crunched down a few chips.

"You can't even tell me if you're close to an arrest? I'm hardly the general populace, after all. I'm the owner of the place where her body was so unkindly left."

He shook his head so slowly it looked like he was underwater. Then he leaned toward me. "We had

Tiffany Porter in yesterday," he said in a low tone. "She really didn't like Erica none."

"Apparently nobody did except Erica's immediate family. And even they say she was difficult. But do you think Tiffany killed her?"

"Ain't up to me to decide. Them staties have taken over. They got their evidence and all." He scrunched up his face and squinted through one eye for a second, then let it go. "I can tell you it was your press which whacked her upside the head. Or one of the things that whacked her. They found the press in a Dumpster."

"Really? Octavia didn't tell me. Where was the Dumpster?"

"Over in the alley on Morgan, behind the row of stores where Tiffany's store sets." He swiped at a dollop of ketchup next to his mouth.

"Which is bad for Tiffany, I'd guess."

"Could be." Buck finished the last bite on his plate. "Say, when are you going to start offering pies around here? I'd sure love me a piece of sugar cream pie." Buck got a dreamy look in his eyes as the door jangled.

"I can ask Phil if he'd rather bake pies, but I think he likes the easy desserts where you can do a whole pan at once." I rose and waved in several customers. "Sit anywhere," I called. I leaned in toward Buck. "Let me know if you find out anything else?" I said low enough so only he could hear me. "At least about my press?"

"I'll do what I can," Buck said. He handed me a twenty and fitted his hat back on his head.

I dug in my apron and handed him his change. He ambled over to the Tips jar and slid it all in.

"Buck, you're too generous." I smiled.

"Got to keep the cook happy."

"Well, thanks." I grabbed menus and carried them to the newcomers, hearing the bell jangle behind me as Buck left.

As I headed back to the kitchen area to get their waters, I saw Sue Berry standing in front of the door holding a dripping umbrella. She must have come in right when Buck left. Her blue thigh-length jacket was also wet.

"Sue," I said, walking toward her. "How are you doing?" She looked so forlorn, I took her free hand and squeezed it. "You want to sit down? Are you here for lunch?"

"No, thanks, hon. Well, actually, I could use a cup of coffee." She glanced around. "What should I do with my umbrella?"

Another local way of speaking was the way folks said *um*brella, with the stress on the first syllable. I pointed to the cylindrical can near the door. "That's an umbrella stand; you can pop it in there."

She deposited it, shrugged out of her jacket, and took a seat at a table away from the other diners. I hurried to pour her a mug of coffee and took it over.

"Let me grab those people's orders and I'll be right back."

"You take your time, now." Sue barely looked at me.

After I'd jotted down what the customers wanted, I threw two turkey burgers and a beef patty on the griddle and set up three plates before I returned to Sue.

"You're not doing too well," I said in a low voice.

"I'm not. Not at all. And the heavens are crying for Erica today, too." Her eyes were reddened and her nose was red, too. "But I came by to tell you Erica's funeral will be tomorrow afternoon at one o'clock at Our Lady of the Springs. We're going to have a gathering at the house afterwards, too, and I sure hope you can come."

"I'll be there." If I could get someone to help Danna, that is. "Do you need help with the food?"

"You're real kind. But no, a friend from church does catering and offered to do up the refreshments for us.

"Is there a viewing?"

She shook her head.

I waited. I needed to get back to the griddle, but I wanted to let her say what she needed to.

"I'm so glad we threw that party for her." She gazed up at me and swallowed. "We need to appreciate the living while we have them."

Chapter 14

Lunch ended up as busy as breakfast had been. Danna and I had cleaned up after we closed at two thirty, and she'd headed home at three, as usual. I could have used a nap, but I wanted to get the day's considerable cash to the bank, and realized I still had Sue's check from the party on Saturday to deposit, too. In my apartment, I changed into clean jeans unspattered by pancake batter and beef grease, and threw on a fleece sweatshirt. Pulling aside the bedroom curtains, I saw it was still raining. *Ugh.* And my indoor-outdoor thermometer said it was barely fifty degrees, to boot. *Double ugh.*

But the bank was only a few blocks away on Main Street, and it didn't make much sense to drive. I needed some fresh air, anyway. I pulled on hiking boots and my yellow rain jacket, and grabbed my wallet and keys. As I reached for the extra-large umbrella I'd gotten from First Savings Bank when I'd opened my business account, Birdy ran over and mewed at me.

"Sorry, buddy. I don't have a kitty-sized *um*brella

for you." I laughed as I reached down to pet him. "I don't think you want to go for a walk in the rain, anyway."

He cocked his head, and then with great urgency began to wash his tail, biting at a spot before licking it over and over.

Outside I snapped open the green-and-white umbrella and made my way to the bank. As I filled out the deposit slip, I glanced at the date they so handily posted in big letters and numbers in a metal case. I wrinkled my nose. Tomorrow was December first. Adele's birthday, for which I was completely unprepared.

I waited in line at the bank to make my deposit. A slender woman with a blond ponytail threaded through a ball cap finished her transaction and turned toward me.

"Christina," I said with a smile. "What are you doing in South Lick?"

"How's it going, Robbie?" She gave me a hug and then stepped back. "I'm cooking at the new restaurant in town, Hoosier Hollow. I'm head chef, in fact. Didn't I tell you? "

"You didn't. I heard about the restaurant opening, of course."

"You should come eat. I'll comp you an appetizer or something."

"Sounds like a plan. What kind of cuisine are you featuring?"

"Elegant Indiana fare, if that isn't an oxymoron." Christina laughed. "Gotta get back to it. Hey, the restaurant is closed on Mondays just like yours. Let's have some fun next week, okay?"

"You bet." Good for her. She'd taken over my slot as chef at the Nashville Inn last winter after I left to work on my store. I imagined the fare at this new place would be a more interesting challenge for her. She'd grown to be one of my best friends in the area, but our schedules had clashed for the last year. Monday fun was going to be perfect.

After I made my deposit, I hesitated in front of the bank. I needed to get Adele a present, but what? She was in her seventies and didn't need more stuff. She read books, but we didn't have an independent bookstore in town and it was too late to order anything online. She didn't wear scarves, and she already possessed plenty of sweaters she'd knitted out of her own lovely yarn. As far as I knew she didn't use perfume or scented anything.

I kicked myself for letting the date sneak up on me. She did so much for me, and hadn't forgotten my birthday once in twenty-seven years. Rain dripped steadily off my umbrella and caught the colored light from a store across the street, so it almost looked like flowing blown glass. I snapped my fingers. Adele's one personal indulgence was earrings. She wore her hair short and sensible, but she loved long, dangly earrings. The more exotic, the more brightly colored, the better. Tiffany's jewelry shop was right over on Morgan Street. She must have earrings for sale. Handmade and local were a plus. And maybe she'd talk more about Erica. I couldn't stand having the puzzle of Erica's murder not solved.

I stood in front of Porter Jewelry and Gifts a few minutes later gazing at windows decorated for

Christmas. Silver garlands and puffy white cloth showed off colored glass ornaments, racks of bracelets, and wrapped gift boxes. The shop was housed in a row of stores in a restored Art Deco building, the style of many of the downtown structures, and I realized it was only a block away from where Jim lived upstairs in a similar building.

I pushed open the door of Tiffany's shop and a single chime sounded. Tiffany stood behind a glass display case at the back of the space arranging something inside it. The inside of the store was as festively decorated as the front window, but she had such a lovely array of wares for sale it would have looked celebratory even without the twinkling lights. Small figures of women in fanciful dresses flew on fishing line from the ceiling, as did brilliantly colored enameled butterflies. The walls featured glass shelving holding vases, picture frames, and painted boxes. Framed artwork and mirrors with decorated frames lined the rest of the wall space. A counter was lined with racks of earrings and bracelets, and the air smelled faintly of vanilla.

"Welcome," Tiffany said without lifting her head, and then glanced up. "Hi, Robbie."

I returned her greeting. "What wonderful things you have. I can't believe I've never stopped in here." I gazed up at the flying women. One wearing a blue sundress held a yellow kite, the kite's wire tail decorated with bows in all colors. Another figure flew with an unfurled green umbrella in one hand and a tiny open book in the other.

"Thanks. Aren't those great?" She shut the display

case and pointed to the figures. "They're called Annie's Angels."

"I love them. How long have you had this store?"

"I've been here about five years." Tiffany straightened a small basket of tiny silver Buddhas on the counter, righting one after another back to sitting.

"I guess I haven't been out shopping much. I only moved here last winter. I was pretty immersed in renovating my store and then opening early last month."

"Your store is a great space," Tiffany said. "You did a good job with it. Now, what can I help you with?"

"I need a birthday present for my aunt."

"Adele?"

"You know her?"

Tiffany pointed to a hat tree in the corner covered with rainbow-striped knit caps in several designs. "I've been selling the hats she makes for a few years."

"I shouldn't be surprised. She does seem to know everyone. I think I want to get her some earrings."

"These would look great on her, with her short hair and all." She showed me a row of long earrings worked in three metals, with colored glass beads added in. "I make them myself, you know."

"Those are really pretty. Now I see them, I think one of those angels would be even more perfect for her." I pointed to the ceiling. "Do you know if she already has one?"

"I don't think so. She always admires them but says her budget doesn't go as far as buying herself indulgences."

"Sounds like Adele through and through. Then

I'll indulge her." I pointed to the one with the kite. "I'll take that one. I love how she looks like she's flying." The figure's back was arched and her feet kicked up behind her.

Tiffany brought out a stepladder and used a special pole to gently lift the loop of clear plastic line off its hook. A minute later she had the figure carefully wrapped in tissue and packaged in a white box with her store logo on the side in gold. A row of bangles on Tiffany's arm jingling, she deftly tied silver and gold ribbon around the box and curled the ends.

"Perfect." I handed her my credit card. I didn't even care how much it cost. "Now I don't have to wrap it."

"We're a full-service gift shop." Tiffany smiled back as she ran the card through the reader.

"So, I heard the police questioned you about Erica's death. How'd that go?"

The smile slid off her face and her nostrils flared. "Who'd you hear that from?" She slapped my credit card down on the counter.

"Buck Bird told me. I think he only said so because I'd told him on Monday I'd seen you in Bloomington the day before. He didn't tell me about the conversation or anything."

"I can't believe they think I'd kill Erica. She was a manipulative, unscrupulous person. She stole from me and lied about it. But I didn't bash her head in, and I told the Slade woman as much. Over and over."

"It's good they didn't arrest you," I said, watching her.

Tiffany shifted her gaze away from mine. "Thing is, I live alone. I was home in bed, but I don't have any way to prove it. Living by myself, on top of being furious with Erica at the party when I saw her wearing the bracelet she stole, is making the detective suspicious. But there's no evidence against me. At least not that she said."

I stepped out of Tiffany's with the handled bag she'd placed the gift in. So that made three of us—Tiffany, Phil, and me—who were home alone with no alibi the night of Erica's murder. I swore. It was raining even harder now. I huddled under the shallow overhang while I fumbled with the umbrella, finally getting it all the way open.

"Watch it, now," a deep voice said from next to me.

I tilted the umbrella and craned my neck to see Max standing a little behind me to my right. "Sorry. Did I poke you?" *Where had he come from?*

"Almost." He wore a brimmed hat and the collar of his overcoat was turned up. He held the handles of a black canvas bag that looked like a cross between a briefcase and a tool kit.

"I can't see much under this umbrella," I said.

"Been doing some shopping?"

"I did." I held up my bag. "Tiffany has beautiful stuff in there."

"She does. Hey, hope you'll be able to make it to Erica's service tomorrow."

Max seemed to have changed personalities from when I'd first met him. A change coinciding with Erica's death. Maybe she'd been like a thorn in his foot and life seemed cheerier without her. It was an awful thought, that it might take someone's death to improve a person's mood.

"Sue came by and told me," I said. "I'll be there. One o'clock, right?" A car drove by and nearly sprayed us both when it drove through a puddle. "I'd better be going before it rains any harder."

"Can I give you a ride somewhere?" he asked. "It isn't much weather for walking." He pointed to a big green pickup truck parked a couple of spaces down.

"Thanks so much. I'm headed back to the store only a couple of—"

"I know where your place is, Robbie." He held out his keys and clicked the fob at the truck, which beeped and blinked its lights. "Hop on in."

I climbed into the passenger seat and laid my wet umbrella on the floor. It seemed like a fairly new truck, but the dashboard was littered with odd bits of tools and cylinders of locks that looked naked outside the doors they belonged in. The floor mat sported a collection of crumpled White Castle bags, some bearing stains of ketchup and mustard from the hamburgers they'd held. An empty fries box lay there, too, with the chain's tag line of WHAT YOU CRAVE in white letters on orange. I should probably come up with something equally snappy for my restaurant.

As we rolled down the street, I said, "Were you shopping somewhere, too?"

"Not shopping." He laughed, a low rolling chortle. "I work right back there."

"At the men's store?"

"Heck, no. I'm a locksmith. Guess you didn't know." He glanced at me with a smile, then back at the road.

"Right. My aunt told me and I forgot. Have you been doing it long?" I turned a little sideways to face him.

"Most of my adult life, since I got out of the Army, anyhow." He pinched the bridge of his nose. "Actually, it was the military who trained me in the trade."

"You must have to pick locks for people who lock themselves out."

"All the time. Or they go ahead and lose the only key. Who doesn't get copies made?" He shook his head and patted the canvas bag, which sat on the console between us. "I'm off right now to install a dead bolt for a lady who got her house broke into. Burglars got in with a credit card. Shee-it."

"I've heard of that happening."

We rode in silence for a block, then he said, "Somebody told me you're one of those crazy bicyclers." Max glanced over. "The ones who ride around in a pack wearing ridiculous colored outfits, who take up the whole road."

"I hope I'm not crazy. And actually I rarely ride in a group. I just like the exercise. And it clears my head."

"I don't get the attraction."

"How's Paula doing?" I asked.

"She's awful torn up about Erica." He pulled his mouth to the side as he pulled up in front of Pans 'N Pancakes.

"Was she able to remember anything about Erica leaving the house that night?"

"I told you, she's a solid sleeper. She says she didn't hear anything. And having to be questioned by the police after her sister was killed really sent her over the edge."

"What a shame."

"It wasn't any fun. They took us all in separate, too." His right index finger beat a rhythm on the steering wheel.

"I'm sure the police were only doing their job. Did they give you any clue about how the investigation is going?"

He cast a sideways look at me. "No," he scoffed. "Why would they?"

"Just curious. I'm trying to figure out who would have killed Erica, although I'm not making much progress."

"Really? You don't trust the police?"

"I'm sure they'll find the killer. But it's bugging me they brought my friend Phil MacDonald in for questioning, too. I know he never would have hurt her."

"My sister-in-law rubbed folks the wrong way. All the time."

"Apparently. Even Tiffany Porter," I said.

"You could say that again. The two of them were arguing something fierce last week. Right out on the sidewalk, too. Airing their dirty linen in public." He looked disgusted. "Normally Tiffany is as smooth as chocolate pudding with all those men she goes out with."

"What do you mean?"

"Everybody knows Tiffany likes to be shown a good time. She's always at one fancy restaurant or another. And with a different guy every time. Not locals for the most part."

"I'm not surprised. She's an attractive woman." I stared out at the rain, then back at Max. "That guy, Vince. When did he arrive in town?"

"What are you asking about him for?" Max narrowed his eyes.

"It seems like a long drive to make. He must have been close to Erica."

He snorted. "He couldn't stand her, to tell you the truth. He told me he was closer to her husband. Not quite sure why he came down. But he seems like a decent enough guy, and it made Sue and Glen feel warm and fuzzy he made the effort."

"I guess I'm going to have to trust the police to solve the puzzle of the murder. I sure can't figure it out, at least so far." I laid my hand on the latch. "Well, I'd better get inside. Thanks for the ride."

"Not a problem. And I apologize for Paula's outburst yesterday. She's not herself. Anyhow, we know you didn't have anything to do with the murder. Just like none of us did, either."

Chapter 15

I jabbed the red phone icon that evening, setting my phone on the kitchen table with a little too much force. I glanced at the clock, which already read eight. I'd completely struck out trying to find someone who could work with Danna while I attended the funeral. Adele wanted to go to the service herself, as did Samuel. Jim? I didn't even want to ask him. His real-estate law practice was a busy one. *Shoot. Who else could I call?* I should have started calling earlier, but I'd gotten absorbed in a puzzle while I ate dinner and two hours had slipped away.

On the off chance Phil didn't have to work tomorrow, I pressed his number and said hello after he picked up.

"Phil, I'm in a bind tomorrow. Remember last month when you filled in for me so I could attend Stella's funeral?"

"And tomorrow is Erica's. Sorry, Robbie, but I have a new boss in the music department. She frowns on people taking too much personal time. I'd rather come work with Danna again, but . . . "

"That's okay. How are you doing, anyway?"

"Well, they forced me to go to the police station again yesterday, which did not make my boss happy, as you can imagine. And the interview was one more sham, one more travesty." Phil's rich baritone sounded angry. "Once again they let me go, of course. But the ever-vigilant Detective Slade told me not to leave town. She sounded like a bad police show."

"I'm so sorry. I wish they'd find the actual murderer so we can all relax and get back to normal."

"Agree a hundred percent. Speaking of normal, I owe you some more desserts. And they're in the oven now."

"You're a dear."

"I love doing it, as you know. I'll drop them off early tomorrow."

I thanked him and hung up. I'd better start training a part-time worker. What if I had to go away somewhere? Which, come to think of it, I was planning to do after Christmas. Or, heaven forbid, what if Danna or I got hurt? Danna. Maybe she had a friend who could help. I pressed her number.

After she greeted me, I said, "Do you happen to have any friends who have experience cooking?"

"Why?"

"I wanted to go to Erica's funeral tomorrow. It's at one o'clock. And I haven't found a substitute."

"I can handle the restaurant alone," Danna said.

"If it's quiet, I'm sure you could. But what if we got a rush? There's no way you could manage. And the business is still so new, I don't want any customers to have a bad experience."

"I guess. Let me think." She fell silent for a moment. "There's one guy from high school. He liked to cook as much as me."

"Do you think he's free?"

"Problem. He went away to college. He's back East somewhere. Yale, maybe."

"And there's nobody else?"

"Nope. I didn't have a big circle of friends in school, and the ones I still hang with think it's weird how much I like making food. They're always getting fast food, or nuking frozen stuff." I could hear the disgust in her voice.

"I don't suppose Corrine could help out for a couple of hours? I mean, I know she's the mayor, but—"

"Not going to work. Remember? Mom's out of town."

"Right. I guess I'll skip the service," I said. "I didn't even know Erica, but Sue seemed to really want me to go."

"Sorry, dude."

We disconnected. Maybe I could still make it over to the Berrys' house after the funeral for the reception, or gathering, or whatever Sue had called it. Danna wouldn't mind handling all the cleanup herself. My gaze fell on the bag from Tiffany's. How was I going to work Adele's birthday into the day, too? I thought for a minute, then pressed her number.

We chatted for a couple of minutes before I said: "I'd like to have you and Samuel over for dinner tomorrow. Can you come?"

"Hang on, I'll ask him." After a few moments of

muffled noises, she came back on. "Splendid. What time?"

"Come at six, okay?"

"We'll be there. Love you."

It would be fun to have Jim join the group, too. But I didn't feel like talking to one more person, so I texted him the invitation, and he texted back almost immediately he would be there with bells on. Whatever that meant. I poured an inch of bourbon into a squat glass and sat again, pulling today's puzzle toward me. Only the bottom left quadrant remained, and I had two of the words. But *an author named Bagnold* had me stumped, as did *an Adriatic peninsula.* I took a sip of the whiskey, savoring the warm, smooth feeling as it went down. *Without rival* was a clue for a four-letter word. I stared at it for a while, finally writing in *lone.*

I gave up on the puzzle for now. After I transferred a load of restaurant laundry from the washer to the dryer, I moved to the computer. I'd set up a Facebook page for the store, which was a pain because now I needed to keep it current all the time. Had I planned a special for tomorrow? I could whip up some apple-spice muffins. Customers loved something a little sweet with their breakfast. I wrote an entry, searched for a public domain picture of a muffin, and put it up with the text. I checked my news feed, but since I spent as little time on social media as possible, I had almost no friends. I noticed the little person icon at the top had a red bubble on it, so I clicked it. *Oh.* Abe O'Neill wanted to be friends. *Cool.* I confirmed it, and almost instantly a message from him appeared down in the right-hand corner.

Nice to see you on here. Did you hear about the funeral tomorrow?

I typed, Hi, Abe. Yes, but I can't go. Nobody to help Danna in the restaurant.

A moment passed, then I can do it. Wasn't going to go to the funeral, anyway popped up.

My eyes bugged out. Really? Do you, um, know how to cook? I softened the message with a winking emoticon.

I'm not a pro, but I love making food. Have tomorrow off work. And I AM a pro dishwasher . . .

You're hired, I typed. Come at noon so we can over-lap. I'll pay you. I couldn't believe my good fortune.

No pay. C U tomorrow.

Thanks! I stared at the screen. What a guy. I'd have to think of some way to pay him back. Free meals for a week, maybe?

Chapter 16

The apple-spice muffins went together easy as pie the next morning. I slid four pans into the oven, one after another, as Danna strolled in at six thirty.

"Hey, I found somebody to help out this afternoon." I smiled at her, setting the timer for twenty minutes.

"Who?" After she hung up her coat, Danna slid an apron over her head and tied it, then scrubbed her hands. Her dreads were held back by a multicolored knitted band this morning, and she wore a faded flowered cotton dress over a ribbed sweater and leggings, both in black.

"Abe O'Neill said he'd be happy to," I said. "And I got the feeling he knows how to cook."

"Sweet. He's a nice guy. Where do you want me to start?"

"Table setup, then the pancake batter. I already started the coffees."

She saluted. "Yes, ma'am," and hoisted the box of silverware rolled in blue cloth napkins.

I erased the Specials blackboard and lettered

Apple-Spice Muffins onto it, then headed into the cooler for sausage, bacon, and more.

"The rain must have stopped overnight," I said when I emerged with my arms full of meat, milk, and eggs. Danna hadn't appeared at all wet when she came in.

"It did. It's clear out but it's cold." She shivered. "Feels like winter."

I switched on the strings of lights. "Does that help?" I'd forgotten to leave them on all night yesterday.

"It does, sort of." She laughed. "Those sure look pretty. You did a super nice job with all the decorations."

"Thanks. So, if your mom is out of town, you're all alone in the house. You okay?"

"I'm cool. Kind of nice to have the place to myself. I can play music as loud as I want without her telling me to turn it down. I've stopped freaking about strange noises, too." She finished laying the tables and started measuring flour, brown sugar, and other dry ingredients for the pancakes.

Bananas. Oops. "Darn. I think I forgot to order bananas." What was up with my brain this week? Too much else on my mind, that was what.

"Don't we have some frozen blueberries? We can make it seem like we planned it that way." Danna grinned as she strode to the Specials board and added Blueberry Pancakes to it, then drew out a couple of bags of berries from the freezer.

We worked in silence for a few minutes.

"You know, I read something last night you might

be interested in," Danna said, cracking eggs into the mixing bowl.

"What's that?"

"I was noodling around on the Internet, looking for information on Erica."

"Why?"

"I thought I might find something new. And because her body was in your store." She beat the eggs with a whisk.

"Did you find anything?"

"Sort of. I saw a column from a Chicago news site speculating her husband didn't commit suicide." She measured milk into the bowl and then oil. "That he was murdered."

I felt my eyes go as wide as they got. "You're kidding."

"No. This guy was actually looking into police corruption. Which they have a real problem with up there, apparently. And the officer who declared Jon Shermer committed suicide was under investigation himself."

"Did the article say who would have killed Jon? And why?" If it was true, then there was a killer at large in Chicago. But it also might soothe Jim's heart to know his brother didn't cause his own death.

"That's where Erica's name came in. The guy suspected she was having an affair with this unscrupulous officer."

I tilted my head. "You mean, the writer implied Erica killed her husband?"

"Yeah." Danna stirred the flour mixture into the liquids and set the beater to rotate on low.

"That's really incredible. Will you send me the link after you get home today?" I asked.

"For shizzle."

"Huh?"

"Translation: for sure."

I laughed. "You're making me feel old and I'm only twenty-seven." I glanced around the store, making sure the tables were ready, and my gaze fell on the garlands. I laid down the knife I was cutting fruit with. "Shoot. The tree."

"What tree?"

"I cut a Christmas tree on Monday at the place where I got the garlands. But I forgot all about decorating it. It's outside in a bucket of water. I better go check and make sure it isn't dry." I headed for the service door. It was indeed cold out, and I was only wearing a long-sleeved T-shirt. Once outside, I hugged myself. And then stared.

Where was the tree? I'd put it in a bucket of water on Monday right here, right beyond the trash cans. There was the bucket. But it was empty. *What?*

I strode out and all around the area. Sure enough, pine needles littered the ground around the bucket. I checked around the back at the small brick patio outside the back door of my apartment. No tree. I looked in the barn. No tree. I stomped around to the front porch. No tree.

I couldn't believe it. Who was so small-minded they would steal a Christmas tree? Could anyone be desperate enough to do such a thing? I headed back around the side and slammed the service door behind me. Danna looked up from the griddle where she was turning sausage links.

"What's up?" She frowned.

"Somebody stole the tree. My Christmas tree is gone. The one I cut myself! Someone stole it." I strode the length of the store and back.

"That totally rips. Who would steal a tree?"

"My sentiments, exactly." I wanted to grab a cast-iron skillet and throw it on the floor. Which would not help, exactly. I glanced at the clock and swore. It was getting near opening time, so instead I hurried to the sink, washed my hands, and picked up the fruit knife.

"Are you going to call the police about it?" Danna asked, wrinkling her nose.

"I don't have time right now. Buck will probably come in for breakfast, anyway. He usually does." When the timer dinged, I extracted the pans of muffins. I slid the nutty brown puffs out, grateful as always for the non-stick pans, and lined up the muffins on a cooling rack. I quickly rolled out the prepped biscuit dough and cut out a couple of pans' worth of disks. As I opened the oven door, the bell on the front door jangled. I groaned before looking up to see my regular chess players.

"Morning," I called, pasting on a smile.

The women, two taciturn senior citizens, said hello and headed for the square table I'd painted with a chessboard. They always brought their own playing pieces in a quilted bag, but I kept a set available for less-particular customers.

After I put the biscuits in the oven, I brought over a pot of coffee and said, "The usual?"

"Yes, please," the taller one said. A rare smile lit

up her deeply lined face. Her build was all angles
and she wore salt-and-pepper hair pulled up on top
of her head in a bun.

The shorter one, with rounded, rosy cheeks and
a sensible cap of snow-white hair, glanced at me.

"Sorry we didn't get in yesterday, hon," she said.
"We heared you was closed. Didn't realize they'd let
you open up again, after the murder and whatnot."

I smiled. "No worries. I'm glad you're here today."

"Give us a couple of them special muffins, too,
would you?" The taller one pointed at the blackboard.

"And a side of bacon," the other one added.

"You bet." I bustled off.

The place filled up, and Danna and I didn't get a
chance to breathe until eight thirty. Phil dropped
off the desserts on his way to work and I barely had
time to say hello. A number of customers remarked
on how cheery the place looked all decorated. Too
bad I didn't have a tree to go with it. A couple of
regulars didn't show, but maybe they were simply
out of town instead of staying away because of a
dead body. Buck ambled in at about eight forty-five
carrying a piece of green paper.

I poured his coffee and said, "Don't tell me. You
want both specials, two biscuits with apple butter,
and two fried eggs with sausage." I knew his hollow
leg as well as my own.

His nod was slower than pouring molasses in the
middle of winter. "But first you think I might could
pin this here notice up on your bulletin board?" He
showed me the paper, which advertised a police

department toy drive for needy children. "Does the boss approve?"

"Absolutely. Do you want me to put a big cardboard box under it for toy donations?"

"If you got one, sure. Or we can take and drop one by." He ambled over to the community bulletin board I'd hung near the door and tacked up the poster.

There was that *take and* phrasing again, which only accentuated that Buck was definitely from around here. It only took a couple of minutes to put together his order. After I set it in front of him, I glanced around the place. Two tables were occupied with hungry townsfolk tucking into their breakfasts and nobody seemed to want anything right now. I sat across from Buck.

"I need to report a theft."

Buck's eyes went way wide, but he forked in a mouthful of pancakes before answering. "You got burgled?" he mumbled, a speck of blueberry in syrup dribbling down his chin.

"Yes. I cut a Christmas tree on Monday and left it in a bucket of water outside. I went to check it this morning and it's not there. Not anywhere." I folded my arms. "Who in heck would be so rotten?"

He turned down the corners of his mouth. "That seems downright mean. When's the last time you seen the tree?"

I concentrated. "I don't think I went out there yesterday. We got a delivery, but the guy brought the stuff in. So I guess I haven't seen the tree since Monday."

"Think the delivery man might coulda taken it?"

"I sure hope not."

"Give me the name and number of the delivery company. I'll check it out. Don't suppose you can describe the tree?"

I hurried over to my desk and jotted down the information on a slip of paper. I handed it to Buck. "I don't know the name of the variety. But, actually, I ran into Abe O'Neill at the tree farm. He helped me bring it to my car. I can ask him if he knows what kind of tree it was."

"I'll keep my eye out around town. Except, you know everybody's getting their trees these days. Don't get your hopes up."

We experienced another minor rush at nine, but by ten it was quiet again. I carried a load of dishes in my arms and was headed to the sink when I glanced at the wall calendar. Wednesday popped out at me like a pileated woodpecker hammering a dead tree, as Adele was fond of saying. I was supposed to pick up the glass for the door today.

"Danna, I have to run over to the hardware store to pick up the replacement glass for the door. It'll only take me a few minutes. Okay?" I slid the dishes into the sink.

She waved me away. "No probs. I'll get started on lunch prep."

I thanked her, pulled on my coat, and went out through my apartment so I could grab my bag. Normally I'd walk, but I'd have to haul the glass home, so I hopped in the van and drove the three blocks, which gave my brain enough quietude to let what Danna had said float back up to the surface. Erica by all reports was manipulative and unscrupulous. But to have an affair with a cop, then kill her husband and have the cop cover it up? That was a stretch.

Barb greeted me with a big smile when I walked into Shamrock Hardware.

"Hey, there, Robbie. Everything back to normal now?"

"Pretty much." I wasn't going to go into details with her, not with a half-dozen town residents milling around inspecting extension cables, picking up boxes of screws, ordering paint.

"What did you decide about the gingerbread log cabin? I'd sure love to see what you come up with."

I laughed. "Actually, I decided to enter and I baked the walls last night. My friend Phil is going to help me create it Friday night. You said you're good at using icing, didn't you?"

She beamed. "Heck, I'm better at prize-winning roses made out of sugar than the Queen of England. You just call on me, hon."

"Perfect. I might have to." I high-fived her.

"You know you got to use royal icing to glue it all together. Sugar and egg whites."

"Got it. Any idea if my glass is ready? I guess I should have called first."

"Go on back and ask Don. He's the one who knows."

I thanked her and headed to the rear of the store where Don was on the phone. He held up a hand, signaling for me to wait, so I stood there, hoping it wouldn't take long. The restaurant could get another flood of customers at any moment.

I snapped my fingers. I'd meant to bring the tool thingy in and ask Don what it was. I strolled over to the tools area and strolled down the aisle, peering at the selection of screwdrivers and drills. There were wrenches large and small, and pliers from needlenose to vise-grips. Nothing that matched what I'd found, though.

"Robbie?" Don called.

I turned around to see him holding a large flat package wrapped in brown paper. "Here's your glass, and you already paid for it. You got your putty, your glazing points, your glazing tool?"

"I'm all set, thanks."

"Assuming you drove on over?" When I nodded, he went on. "I'll carry it out for you."

"Thanks."

After he'd carefully laid the glass on the floor in the back of the van, he straightened. "How are things going, you know, with the murder and all?"

"I don't know anything. Except they haven't caught the killer. And somebody stole my Christmas tree from outside the store."

"What a crying shame, Robbie. They just up and took it?"

"It was in a bucket around the side by the service door. I cut it myself on Monday." I shook my head.

"Probably not much chance of finding it, this time of year."

"I know. Hey, Don, this isn't related to anything, but I found a strange little object in my store. It looks like a tool, but I didn't see one like it in your store. It's got two little, like, levers or something. About yay long." I showed him the size with my fingers. "I guess that's not much of a description. I meant to bring it in and show you."

"It doesn't ring a bell. But do bring it in next time, and I'll see if it looks familiar."

"Thanks." I headed around to the driver's side as he turned to go back into the store. "See you at the funeral this afternoon?"

He shook his head. "I didn't know her. And even if I did, well, God rest her soul."

Chapter 17

When I hurried back into Pans 'N Pancakes with the glass in my arms, every table was occupied and Danna shot me a desperate glance from the griddle. This was crazy. Who ever heard of Wednesday at eleven bringing on a rush of hungry customers? I shook my head as I carefully set my load down by the service door, then quickly washed my hands and slipped on a clean apron. A crowd was great for the bottom line, but it made for a hectic morning.

"Want me to cook or do tables?" I asked her.

"You cook, I'll do the front." She headed toward a table full of folks who were looking impatient. "And we're almost out of biscuits," she called over her shoulder.

"I'm on it." I checked the order slips clipped into the rack at eye level. I laid six strips of bacon on the griddle and poured twelve perfect circles of pancake batter, the blueberries sticking up like little round boats in a pond. After I stirred the meat gravy, I laid two biscuits on a small plate and ladled gravy on top, the crumbles of sausage bumpy under the sauce. A kitchen-sink omelet, three bowls of fruit salad, and an order of two eggs sunny-side up later, I slapped the little bell we used to indicate orders were ready.

When Danna picked up the plates, I said, "How'd lunch prep go? Did you finish?"

"I think we're all set."

I rolled out the last of the biscuit dough and slid a panful into the oven. It was getting near lunch time—even though we cooked breakfasts all day, we didn't offer the lunch menu until eleven thirty—so I loaded up the warmer with buns. And the rush never let up. Lunch customers started ordering burgers at eleven thirty sharp. The air was redolent with the mixed aromas of berries sizzling next to beef patties doing the same. When Abe materialized at my side at noon, the griddle in front of me was full and a couple of parties were waiting for tables.

"Popular place today," he said with a grin, his big brown eyes smiling, too. "Where do I start?"

"Wash your hands and grab an apron." I pointed to the box of clean store aprons. "Then I'll show you where we keep things. You and Danna can decide if you want to cook or work the front, which means taking orders, delivering food, and busing tables."

"Your wish is my command, madam." He stuck one foot out and bowed, making circle waves with his hand toward the floor before straightening and heading for the sink.

I laughed. "I really appreciate your help. I'll finish this batch of burgers and then go get changed." I flipped all the patties on the griddle and added slices of cheese to the two black bean veggie burgers and to one of the turkey patties.

From the sink, Abe said, "Looks like you didn't get your door fixed yet." He gestured with his head toward the front.

"I know. Picked up the glass from Don this morning but haven't had a free second to install it. It's over there by the side door. And speaking of the side door . . ." I told him the story of my stolen Christmas tree. "The very one you helped me carry to my van on Monday. Can you believe it?"

"Awful. Criminal. You reported it, I assume."

"I did." I slid the cooked patties onto bottom buns on which I'd laid lettuce and tomato. "Do you remember what the variety was? What kind of tree? I didn't pay any attention to the name."

"It was a Fraser fir. You gonna go get another one?"

"Maybe. If I ever have time. Which probably won't be until next Monday, but that's okay. If I get it closer to Christmas, it won't dry out as much. I thought it'd look pretty in here."

"The place looks great already the way you've decorated it." Abe smiled.

There was something about a dimple in a man's cheek that made my knees go weak. I cleared my throat. "Here's where we keep the meat and cheese. Veggie burgers are over here so vegetarians won't think they've been contaminated by meat." *Jim's suggestion.*

"But you cook them on the same griddle as the meat."

"I know, it's kind of silly. We warm the buns in

here." I pointed to the warming oven, and then to the cooler. "The walk-in is over there if you need to resupply, and Danna knows where everything is, anyway." I dinged the bell again.

"The ready bell?" he asked.

"Sure is." Danna said as she walked up. "Hey, Abe. Thanks for helping out."

"I'll leave you guys to it, then," I said. "See you in the morning, Danna. And Abe, I owe you one."

"I won't forget to take you up on it." He locked his gaze on mine.

Oh, boy.

I parked my van at the end of a row of a dozen or more cars in front of the Berrys' house and sat for a moment. The funeral had been sparsely attended, which surprised me. Sue and Glen Berry were both from South Lick themselves and had lived in town their whole lives. I would have thought the church would be packed. The paucity of attendees had to be a testament to Erica's difficult nature. Jim was there with the family, of course, and a number of people I didn't know. Octavia stood in the back. I chose not to sit up front with Jim, instead deciding to take a seat toward the rear. After I spied Adele and Samuel, I slid in next to them. The service blessedly didn't run on too long, and the priest managed to find some positive things to say about Erica.

I climbed out of the van and made my way into the house, handing my good coat to a teenage girl who said she'd take it upstairs. I was a little worried Paula would accuse me of the murder again. Maybe I could find a way to talk with her alone. I followed the noise of voices, laughter, and glasses clinking to the same kitchen-sitting area where I'd visited with the family on Monday. The island was now spread with platters of finger food like meat pastries, tiny meatballs, deep-fried shrimp, Buffalo wings, something looking like it might be little catfish cakes, and more. Not a fruit or vegetable in sight, but I'd gotten used to that in Indiana. Lots of Hoosiers really liked their meat, at least in this area. A table, next to a side wall, was set up as a full bar, and by the looks of the crowd almost everyone was partaking.

I spied Paula sitting with her back to me in the corner of the sunroom. I wasn't going to bother her right now. Adele had said she and Samuel weren't going to be able to come to the gathering, as they needed to get the sheep in before coming back to town for my dinner. After Jim waved to me from the other side of the dining room, I helped myself to a glass of Chardonnay, slid a few meatballs and shrimp onto a small plate, and headed in his direction.

Sue turned away from the cluster of women she'd been talking with as I passed. "Aw, Robbie, thanks for coming to Erica's service, hon." She laid her hand on my arm. "And we're so glad you could join us here, too." Her skin was puffy under watery eyes and the glass she was holding shook, making little whiskey waves.

"It was a lovely service, Sue."

She started to speak, then clamped trembling lips together. She squeezed her eyes shut and took a deep breath, then opened them. "My baby's dead. But we have to move forward, don't we?" She pasted on a steely smile as she lifted her chin. "Now you go ahead and have a fine time, hear? You got yourself something to eat and drink, good." She patted my arm and turned back to the women.

It wasn't right, for a mother to lose a child. I wove my way over to Jim, my own eyes suddenly filled with tears, grateful he stood alone. I set my drink on an end table, tucked my hand through his arm, and squeezed.

"You all right?" Jim peered down at me. He took a step back, effectively disengaging my arm.

I swallowed hard. "Feeling sad for Sue all of a sudden." And wishing for the comfort of his arm. I swiped my eyes, and took a sip of wine.

"I know. Doesn't matter how prickly Erica was, she was still their little girl." He gazed at Glen, then at Sue.

We stood there without speaking for a couple of minutes, watching guests and family talking, eating, pouring drinks. Paula sat on the couch with a couple of other women her age, and Max, holding a plate of food, was in an animated conversation in the far corner with Vince and several men I didn't know. I watched as Max lifted his fork with his left hand and took a bite.

"What are you making for this birthday dinner tonight?" Jim asked.

"Not sure yet. It's going to be easy and fast, though." I glanced at a wall clock. "It's only three, but I shouldn't stay long." I looked at Jim through narrowed eyes as I thought of what Danna had told me. "But before I go, I want to run something by you. Let's go find somewhere quieter to talk."

He cast me a look I couldn't interpret, blinking fast a few times. He glanced around at the room, but finally followed me out through the hall to the small living room in the front, which was blessedly empty. I sat on the couch and patted the cushion next to me.

"What's the mystery?" he asked as he sat, but at the other end of the couch, instead. He jiggled his right knee up and down like a reciprocating saw, at a rate slow for a saw, but fast for a knee.

Why was he sitting way down there? "Well, Danna . . ." *Wait.* Bringing up Jon's death right now could be a painful thing for Jim. A clock ticked on the mantel.

"Danna what?" He waved a hand as if to bring me back.

I let out a breath. "She was looking for information about Erica on the Internet."

"Trying to figure out who killed her?"

"I guess." *What the heck.* Jim might already know about the corrupt police officer. "She found a news story about the police officer who was investigating your brother's death. Well, not investigating, but the one who—"

"The one who declared it a suicide?" Jim's mouth looked like he'd tasted spoiled tofu. "The corrupt one?"

"Exactly. This reporter was digging into the officer's story. Danna said the article speculated your brother was murdered, that he didn't commit suicide."

Jim looked horrified. "Why didn't I ever see this article?" He shuddered.

"Maybe it came out after you'd come back down here. After his funeral."

"Does this reporter think the officer killed Jon?" His low, urgent tone matched his lowered brows.

"I don't know. I haven't read it yet. But get this. The reporter also implied Erica might have been having an affair with the officer."

Jim stared at me. The noise from the back of the room floated into our bubble of silence, a buzz of talking punctuated by a laugh here, a clink of glass there.

"And that she killed my brother. Her husband. The only one who adored her." His nostrils flared and his eyes were grim gems.

I nodded slowly.

"I always thought it didn't make sense. Jon's death. He never would have killed himself. Never." He pushed himself to standing, then paced to the opposite side of the room and back. "Good thing I didn't hear about this earlier. I would have killed Erica myself."

"What did you say?" Max bellowed. He stood in the doorway with clenched fists.

Oh, crap.

"Did you just say you killed Erica?" Max took two strides into the room.

Jim held his hands up. "No, of course not. Back off, now."

I stood, too. "We were talking about something that happened in Chicago, Max. A long time ago." I kept my voice light. "Jim was joking."

Max stared at Jim, but he relaxed his hands. "You don't joke about murder, man. You just don't."

Chapter 18

I unloaded two cloth grocery bags full of food, including various candies for the gingerbread house, in my apartment kitchen before flipping on the radio in time for the five o'clock news. I needed to get going on dinner. But after I'd delivered the news bombshell to Jim, I couldn't very well simply get up and leave. He'd been stunned by the allegation Erica might have killed his brother, and after Max left the room, Jim made me promise to send him the link after I got it from Danna. He'd kept a physical distance between us, though, which wasn't like him. And come to think of it, he'd been acting a little odd even before I talked to him about the article.

At any rate, I hoped he'd be calm enough to enjoy the dinner tonight. Which we wouldn't be having if I didn't get busy.

I took a minute to check out the store, but all was well there. Danna and Abe had cleaned and tidied everything, and the tables were even set for tomorrow. They'd left the holiday lights on, so the place sparkled in more ways than one. Even the glass in the door—the glass in the door! Abe must have installed it. What a great guy. I hurried over to check it out. Perfect glazing, and not a fingerprint in evidence, so he'd cleaned it, too. Now I owed him double. I whacked the *Total* key on the antique cash register and lifted out a nicely full till. I transferred all except the starting cash for tomorrow to a zippered bank bag and carried it back to the safe in my apartment. I didn't bother to lock the door between my apartment and the store, since nobody but me would be in the store before I opened up again in the morning. Now it was time for shrimp bisque.

After chopping and sautéing shallots, celery, and garlic in the Dutch oven, I added half a cup of brandy and let it cook down for a couple of minutes. I stirred in uncooked white rice and tomato paste, followed by a bottle of clam juice and a quart of shrimp stock I'd taken out to defrost this morning. As I waited for the pot to come to a boil, I poured the end of a bottle of Chardonnay from the fridge into a glass and took a sip, then minced a red sweet pepper and threw that in the pot, too. I was itching to read the article by the investigative reporter, but that would have to wait. What if his ideas were correct? Who could follow up on them? The police usually protected their own. They probably weren't going to investigate. And now that Erica was dead, she couldn't be questioned or made to testify.

Maybe the police officer himself killed Jon, or worked with Erica to make it happen.

I stared at the blue enamel of the Dutch oven, and at the concentric circles in the lid. Maybe the police officer came down here and killed Erica. What had I thought at the Christmas tree farm when it had seemed someone was after me? *Kill once, kill twice, what's the difference?*

Steam and the busy sound of boiling brought me back to the present. I shook off thoughts of murder in Chicago as I turned down the heat under the pot. After I drew out Mom's handmade salad bowl, featuring strips of wood in all different shades, I dumped in a bag of mixed baby greens. On top of the greens went a sliced avocado drizzled with fresh lime juice so it wouldn't brown before the guests arrived. I'd been lucky to find a ripe avocado at the store. I halved cherry tomatoes and grapes and added them to the salad.

What else? The cake. Or the cheesecake, more precisely. I knew I didn't have time to bake, and since the grocery store stocked Bake My Day cheesecakes anyway, I figured why not? It was the marble variety with a chocolate-cookie crust. And if Adele liked anything, she liked chocolate. But there was no way I could fit seventy-one candles on there. Instead I stuck seven around the perimeter and put two in the middle, including the all-important one to grow on.

I checked the clock. Five thirty. I was in great shape. I dashed into my bedroom to swap out the gray skirt for a pair of snug jeans, but left my black cashmere sweater on. I paused in front of the framed picture of Mom and me on a hiking trip when I was ten. She was smiling into the camera with her arm around me, and I was giggling about something. We wore our matching Sequoia National Park T-shirts picturing giant redwoods, the same giant redwoods that reached skyward behind us in the photo.

"Wish you could come to the birthday party, Mom." My throat thickened as I reached to pick up the frame. "I wish—"

The picture frame slipped out of my hand and crashed to the floor, accompanied by the tinkling of splintering glass. Swearing, I knelt and gingerly lifted up the frame. The photograph was intact, but glass now littered the floor to the side of my dresser. I held the frame by the stand and laid it face down on the top of the dresser, sliding back the clips securing the back. When I lifted it, a folded piece of paper lay between the back and the picture.

I froze. My name was written on the paper. The handwriting was Mom's.

Switching on the lamp next to my bed, I slowly unfolded the note in the light. I read it even more slowly. She'd written it that same summer I was ten, and she laid out the facts about my father I now knew to be true. The facts I'd discovered in October, which she'd never told me. Not once.

At the end, she wrote, *I plan to tell you about Roberto when you're ready. Maybe when you turn twenty-one, or maybe when you're the age I was when I was so overjoyed to give birth to you. But if something happens, I know you'll find this when the time is right. All my love, Mom.*

I sank onto the bed, tears dripping onto my lap. I stared at the letter, purple ink on pink paper, Mom's strong, sure hand letting me in on a secret I'd already discovered. The one secret she didn't tell me was why. Why she'd never told me I even had a father on this earth.

Chapter 19

At the sound of my cell ringing in the kitchen, I swiped my eyes, closed the bedroom door tight to protect Birdy's feet from the glass, and dashed into the kitchen. I could clean up the mess later. The caller ID said ABRAHAM O'NEILL.

After I said hello, Abe greeted me.

"Abe, I can't thank you enough for installing the glass in the door for me. You went way above and beyond." I tried to quietly sniff back my tears.

"It was no problem. Installing glass is as easy as sliding off a greased log backwards, you know."

A laugh bubbled up in me. "I know. What wasn't easy for me today was finding the time, so I really appreciate it."

"It looked all right?"

"It was perfect. How did the lunch rush go?" I asked.

"Also perfect. A good steady stream of customers. Nothing broke. We didn't burn anything. And Danna's a hoot to work with."

"She's awesome and so are you. I can't thank you

enough for filling in and then also fixing my door. Are you sure I can't pay you?"

He made a scoffing noise. "Of course not."

"Well, your next week's worth of meals is on the house. Totally."

"You could let me take you to dinner sometime." The smile in his voice was obvious.

"You're not going to give up on dinner, are you?" I asked.

"Nope. You take care now."

"You, too. See you around." I disconnected. *What a great guy.*

Steam emerged from the Dutch oven, and it was ten before six all of a sudden. I didn't have a second to think about Mom's note. If I got a chance, I'd tell Adele. But the note had waited seventeen years. It could wait another day or two.

I spun into high gear. I flung a tablecloth on the kitchen table, which was all I had for a dining room. I hastily unwrapped a round of Brie and a log of goat cheese onto a wooden plate, threw crackers in a basket, and uncorked a bottle of Merlot and another bottle of chilled Chardonnay. I set them on the table along with three glasses as I heard a knock at the back door. I hurried over and unlocked the door when I saw Adele through the glass.

"Anybody home?" Adele bustled in, Samuel right behind her. "Lordy, it smells good in here," she said after kissing my cheek.

"*Mmm-hmm,* it surely does." Samuel drew me in for a one-armed hug, then brought a bunch of flowers out from behind his back.

"Thank you, Samuel." I stuck my nose in for a

sniff. "They smell so good, too." Baby white roses mixed with red carnations and pink alstroemeria, with the obligatory baby's breath and fern fronds also in the bunch. "And look at your tie. It matches the flowers."

He smoothed down his silk tie, which featured an abstract design with swirls of pinks and reds. Adele pulled out a chair and sat.

"Have a seat, Samuel," I said. "Help yourselves to wine, and to cheese and crackers while I cook. I'm afraid I'm running a little behind. Happy birthday, Adele." I lifted my nearly empty glass toward her.

"Thank you, honey. Kinda thought you'd forgotten." She winked at me.

Samuel sat, too. After he poured red for Adele and himself, he beckoned for my glass and filled it, too. They both raised their glasses and the three of us clinked.

"Here's to many more years." I smiled.

"My thoughts exactly," Samuel said. He leaned over and planted a kiss on Adele's lips. "I plan to share every single one of them with you."

She covered her heart with her hand, then blew him a kiss off her fingertips.

I stirred the pot and made sure it was on the very lowest flame before covering it again.

"Who's the other glass for?" Adele asked.

I glanced over at Adele. "Jim is going to join us, too. That's okay, right?"

"Any beau of yours is a friend of mine," Adele said.

I turned back to the counter, and began to finely chop fresh thyme, parsley, and chives. Yes, he was my beau. Which someone once told me translated to *good looking*. My good looking. He was that, for sure. But did I also want him to be my love?

By six forty Jim still hadn't arrived. I'd pureed the bisque base and stirred in the heavy cream and herbs. The baguette was heated up and sliced, we'd set the table with napkins and Mom's silver, and the cheese plate now held only a smear of chévre and a memory of the Brie.

"I guess I'd better call him," I said. I'd just pressed his number when Jim flung open the door and hurried in, bringing a wave of fresh cold air into the almost overheated kitchen, his knee-length coat flapping open.

"I'm so sorry, Robbie. I got hijacked at the reception by a friend of the Berrys who wants to put his house on the market." Jim spoke fast, like he'd had too many cups of coffee. His hair was more unruly than usual and his breath smelled of mint. "He chewed my ear off for way too long, and then insisted we go look at his house together. Glen asked me to do it as a favor to him. I kept telling the guy he should be talking to a real-estate agent, not a real-estate lawyer." He shook his head and finally glanced around the room.

"Adele, happy birthday." He took two steps and leaned down to give her a hug, then shook Samuel's hand. "I apologize for being late to the party." He turned to me and kissed my cheek. "Forgive me? I even come empty-handed. I wanted to bring wine or something, but . . ." He shook his head.

I sniffed and caught a whiff of something a little sweet. Jim didn't usually wear aftershave or cologne, and men's scents weren't usually sweet, anyway. It must be something from the Berrys' house, maybe a perfumed soap. *Or perfume?* A mean little thought popped up in my brain, saying maybe Jim was lying about the guy and his house. Maybe he'd been renewing his acquaintance with Octavia instead. He still hadn't told me the details of his past with her, other than that they had dated. My girl-sense told me it was more than that. I slapped the thought down like a pesky mosquito. I'd never known Jim to lie about anything. He was a straight arrow and a kind one.

"Don't worry," I said with a mustered smile. "Sit down and have some wine while I cook the shrimp. I didn't want them to overcook." I emptied the bag of shrimp into a sauté pan and stirred as I checked the time. "They'll only take a couple of minutes."

Adele poured for Jim. Samuel asked him how his work was going. I let the three of them chat while I readied the dishes. Five minutes later I distributed the shrimp into four wide, shallow bowls and ladled bisque over them, adding a dollop of sour cream and a sprinkle of chopped chives and thyme on top. I set each bowl on a salad plate and handed them to the table one by one. "Jim, would you light the candles?" I handed him a box of matches before switching off the overhead light. I kept the lights on under the cabinets. Jim struck a match and lit the tapers on the table.

Sighing, I sank into the remaining chair. "Well, dig in." I picked up my soup spoon.

"I'd like to say a blessing if you don't mind, Robbie," Samuel said.

Oops. "Please do, Samuel." I set the utensil down and folded my hands.

"Dear God, please bless this wonderful meal our dear Robbie has made. We thank you for your abundance and your grace. Please keep us, your children, safe from harm and assist the police in finding the troubled soul who took young Erica's life from her. May that person be well and find his path to you, Lord. In Jesus's name, Amen."

A murmured chorus of "Amen" followed. I sure hoped the police would find that troubled soul soon, whether assisted by God or not. A murderer wandering free on the streets of town was not what any of us wanted.

I lifted my glass. "And a toast to the birthday girl. To a great year ahead, Adele, and many, many more."

"I second the motion," Jim said.

Samuel simply beamed at Adele with a smile capable of powering a village as we all clinked glasses.

"I thank you all most kindly," Adele said. "Now let's eat." She lifted a spoonful of the thick, creamy soup to her lips and savored it. "My, my, Robbie, you've outdone yourself."

"Heavy cream makes anything taste great, doesn't it?" A birthday dinner was no place for a diet, to my way of thinking, which was why I'd also pulled out the Irish butter. I spread a thick layer of it on a slice of bread and savored the rich, creamy flavor, imagining happy, frolicking, grass-fed Irish cows.

We ate in silence for a few minutes, with only the clink of silver on china and the sounds of quiet chewing as accompaniment. I glanced at Jim. He met my gaze and then looked quickly away. Something was definitely up with him.

"You weren't even in this apartment a year ago, Robbie," Adele said after a sip of wine. "Just look at all you've accomplished."

Samuel nodded. "You're a real go-getter. And the best cook in the county, to boot."

"No way," I said, feeling a blush rise up my neck. "I simply enjoy making food that makes people happy. Now, who's ready for seconds?"

Adele inhaled deeply before blowing out all nine candles an hour later, and we clapped to the brief smell of smoldering wicks. I handed her the box from Tiffany's store.

Her eyes widened. "You didn't have to get me a present, honey."

"Just open it," I said. I brought small plates, dessert forks, and a knife to the table.

Her face when she drew the angel out of the box made the purchase price worth every penny.

"How did you know I love these?" She held it by the string and watched the kite flyer spin, dancing in air.

"An angel told me." I cut four generous portions of cheesecake and passed them around. "Coffee or decaf, anybody?"

"No, thank you," Samuel said.

Adele and Jim shook their heads, too.

"A spot of whiskey? I have a nice one, made right over the border in Kentucky."

"Four Roses Bourbon?" Adele waggled her eyebrows. "Thought you'd never ask. You're driving, right, Samuel?"

"I am," Samuel said. "So you go right on ahead, sweetie."

After Jim and Samuel both declined, I poured two shots, sprinkling a few drops of water into each glass.

"What did you think of Erica's funeral?" Samuel asked.

Adele looked expectantly at Jim and me even as she swallowed a forkful of dessert. "*Mmm*, this is good," she murmured.

"I was glad to hear the priest say some nice things about Erica," Jim said.

"Me, too," I added. "But I was surprised at how empty the church was. Or maybe not, considering how she rubbed most folks the wrong way."

"Darn tooting she did." Adele snorted, then cast a quick glance at Samuel. "May she rest in peace."

"Robbie heard something very disturbing about Erica from Danna this morning," Jim said with knit brows.

"Oh?" Adele said.

"Danna told me she'd discovered a Chicago-area investigative reporter looking at a corrupt police officer up there," I said. I chased a bite of cheesecake with a small sip of bourbon. "The reporter suggested the officer might have been having an affair with Erica, and that Jim's brother's death might have been murder, not suicide."

"Lands sakes alive, that's some suggestion." Adele

narrowed her eyes. "Murder by this officer, or by Erica?"

"No way of knowing from here," Jim said. "Unless they were in it together, because Erica couldn't do the honest thing and just leave Jon." His eyes dragged down at the edges, and his mouth matched. He took a deep breath and let it out.

"I had the same thought earlier, Jim." I covered his hand with mine, but after only a moment he slid his out and laid it in his lap.

"And if there's corruption in the police, this reporter can't very well go to them to find out, then, can he?" Adele asked.

Jim shook his head slowly. "They're not all corrupt, I'm sure, but it might be hard for the reporter to figure out who is and who isn't."

"Jim, will it be a solace to you if you learn your dear brother did not take his own life?" Samuel's somber gaze focused on Jim.

Jim, sitting slumped, returned the gaze. "Yes. It would be a comfort, odd as it sounds."

"We sure can't ask Erica about it now, though." Adele swiped the last smear of cheesecake off her plate with her fork.

"No, we can't. There has to be a way to dig deeper into this thing," I said. I tapped my fork on the edge of my plate.

"My nephew William lives in Chicago, on the South Side," Samuel said. "You know, Adele, my brother's boy? Retired army, he is. And he happens to be a private investigator."

Jim sat straight up. "He is?"

"Yes, indeed." Samuel tapped his glass with one

finger. "I bet he could help this reporter fella look into the matter more deeply."

"I'll pay whatever it takes to get the truth about Jon." Hope played on Jim's face now, and determination.

"I had one more thought while I was cooking," I said. "It's probably a long shot, but what if the officer came down here and killed Erica? Maybe she was blackmailing him about Jon's death."

"Goodness, all these ideas. All these evil people." Adele pursed her lips.

"They are children of God, sweetie, every one of them, and surely they are troubled souls," Samuel said.

I caught the smallest rolling of eyes from Adele.

"You're absolutely right, Samuel," she said. She tossed back the rest of her whiskey and stood. "Now I've got to get these seventy-one-year-old bones home and into bed. Thanks for the perfect birthday party, sugar." Adele pulled me in for a hug.

Samuel stood, too. "I'll have Adele email you my nephew's phone number and email address," he said to Jim. "I think I have it written down somewhere. Not that I could use the email. Like I don't use the Google." He laughed. "Computers these days baffle me. They always have. I leave it to you young folks. My sweetie included." He slung his arm around Adele's shoulder.

"Thank you, sir." Jim rose and extended his hand to Samuel. "I really appreciate your help."

"Don't forget your angel," I said to Adele, but she was already wrapping it in the tissue.

"It was a perfectly delicious dinner, Robbie," Samuel said. "We're much obliged to you."

"Totally my pleasure. Easy and fun." I glanced at Adele. "Now let me give you the rest of the cheesecake to take home, too."

She made a stopping gesture with her hand. "You keep it. It's far too rich for us old folks to be having more than one piece a year."

"You sure?"

Adele looked at the half-empty platter and back at me. "What the hey. You only live once." She grinned.

Chapter 20

I wiped my hands on the dishtowel and hung it on the hook next to the sink. "Thanks for helping clean up," I said to Jim, giving one last swipe to the drainboard with the dishrag. We'd done the dishes and pots in near silence. Every time I tried to comment on the dinner or the murder investigation, I got a monosyllable in return and finally gave up.

"Not a problem." He rolled his sleeves back down and buttoned the cuffs with quick movements. "Think we could take a look at the article?" he asked.

So that was why he'd stayed. It sure hadn't been for the conversation. Something was going on with him, no question. I supposed I could simply ask him. But no, I'd let him tell me when he was good and ready.

"Sure, if Danna sent the link. Come on in here." I gestured for him to follow me into the living room. It wasn't a big space, but I loved the tall windows looking out onto the old barn and the woods beyond. I'd furnished it with my desk, a small sofa, and an easy chair. The wood on the sleek coffee table and end tables shone, partially from the love Mom had put into crafting them for me. A big split-leaf philodendron I'd nurtured since high school reached for the ceiling in the corner of the room. Birdy, who'd made himself scarce when we were eating dinner, lay on the back of the sofa curled up in a sleeping ball of black and white.

I sat and scrolled through my email until I saw one from Danna. "There it is." I clicked the link and pointed to the article on my laptop screen.

Jim sank to his knees on the floor next to my wheeled chair, his left arm around the back of the chair. His face came right above my shoulder and I was stunned by how intimate it seemed sitting this way. He smelled like himself again, but I still caught a faint trace of something sweet. I wanted to take his head in my arms, kiss it, stroke it. I know earlier I was doubting my feelings, but not in this moment. I wanted to—

He reached over to the touchpad and scrolled down in the article. I cleared my throat a little to calm down. This feeling obviously wasn't mutual. At least not right now. When he reached the end he sank back on his heels and then sat on the floor, knees up, resting his arms on them.

"Not much more than Danna told you." He swore and shook his head. "Did Samuel send his nephew's name yet?" He gazed up at me.

I checked. "No, not yet. But they probably just got back to Adele's, and I imagine he has the informa-tion at his own house."

"So I won't get it tonight."

"I doubt it. I'm sure Samuel is staying over at

Adele's. They do sleep together, you know," I said. "But I'm sure he'll send it along tomorrow. Or have Adele do it."

He looked at the floor again.

"Let me do a search for the reporter's name." I tried several options, but didn't see anything new. "No luck there."

"I'll have to wait," Jim said.

"So." I swirled the chair until I faced him. *The heck with waiting.* "You really never told me about your past with Octavia. Will you now?"

"You don't want to leave that alone, do you?" He shoved himself up to standing and stuck his hands in his pockets, gazing down at me. He didn't smile.

"No." I smiled, instead, to soften my refusal to let go of the topic. "Did something terrible happen? Did you guys conspire to kill her husband or something?" I said lightly.

He let out a groan and sank down onto the sofa. "I told you we dated about ten years ago. She was going through her state police training in Bloomington. I'd recently moved back here and opened my practice after law school. We met at the contra dance and I fell really hard in love with her. Really hard. She's very smart, and she has a passionate side hidden behind her all-business all-the-time attitude." He took off his glasses and rubbed at the bridge of his nose.

I winced. Like I wanted to hear about Octavia's passionate side. I watched him. So they'd met at the contra dance. Maybe Jim kept going to the dance hoping Octavia would show up again. Or out of nostalgia. I wished he hadn't taken me to the same dance. "What happened?"

"She was in love with me, too. We were both busy, but we spent weekends together, and that summer we went up for two whole weeks to Michigan's Upper Peninsula and stayed in a cabin her family owns." He gazed at the dark window as if he could see the six hundred miles to Sault Sainte Marie. "I knew our time was short there, and I didn't even want to go to sleep because I knew it would mean I would miss out on hours of being with her."

I waited. I was getting a bad feeling about this. But I waited.

"What happened was she was married when I met her," he finally went on. "And she decided to go back to her husband. She's a few years older than I am—she must be forty by now. Her husband was twenty years older than her and wasn't in good health. She didn't feel she could leave him." He finally met my eyes. "It broke my heart. I'd never loved anyone like that."

"You're still in love with her." It seemed so obvious I didn't know why I hadn't seen it before.

"I don't know. I've always wondered if it would have worked out between us once we'd gotten over the giddy phase. We never had the chance to try."

"Have you seen her this week?"

He sank his face into his hands. After what seemed like a year, he raised his head and patted the couch next to him.

"Come and sit?"

The dread in my stomach was cold and hard, but

I went to the sofa and sat. Not right next to him, but a foot away. I twisted to face him.

"I really, really like you, Robbie. You know that, right?" He reached for my hand.

I nodded without speaking. I let him hold my hand, my fingers shorter and broader than his long, slender ones. A faint haze of fine red hair coated the back of his freckled hand, a contrast to my smooth olive skin.

"I like the way we are together. I admire you and I love spending time with you." He studied our linked hands, then looked up. "When you said Octavia was in town it stunned me. I hadn't seen her or heard from her in a decade, but all those old feelings gushed up like it was yesterday."

"Have you seen her this week?" I couldn't help my voice coming out as if it were crafted of cold steel. I drew my hand away and rested it in my lap.

He gazed at me with sad eyes, then set his hands on his knees and sat up as straight as a piece of reinforcing bar. "I lied about the real estate guy."

Guess I called that one right.

"Octavia spoke to me after Erica's service. I met her in Nashville for a quick drink after I left the Berrys'. That's why I was late getting here."

"I thought you smelled like a woman's scent." I clamped my lips together.

"All we did was have a drink, Robbie."

And some kissy face, too, no doubt. I've never yet met a bottle of beer that gave off a sweet aroma.

"Does she know you've been seeing me?" I didn't let my voice wobble.

"I didn't tell her."

"Nice." I narrowed my eyes. "Is she still married?"

He examined his hands. "Her husband died last year."

Birdy slept next to my right ear. He stirred a little and gave out a soft sigh in his uncomplicated feline dream. "Well, how lovely for you." I stood, my very complicated feelings roiling inside me. Birdy opened his eyes and leapt to the floor in one movement, tearing into the kitchen.

"Robbie . . ." Jim reached for my hand, his eyes imploring me, but I took a step back.

"You go on and figure out what you want. Who you want. It's been nice knowing you." I turned and followed Birdy. I didn't know if I was going to start bawling or smash a dish on the floor. Maybe both at the same time if he didn't get out of my house.

Chapter 21

I sat at the kitchen table with another finger of bourbon in a glass, the microwave clock reminding me with its 9:01 reading that I hadn't done any prep for tomorrow. Jim had slid toward the door as I faced the kitchen window, my hands gripping the edge of the sink.

"I'm so sorry, Robbie," he'd said. "I'm so sorry."

I hadn't turned to watch him leave.

Birdie sidled out of the hall and rubbed against my legs. Funny how things happen. It was only a couple of days ago I'd started wondering if Jim was the right man for me. Maybe I'd picked up his rekindled feelings for Octavia in the energy layer or whatever goofy New Age thing was most recent. I'd never been the kind of Californian to look for auras, or believe in crystals or homeopathy. Maybe there was something to feelings traveling in the public airspace, though. South Lick was a pretty small town, after all. Or maybe it was the rush of hormones aimed in someone else's direction. He'd seemed totally normal and attentive in Bloomington

Sunday night. I realized I hadn't seen him again until today. He'd seemed kind of standoffish at the Berrys', come to think of it. And that was even before he'd hung out with Octavia. But, no, he'd said they'd talked after the service.

My doubting problem was solved for me, at any rate. My heart hurt, but not as much as it might have. At least he'd had the decency to tell me right off the bat, unlike what my rotten ex-husband had done while we were still married. And now I had another problem, hashing over why Mom had decided not to share my father's identity with me. Not before she died, not in the note, and not even in her will. She didn't expect to pass away in her fifties, of course. Who does? I carried the dustpan and hand broom into the bedroom and swept up the shards of glass, making sure no slivers remained to cut either Birdy's or my feet.

After I dumped the glass into a paper bag and put it in the trash—if only it was so easy to discard life's problems—I sat at the laptop again. I forwarded the link to the article to Adele and to Jim without any additional message. I was dying to read the article in depth, but I had prep to do. I took my drink into the restaurant, and let Birdie come along. Normally he wasn't allowed in the store—the Board of Health would have a cow, or worse, if they knew—but I could use the company right now. Birdie was delighted and began exploring every corner. The glow of the holiday lights gave him shadows to play with. And reminded me I still didn't have a replacement tree.

As I stood in the walk-in with my shaken-up life,

I decided to shake up the menu a little, too. I spied a few baguettes I'd gotten for the party in case we ran short on food but I hadn't used them. I could offer a special French toast bake in the morning. Slightly stale bread was perfect for French toast. I pulled out the bread and eggs, then returned for half-and-half, butter, and pecans.

The repetitive motion of sawing the long loaves into inch-wide slices calmed my brain and helped me get Jim and Octavia out of there. No puzzle solving was going to change that situation. I wanted to think about the much more urgent question of murder, instead. It was already Wednesday night and no arrest had been made, as far as I knew. Unfortunately, instead of seeing the puzzle pieces in a clear, still pond, my thoughts were a murky roiling river after a downpour, with the muck stirred up after the storm topped by opaque, dirty foam.

I washed my hands and cracked eggs into a big bowl, enough for three large pans. I could triple a recipe in my head by now. I ran through the possibilities as I worked. The corrupt cop was new on the list of suspects. Vince was right up there, too. Tiffany and her argument with Erica qualified her. Who else? Max, maybe, although I didn't think he would do anything to imperil the life of his unborn baby, and for Paula to find out her husband had killed her sister would be a huge shock. *Paula.* She was the last person to see Erica alive, except for the killer— unless she murdered her own sister. Phil might still be under suspicion, but I would bet my entire business on his incapacity to harm anyone.

After I beat the eggs with the half-and-half, I

added sugar, vanilla, cinnamon, nutmeg, and salt and mixed it well. I reached for the Grand Marnier and added that, pouring a little into a glass for me to sip, too. When Birdie came over to investigate, I poured a bit of half-and-half in a saucer for him and set it on the floor. I was probably setting a bad precedent, but tonight I didn't care. I sipped the orange-flavored liqueur, then buttered each pan and began dipping the slices in the egg mixture. I arranged them, overlapping, in one pan after another. Too bad I couldn't line up all the suspects in an overlapping row and pick out the guilty one. I stilled my hands.

Wasn't Jim a suspect, too? He was also family, after all. The thought hadn't even occurred to me while I was feeling connected to him, fond of him. It was pretty obvious why it had now. But if he and Octavia were a number, that would be a major conflict of interest. Wouldn't it? Even without their having a drink earlier today, the simple fact of them having a past together should disqualify her from investigating him.

I resumed working, finishing off the three pans quickly along with the Grand Marnier. The comforting smell of cinnamon didn't do much to dispel the unease of an unsolved murder. I sprinkled chopped pecans over the top of the bake, covered the pans with foil, and carried them one by one back into the walk-in. As I cleaned up, I glanced at the clock and groaned. I should talk to Buck about Jim's relationship with Octavia as it pertained to the murder investigation. But it was almost ten o'clock. It wasn't an emergency, and I needed to get to bed. Calling him would have to wait for tomorrow.

The first customer to walk in the door the next morning, at seven sharp, was Octavia. *Just my luck.* Danna was about to wait on her when I held up my hand.

"I've got it." Maybe I could slip some poison in her coffee. I grabbed the coffee pot in one hand and a menu in the other, and headed for the small table where she'd taken a seat. Octavia removed her jacket and hung it on the back of her chair. The first pan of French toast had finished baking and the warm cinnamon-spiced air smelled like anything but poison.

"Good morning, Octavia." I handed her the menu. "Coffee?" I could rise above petty feelings with the best of them. At least for a while, and certainly for the sake of my business.

"Please." She returned the menu. As with every time I'd seen her, her hair was a perfect cap, and she wore the same sensible slacks and blazer with her sensible black sneakers. Sure didn't look like a passionate package to me. "Can I get two poached eggs with whole wheat toast, no butter? And a bowl of fruit, whatever you have." She gave me a half smile.

"Of course." I poured her coffee and headed for the cookware shelves. Poached eggs. First customer ever to ask for that. Good thing I had a vintage egg poacher somewhere around here. I spotted it and carried it to the kitchen area. After I scrubbed it, I set the eggs to poaching, grumbling in my mind about prissy people who didn't think eating fat was good for them.

A couple of minutes later I set her order in front of her. She was focused on her phone, but I stood there until she glanced up and thanked me.

"How's the case going?" I asked.

"I can't discuss it with you, Robbie."

I glanced around the store. Nobody else had come in yet. I sat opposite her. She gave me a disapproving look before dipping a corner of toast into one of the eggs.

"I learned something I think you should check into." I rested my forearms on the table and leaned forward. "There's a corrupt police officer in Chicago who might have been having an affair with Erica. And they might have killed Jim Shermer's brother together."

She blinked fast several times. Jim's name got her attention. "The brother who committed suicide. That's a lot of *mights.* How would it relate to Erica's murder?"

"What if Erica was blackmailing the cop about the murder, and he came down here and killed her?" I sat back, wondering how she knew about Jon's suicide if she hadn't been in touch with Jim for a decade. Wondering if Jim had lied to me about that, too. But no, of course she'd know. Because of Erica.

"How did you learn about this officer who might have known Erica and might have killed her husband?" Nothing seemed to ruffle this woman.

I stood. "There's an investigative reporter in Chicago looking into it. Ask Jim." I headed back to the kitchen area glad I hadn't throttled her. Which would be wrong and illogical, of course. Jim wanting to be with her wasn't her fault. It wasn't anybody's fault. But the heart is rarely logical. For example, hadn't I doubted my feelings for him only yesterday? So why was I taking this thing so hard?

Abe pushed open the door and breezed in, followed by three other men. "Hey, Robbie," he called with a big smile. He removed his white hard hat and waved it at me.

I blew out a breath. Time to focus on my livelihood. Customers. Food. Even handsome workmen. "Hey, yourself. Hi, guys. Sit wherever you want."

The men, all electric company employees in work boots and green uniform shirts with the REA logo on the pockets, pulled out chairs, setting their hard hats on the floor next to them. Octavia glanced up from her phone and then looked away. I brought the coffee pot over to the guys along with four menus.

"Got the early shift today?" I asked as I poured.

"Sure do. Pole over in Gnaw Bone got hit by a car." Abe shook his head. "Driving drunk on a Wednesday night. Go figure." He glanced up at the Specials board. "French toast bake sounds perfect." He wiped the corner of his mouth and grinned. "Got to clean up the drool. I'll take the special with two fried eggs and sausage. Please."

I smiled right back. "You got it. How about the rest of you?"

Two of them ordered the same, except with bacon. The fourth, a gray-haired man with a sizable belly, slumped in his chair.

"I'll have the granola with fruit and skim milk, please. Doctor's orders."

Abe leaned over and elbowed the man's arm. "You're a good man, pal. Always do what the doc says."

The man groaned in return. "I pretty much have to. My health needs fixed. I sure don't want to have a heart attack. And he said if I keep up with the meats and fried foods, it'd be like I scheduled one."

"Breakfast coming right up." I walked the orders over to Danna.

A flood of customers kept us busy for the next half hour. Octavia paid and left, and a couple who'd been waiting occupied her table as soon as I wiped it down. The place was full when Abe's group finished and pushed back their chairs. Abe brought the bill with a handful of dollars up to the register.

"How was the bake?" I asked.

He rubbed his stomach. "It was out-freaking-standing. Probably too sweet and rich to have every day, but once in a while?" He whistled. "Really hit the spot."

"You're not paying for your breakfast. I owe you from yesterday." I handed him back the cost of his meal. "Here's the change for the other guys."

He promptly deposited all of it in the Tips jar.

I shook my head. "Now come on, Abe."

"You split it with Danna. I want, we all want, this place to succeed." He stuck his hands in his pockets.

"Well, thanks." I took a deep breath. "So, uh, about that dinner." *Now I'd done it.* I could hear my mother's voice in my head warning me about rebound dates.

"Yes?" His eyes twinkled.

"I'd like to take you up on it. If the offer still stands."

"Of course it does. I thought you'd never ask." He turned serious, studying me. "This mean things are off with Shermer?"

"Let's just say I'm looking forward to dinner with you." I smiled.

"Pick you up at six, then. I want to take you to the new place in town, Hoosier Hollow."

"Today?" The word ended on a little screech.

"I like to *carpe* the hell out of the *diem*. So to speak." His dimple was back as he slid his hard hat on.

"*Carpe diem*, it is. See you at six." I watched him saunter out. What was I getting myself into?

Chapter 22

Danna cried out and swore as she jumped back from the griddle an hour later, slapping her hand. I hurried over, trying to ignore the scowls and pursed lips of two carefully coiffed matrons sitting closest to the kitchen area. I could tell they thought swearing was bad form at any time, but especially coming from a young woman.

"What happened?" I asked.

"Grease burn. One of the sausages exploded onto my hand." She uncupped her left hand from the back of her right. A nasty red mark streaked across the back of her hand. She squeezed her eyes shut.

"Ouch. Sorry you got burned," I said. "Go run it under cool water until it stops hurting. You know where the first aid kit is, right?"

She headed for the sink. "At least I'm left-handed."

"Pat it dry and put antibiotic ointment on it. We have some big bandages in there, I think." I hoped. "But cover it loosely, okay?"

I glanced back at the griddle and did my own swearing, except silently. The bacon was burning and so were a half-dozen pancakes. A customer waved one hand at me and pointed to his coffee mug with the other. A party of four appeared through the front door. And something else smelled burnt, too. *Damn.* The last pan of French toast bake. I'd forgotten to set the timer.

Our morning rush had turned into morning disaster. I scurried as fast as I could. I tossed the burned items and laid fresh bacon on the griddle, followed by six new scoops of pancake batter, then quickly pulled out the casserole and set it on the counter. It looked like the middle pieces would be fine but the edges were all blackened. As I carried the coffee pot to the man who'd waved, I almost burst out in a panicked giggle. Maybe I could pass off the dish as Blackened Jamaican Toast.

When Danna approached the griddle again with a big rectangular bandage on the back of her hand, I shook my head. "I'll do the cooking. You okay to serve and bus?"

"Yeah. It hurts, but I'm okay."

"If you're sure. I'm awfully glad it didn't splash into your eye or something. We both have to remember to pierce the sausages before putting them on the griddle." I was once again grateful Danna was neither a wimp nor a complainer. "Let me know if it gets too bad. You can go home any time, okay?"

She bobbed her head as she grabbed menus for the newcomers.

By the time Buck ambled in at around nine thirty, hat in hands, the breakfast crowd had mostly gone. I'd never gotten around to calling him, so he was a welcome sight. He kept his uniform jacket on but unzipped it.

"Sit anywhere, Buck," I called out. "Or, actually, can you come over here for a minute? There's something I want to talk with you about, but I can't leave the griddle."

Buck obliged. As he passed Danna, he said, "What happened there?" He pointed to her hand.

She wrinkled her nose. "Grease burn. Hurts like he . . ." She shifted her eyes to a table of white-haired ladies. "Like heck."

"Sorry to hear it, girl. You might should be careful. Grease is hotter than a hooker's doorknob on payday."

Danna snorted, then headed over to clear a table.

Buck approached the griddle and leaned against the counter to my left. "What's up?" he asked, stretching *up* into nearly three syllables, as usual. He folded his arms and crossed one foot over the other.

I glanced around to make sure nobody was seated near enough to hear. "I was wondering if the investigation has ever looked into Jim as a suspect." I kept my voice as low as I could, not quite believing I'd even said the words *Jim* and *suspect* in the same sentence.

"Shermer?" Buck scratched his head. "Why do you ask that, now?"

I lifted a shoulder, then flipped a couple of pancakes. "Jim's kind of like family with the Berrys, isn't he? Aren't they always the first people you look at?" I straightened four strips of bacon, questioning why I'd even brought it up. Was I trying to exact revenge on Jim for dumping me?

"Now, Robbie. Thinking Shermer killed Erica makes about as much sense as a trapdoor on a canoe. Thought you two were sweet on each other, too. And anywho, you know I can't talk about what Octavia thinks or doesn't think. It's her show this time around."

"That's another problem." I cleared my throat while I tried to figure out the best way to say it.

"What is? That we got a statie in here telling us what all to do?" Buck matched my soft voice.

"Not that, so much. But if Jim is a suspect, Octavia has a conflict of interest. She and Jim are involved. Romantically."

"They . . . what'd you say?" He stared at me.

I squared my shoulders. "They used to go out, like ten years ago, and now they are again. He told me last night." I was horrified to hear my voice wobble and feel hot tears fill my eyes. I blinked fast and took a deep breath. I would not cry about Jim Shermer. I would not.

"Well, tie me to an anthill and fill my ears with jam. Don't that just take all? So he's left you high and dry?" He reached over and rubbed my shoulder for a second. "You poor little thing."

I swallowed. "It appears so. Don't worry about me. I'm fine." Or would be. One of these days. Eventually.

In a bit of a lull, I glanced at the entrance to see Tiffany slide in without jangling the bell on the door. How'd she do that? The cowbell, which hung from a little cast-iron hand and muscled forearm, always rang when the door moved.

Tiffany pulled out a chair at one of the only empty tables, a small one near the cookware shelves, and lowered herself into it with a fluid motion.

I headed in her direction, since nothing was on the grill at the moment. "How's it going, Tiffany?" I handed her a menu, flipping it over to the side with the lunch offerings.

"Fine." She didn't look up at me.

"Can I get you something to drink?"

"Hot tea. And a veggie burger, no bun, with a small salad, no onions, vinaigrette on the side." She handed the menu back, still not meeting my eyes.

"Coming right up." No "how are you?" and no "Please." *All righty, then. Be that way.*

I relayed the order to Danna and watched Tiffany as I assembled the carafe of hot water and a cup and saucer with a tea bag on the saucer. Chin on her palm, she was staring into space. I followed her gaze to the area where the pickle barrel had been. And where Erica's body had lain, now covered by the bench. This had to be coincidence. Didn't it? She couldn't know where I'd found Erica. Unless she'd killed her. I shook my head. It was more likely one of the local cops had talked about the crime scene to a family member and the information spread from there. Word gets around in a town like this. Or maybe Tiffany had learned about where Erica had been found when she was questioned by the police.

As I set down the tea fixings, I said, "Interested in any cookware today?"

She finally glanced up. "Not today, Robbie." Her

usually silky skin looked blotchy and her eyelids drooped as if they'd rather be closed.

"Is everything all right?" She might not want to answer—we didn't really know each other, after all—but it didn't hurt to ask.

Her faint smile only barely lit up her face. "I'm okay. But thanks for asking."

"Hey, Adele really loved the kite-flying angel I gave her."

Now Tiffany put on a real smile. "I'm so glad. I thought she would." Her gaze drifted back to where I'd found the body for a moment, the smile sliding off. Then, as if wrestling her focus away to something else, anything else, her gaze finally landed on the display of Adele's yarn. "How beautiful. Is that Adele's?"

"Right. I'm hoping to sell some for the holidays."

"If anyone comes into my store and asks where they can buy the yarn that goes into the hats I sell, I'll be sure to send them over here," she said.

"Great idea, thanks."

A buzzing sound came from a phone encased in a stylish black and white sleeve on the table. "Excuse me." She turned away, crossing her legs, and picked up the phone.

I headed over to clear a just-vacated table of four, but paused when the cowbell jangled again. A uniformed Wanda sauntered in. She set her hands on her hefty hips and surveyed the room.

"Good morning," I called out, heading her way with a menu. "Take any table."

When Wanda's gaze landed on Tiffany, she bobbed her head once, like she was agreeing with herself. "Well, butter my butt and call me a biscuit," she said, almost too softly for me to hear. She stood near the wall across the room, elbows out and hands on her hips, facing Tiffany's back.

Oh, dear. She'd better not scare customers away. Or arrest Tiffany right here in my restaurant. It didn't look like Tiffany had noticed Wanda's entrance, as involved as she was with her phone. I shook off the thought. No. Wanda wouldn't arrest Tiffany for the murder. That would be Octavia's job. Then why was Wanda so interested in Tiffany? I shook my head again.

"What can I get you, Wanda?" I said, handing her the menu. "You don't want to sit down?"

She shook her head. "Only got time for takeout today. Coffee, cream and sugar, and a couple of your Sloppy Joe hot dogs with everything. To go." She looked around the full restaurant. "You got time? You look busier than a one-legged man in a butt-kicking contest."

I laughed. "I have time. Want coleslaw with your lunch?"

"Nah. Too healthy." She barked out a laugh, but didn't stop looking at Tiffany. "But I'm going to go whole hog today and have some of your French fries."

"Got it. You can sit on the bench to wait, if you want."

"No need." Wanda pointed at Tiffany with her chin. "She been in here long?"

"A few minutes. Why?"

"Just curious."

Danna dinged the bell. I'd turned to go when Wanda laid a hand on my arm.

"Appreciate it if you don't let Ms. Porter know I'm here." She pursed her lips and blinked officiously.

Huh? "Why? Is she a suspect or something?"

"I'd appreciate the favor."

"Well, okay. But I can't help it if she happens to look behind her." What a crazy request in a big, open, public space, with Wanda not concealing herself at all. Not that there would be anywhere to hide except maybe by crouching down behind the kitchen counter, which would only get in Danna's way.

I hurried to the range, handed Wanda's takeout order to Danna, and brought Tiffany her lunch. She hadn't even poured her tea water. She looked up from the phone, which she'd been thumbing with both hands despite her long nails, now painted in a deep turquoise that matched her long-sleeved knit dress.

"Thank you so much, Robbie." She drew out a ten and a five and handed them to me. "That'll cover it, right?"

"Of course. I'll get your change." I perversely wanted to blow Wanda's cover. I glanced over at her, but she gave her head a little warning shake.

Tiffany's phone buzzed again and took her attention away from me.

"Thanks. Enjoy your lunch." I waited for her reply, but she only nodded, eyes and thumbs on her phone.

It took more than our usual quick turnaround before Wanda's meal was ready, since we'd had to start a new batch of fries. When a table opened up near where she'd been standing, Wanda waved me over.

"Any skin off your back if I eat here after all?" she asked.

"Not at all. Your lunch should be right up." And it was, so I carried it over to her.

She thanked me, but she was watching Tiffany the whole time. And because I was at least as busy as a two-armed proprietor-chef with a restaurant full of hungry customers, I didn't wait around to see what happened next. Which didn't mean I turned my radar off.

I was carrying a round tray full of drinks and salads to a table of four right beyond Tiffany's when she wiped the corners of her mouth and stood. She left the change I'd brought her on the table.

"Thanks, Robbie. A perfect lunch." She slipped into her jacket, sliding her bag over her shoulder. When she turned toward the door, I watched as her gaze passed over Wanda. And it stayed there as Tiffany froze in place.

My own gaze zipped to Wanda, who gave Tiffany a little pretend salute. I looked back at Tiffany, like I was watching a tennis match, except slower. Her lips pressed together in a grimace, the kind where your molars are clamped shut so tight they ache. As Wanda rose to standing, Tiffany rushed out the door. The bell tolled after her.

Chapter 23

As soon as I closed up and stuck the till in the safe, I changed into clean jeans and a sweater and headed out to Adele's in my van. I'd made sure Danna would check with her doctor if the burn seemed to get worse during the rest of the day. I hoped she wouldn't have to take the next day off, but if she had to, she had to. I'd cope.

Adele had sent along the email from Samuel with his nephew's contact info. She'd added a note: How's about coming over this afternoon after the store closes and doing some digging with me? Digging on the Internet, not in the garden.

Of course, I typed in return. Not only did I want to dig, I also wanted the kind of comfort only Adele could provide. A kitchen table, open ears, and plentiful hugs awaited me. Maybe I'd grab another Christmas tree on the way back, or maybe I wouldn't. I wasn't exactly feeling in the holiday spirit right now. I dutifully forwarded the private investigator's contact info to Jim, but didn't include a personal message.

I climbed into the van, remembering lunchtime. Wanda clearly had been interested in Tiffany. *But why?* She hadn't followed Tiffany out the door, so it wasn't like she was tailing her. Maybe Octavia had asked Wanda to keep tabs on Tiffany's whereabouts, which would mean the detective was still thinking of Tiffany as a suspect in the murder. I shook my head. Didn't make sense to me, but this week nothing much did.

After I stopped at the bank to deposit the take from the last two days, I aimed the van out of town. I didn't drive by Jim's condo on purpose. It simply lay on the most direct route to Adele's and I was busy thinking about Tiffany and Wanda. I instantly wished I'd gone the long way around. In front of his building, Jim and Octavia strolled hand in hand on the sidewalk, which sent an icicle into my gut. As I passed, they turned into a doorway flanked on one side by the bicycle shop and on the other by my favorite consignment store, both at ground level. It was the doorway leading to Jim's condo upstairs. Watching them, I wasn't watching the road. My right front wheel crashed through a pothole and the entire ratty old frame of the van clunked. I swore, steering out of the hole. When I glanced back, Jim looked over his shoulder directly at me.

I stared straight ahead and drove. Why did that have to happen, right here, right now? He probably thought I was stalking him or something. I pounded the steering wheel. Even with my doubts about us, I guess I liked him more than I realized. The sun, already beginning its descent toward the horizon at barely three o'clock, glared in my eyes as I turned west. These were the darkest days of the year in more ways than one. Why had I ever thought I could trust a man again? Now I wished I hadn't mentioned dinner to Abe. It wasn't fair to him, at all. But canceling at this hour wasn't exactly fair, either. Too late now.

Fifteen minutes later I pulled into Adele's drive. I didn't see Samuel's little red car. *Good.* As much as I liked Samuel, I really wanted to have Adele to myself for a bit. Sloopy ran up to greet me, so I reached back into the van for one of the dog biscuits I kept on hand for him.

"Come on, Sloops. Let's go see Mom." I handed him the biscuit.

He grabbed the treat in his jaws and trotted to the house, pausing once to make sure I was coming. Her door was unlocked, even with a murderer on the loose. Adele probably thought she was safe out here in the country. She did own a gun, after all, and knew how to use it. I called to her and went in. Sloopy plopped down on the old linoleum floor in the kitchen and started crunching.

"In here," she responded. "Dining room."

As often happened when I visited, the house broadcast the yeasty aroma of freshly baked bread. The loaf, already cut into, sat on a board shaped like a sheep, with butter in a dish and a hunk of cheese nearby.

"I'm going to grab a piece of bread first, okay?" I'd eaten lunch, but I'd been so busy on my feet I knew I'd burned up all those calories and then some.

"Of course," she called back.

I cut and buttered a thick slice, and added a wedge of cheese for good measure before I walked through the arched doorway. Adele sat at a laptop computer at the dining table. I'd only ever eaten in here at Thanksgiving or Easter, since we normally made do with the table in the warm, sunny kitchen. I kissed her cheek.

"Whatcha got?" I asked. I took a bite of bread, savoring the texture, chewing the crusty outer layer, before setting my plate on the table. The burnish of its rich red tone in the sunlight from the windows warmed the room, as did the colorful Caribbean paintings Adele had brought back from a trip to Haiti.

"Watch the finish." Adele pushed a cork mat toward me, which I dutifully slipped under my plate.

"Pull up a chair, honey," she said. "This is pretty dang interesting."

I sat next to her. "What is?"

"I read the article. The one Danna told you about." She pointed to the screen. "It's right here."

"I read it last night." The headline read, GOOD COP? OR BAD? I scanned the first couple of paragraphs again. "This reads more like an opinion piece, or something out of a gossip rag, doesn't it?"

"Sure does. But the writer's byline says *investigative reporter.*"

"Maybe he hadn't finished his investigation when he wrote it, but he wanted people to start questioning the cop."

"Could be." She shoved the computer toward me. "Here, you do the searching. I know enough about the computer to do my email and check the few sites and blogs I read every day. But you young folks are better at it."

I laughed and set my fingers on the keyboard. "Let me finish rereading the article first." I focused on the screen, reading and scrolling down until I came to the end. "Not much of substance beyond the cop's name, Bart Daniel. The reporter makes some provocative suggestions, though."

"What's the date on the story?"

I scrolled back to the beginning. "Hmm. Last June. Half a year ago."

"Try to find something more recent."

I searched on **Bart Daniel**. Nothing. **Bart Daniel Chicago**. Zip. **Bart Daniel police**. Strike out. "What's *Bart* short for?"

"Bartholomew."

I typed the full name and hit *Enter*. "Whoa. Look at this." I pointed to the screen. "Guess who's in jail?"

Adele's eyes widened as she read the article I'd unearthed. "Looks like the intrepid reporter accomplished his goal. Old Bart Daniel didn't kill Erica. He's been locked up for all kinds of offenses since October."

I sat back and regarded her. "So he's not Erica's murderer. Wonder who is?"

"It was kind of tempting to want some stranger from away to be the one who did Erica in, wasn't it." Adele tapped the table with a gnarled finger.

"There's still a stranger from away who's a possibility, this guy Vincent Pytzynska. He said he was from Chicago, a law classmate of Jim's brother Jon. Vince came all the way down here to pay his respects to the Berrys, but I found out he's really from Nashville. He easily could have known Erica in high school."

"But why kill her?" Adele asked. "Why now?"

"I don't know. And now Octavia is going to think I'm nuts. I told her about that Daniel guy this morning. She's probably already found out it couldn't have been him, after all. Except she's the last person I ever want to see again."

"Why in heaven's name would you say something like that, Roberta?" Adele cocked her head and watched me.

I finished off another mouthful of bread before I spoke. "Jim told me something last night after we did the dishes." I again felt the thickness in my throat meaning tears were on their way.

Adele pushed the computer into the middle of the table and covered my hand with hers. "About Octavia?"

"Yes. They'd been very much in love about a decade ago, but she decided to go back to her older husband, who was sick. Now she shows up in town. Her husband has passed away. And Jim wants another chance with her." A sob escaped my control. "On my way over, I saw them on the sidewalk holding hands."

"Oh, hon." Adele pulled me in for an embrace.

In the warmth of her arms, I let a few tears bubble up and out. She didn't say a word as she stroked my hair. When my sorrow was spent, I sat up straight and wiped my eyes with both hands.

"I'm sorry. It's just—"

"No sorries around here. You feel what you feel. And right now I feel like a cup of tea with some of that sorghum. It's just wasting space in the cupboard. Come on into the kitchen."

I followed her in and sat, watching as she put the kettle on, brought the bread and fixings to the table, and drew two small glasses out from a cabinet. I knew she and Samuel were fond of this drink, spirits distilled from an Amish farmer's sorghum.

"Too sweet for me. It's almost like molasses," I said. "But I'll bet in tea it's good."

"Yup." She poured an inch into both glasses and handed me one.

When she held hers up, I did too. After we clinked, I took a small sip and set it down. "It's a tough week for me. I want to tell you about something I found in my bedroom yesterday, totally by accident."

Adele tilted her head, but she waited for me to go on.

"I accidentally knocked over a picture frame, one with a photo of me and Mom in Sequoia when I was about ten, and the glass broke. When I picked it up, I found a letter from her to me between the frame and the photograph."

"My sweet Lord." Adele set her elbow on the table and covered her mouth with her fingers, her gaze full of concern.

I took a deep breath and blew it out. "She told me all about Roberto. I know about him now, of course. But what she didn't tell me was why—"

"Why she never told you." Adele waggled her head back and forth. "She never told me, either."

"But you knew he was my father."

"I did. Honey, I think she simply wanted you to be happy. The two of you were so close, and it didn't seem to matter to you not having a dad in your life."

I swirled the liqueur in my glass, watching how it clung to the sides, slowly sliding back down. "I guess it doesn't matter why. I don't have her to ask, but I have a father, and he cares about me."

"That's right. You go ahead and hang onto that, now."

I sat without speaking for another few moments. "You know, it's funny. Earlier this week I was starting to wonder if Jim was really right for me. But now he's decided I'm not right for him, or not as right as the charming detective, it smarts like a bee sting. Or more like a heartache."

"Of course it does. And, for the record, he's an idiot to choose anybody over Robbie Jordan." Adele took a good swallow of the sorghum. "*Whoo-ee.* That goes down just perfect."

I had to smile at her. She could be gruff at times, and was the most no-nonsense and competent woman I'd ever known. But she did like her little nip now and then, and didn't try to hide her appreciation for it. I sipped the drink again, rolling it on my tongue, the sweet liquid punctuated by the sharpness of alcohol.

"I think it grows on you." I sipped again.

"So don't I." When the kettle whistled, she jumped up and a moment later brought cups of herbal tea to the table. "How are we going to get you past this bump in the road called Idiotic Jim Shermer?"

"Well, I happen to have a dinner date with Abe in a couple of hours." I smiled and cleared my throat.

"The younger O'Neill boy? The cute one?"

"The very one." I doused my tea with the rest of my sorghum.

"Way to jump right back in the saddle, honey." She reached over and patted my hand. "If I were forty years younger, I might could go after that boy myself."

Chapter 24

Before I left Adele's, we'd talked more about Erica and the cop, and as I drove home I couldn't get the thought of them out of my mind. There had to be more to the story as far as Erica was concerned. But how could I find out? I could shoot the reporter an email. I could turn it all over to the lovely and passionate Octavia. *Now, Robbie, spite isn't an attractive trait*, I could hear my mother saying. I wrinkled my nose. I sure couldn't talk to Jim about it. I . . .

I slammed on the brakes, pulling to the side of the road across from the Beanblossom covered bridge. One person in South Lick might know all about it. I pressed the Berrys' number and said hello to Sue when she picked up.

"Hey there, Robbie."

"How's it going today, Sue?"

She didn't speak for a moment. "It's only about the hardest thing we've ever had to go through. But we'll be fine. It'll be all right."

"I'm so sorry. I lost my mom last winter, and—"

"Oh, hon. I didn't know about that. My heart just goes out to you."

"Thank you. The pain does get a little less sharp with time. A little." I cleared my throat. "Say, you know your friend Vince?"

"Of course. It was so dear of him to come down and offer his condolences in person."

"Absolutely. I wondered if I could speak with him, please. If he's staying with you."

"He's not here."

Rats. Had he already left town? I watched a bald eagle beat its wide wings toward Lake Lemon, and then glide under a sky that had turned to a steely gray in the last hour.

"He's staying at the Lamplighter Motel," Sue continued. "But he told me he's in town doing a few things."

Whew. "In South Lick?"

"No, he went up to Nashville. Let me give you his cell, okay? You might could catch him or figure out a place to meet."

"Thanks, Sue. Perfect." *Was it?* Abe was picking me up at six and it was already after four.

She rattled off the number after I found a pencil stub and an old receipt among the detritus strewn about my van. I thanked her again, disconnected, and pressed Vince's number.

After I greeted him, I said, "Remember me? I came by with some food on Monday."

"Sure. How's it going?" His voice, scratchy on the cell phone, sounded less jittery than before.

"I learned about something that happened in

Chicago, and I wondered if I could ask you a couple of questions."

"What about?"

"It's kind of complicated. Could we meet in person?" I asked. "Maybe for coffee in Nashville?"

"I guess. But I'm at Brown County State Park checking out some birds. I'm not done yet."

I looked toward the west. Shadows were lengthening, but it was still an hour until sunset. It would take me fifteen or twenty minutes to get there. The talking wouldn't take long. I should be able to swing it and still get home in time to get cleaned up for dinner.

"I'll be there as soon as I can, but it'll be at least fifteen minutes." Would he wait for me?

"That'll give me enough time. If I'm not already in the parking lot, I'll be heading that way on Trail One."

"Thanks so much. I'll see you there as soon as I can." The phone went dark. I had a sudden pang, questioning the wisdom of meeting someone who might be a murderer on a trail in the woods. But no, the park was always packed with nature lovers, hikers, birders, not to mention rangers. I'd stay in the parking lot and wait. I'd be fine.

At the state park entrance, I drove through the double covered bridge, the only one in the state, showed the ranger in the booth my yearly pass, and headed into the parking lot. Where was everybody? I saw exactly two vehicles, plus the state park vehicle near the booth. Must be the difference between early October and late November. The last time I was here, when I thought someone was using me as target practice, there'd been barely an empty parking spot. I glanced over at the Abe Martin Lodge, which looked distinctly unoccupied. I thought they were normally open year-round, but maybe they were closed for renovations.

I definitely wasn't going to head out Trail One to meet Vince. I climbed out of the van. Leaning against the driver's side door, I pulled up the collar of my thigh-length coat and snugged my scarf more tightly around my neck. The sun had sunk below the tree line and the temperature was dropping fast. Slate-colored clouds scudded by and the air smelled of pine with an overlay of wood smoke. Where was Vince?

Laughter came from the opening to the trail and I watched it closely. Maybe Vince had been bird-watching with friends. Instead, two middle-aged women trudged out, hardy in fleece sweatshirts, hiking shorts, and boots, with gloved hands holding pairs of walking sticks. They climbed into a small SUV and drove off, leaving only a tan sedan with Illinois plates in the lot.

I paced circles around my van, glancing occasionally at the trailhead. No Vince. I checked my phone. No message, and now it was quarter to five. Should I call him again? I didn't want to scare him off by being too persistent. I'd give him five more minutes and then I was leaving. If I didn't, I'd be late to meet Abe. I pulled down my e-mail account on my phone, but saw nothing important in my inbox. The scratchy, piercing cry of a raptor made me glance up to see one soaring overhead. It beat its wings to stay in place, and then swooped to the ground in the open field at the end of the lot. When it took to the air again, a field mouse struggled in its powerful talons. My hair prickled, and not from the cold.

"Waiting for somebody?" A reedy voice spoke from behind me.

I held tight to my phone as I whirled. Vince stood behind me with his hands in his jacket pockets. Binoculars hung around his neck over a khaki jacket.

"Where'd you come from?" I asked, patting my chest. "You startled me."

"Sorry. Came around the long way. Was tracking the song of a hooded warbler. Never did see it." His pale blue eyes were bright in his linen-colored face. Even the brisk air didn't bring any natural pink to his cheeks. He wore a black watch cap, with stray strands of reddish-brown hair sticking out over his ears like straw.

"No problem." I shivered again, and this time it was from the falling temperature.

"Want to get in and talk?" He gestured to the van. *No way.* "No, it's okay."

"So you said you had some questions for me." His words came out in a rush, and he rubbed his thumb and fingers together with a rapid motion like he was trying to polish them.

"I do, and thanks for agreeing to meet with me. Did you ever know of a man named Bart Daniel?"

"Bart Daniel." Vince gazed at the woods, then back at me. "Why are you asking?"

"He's a police officer in Chicago." I watched for his reaction.

His face darkened. "The one who called Jon's death a suicide." He shook his head. "I never met him personally."

"Did you know if Erica knew him? Hung out with him, even?"

"Erica did what she pleased." His mouth looked like he'd tasted moldy apple butter. "Husband's dead, why not hook up with the cop who didn't look into why a perfectly happy and successful man would kill himself?"

"So she went out with him? But only after Jon died?"

His nostrils flared. "I saw her with Daniel before Jon's death, too."

"Really?"

"All snuggled up in a booth at a bar across town from where Jon and Erica lived."

"Wow. Did you tell Jon?"

"And destroy his image of Erica as the perfect wife? No way."

"I read today the cop is in jail for corruption." I watched a crow soar across the parking lot and land in a tree.

"Good riddance."

"The investigative reporter might have had something to do with it, getting those questions out into public scrutiny."

He folded his arms. "Why are you looking into all this, anyway?"

"My b . . . my friend Jim is Jon's twin. We heard a reporter up there was looking into Jon's death. The article said it might not have been suicide, and that Daniel and Erica might have been involved. Murder is terrible, but thinking your twin killed himself is almost worse. I was only trying to help."

"Have you told the cops?" Now he watched me, the fingers on his right arm beating a rapid rhythm on his left.

With Jim seeing Octavia? "They know all about it."

Chapter 25

I stood in front of my closet. What to wear, what to wear? Abe said we were going to Hoosier Hollow. Which Christina had described as elegant Hoosier food. Which probably meant dressing up, but it was cold out, so my choices were limited. I decided on a magenta cashmere sweater that warmed my Mediterranean coloring and had a luscious floppy cowl neck. I paired it with a flared short black skirt I loved, pink tights, and knee-high black boots. I let my hair down and brushed it out, then pinned back a swoop with an abalone clip on one side. I slid the gold hoop earrings Mom gave me for my sixteenth birthday into my ear lobes, swiped on dark pink lip gloss, and I was ready. I was blessed with full, dark lashes and didn't really need makeup besides a little color on my lips.

And was I a little nervous? Sure. I knew it wasn't the wisest thing for me to do, jumping into a date the day after I was dumped by my previous guy. The last thing I wanted was to be burned in love one more time. But hey, I wasn't marrying Abe. It was only dinner.

Birdy ran to the kitchen ahead of me to make sure I filled his food and water bowls, so I obliged. The clock on the microwave read five fifty-five. I realized I didn't know where Abe expected to pick me up. Did he even know where the back door to my apartment was? I threw on my black wool coat, grabbed my gloves and bag, making sure my phone was in it, and let myself into the store. After I switched on all the holiday lights, I stood for a moment in their glow. What a dark, mixed-up start to the season, which was already dark enough without crimes and secrets to make it worse. No wonder ancient peoples in northern climes had lit candles and brought evergreens indoors in December to ensure the light would return with spring. I flipped on the outside lights, too.

I headed out and locked the heavy antique door behind me. When I didn't see a vehicle parked in any of the slantwise spaces in front of my store, I perched on the top step. I couldn't miss Abe this way.

As I sat, I thought about Vince and our meeting in the parking lot. So he'd known of the cop, but apparently not about the corruption investigation. Vince had said he knew Erica was seeing Bart Daniel, and had expressed his strong dislike for her. But had those feelings spilled over into hatred, enough hatred to kill her? Once again I wondered why he'd come all the way down here if he hadn't even cared about her. Something was very off about that man.

And speaking of men, where was the one who was supposed to be picking me up for dinner? Every time a car approached I thought it would be Abe, but it always drove on by. I didn't even know what kind of vehicle he owned. I kind of assumed it would be a truck, since he worked for the electric company. Which might have been my preconceived notion speaking, a blue-collar stereotype. For all I knew, he drove a Cooper Mini or a vintage Jaguar.

I yawned. It'd been a full day. Maybe this dinner date had been a bad idea. I'd be doing tomorrow's prep late again. I needed to run a load or two of restaurant laundry. And it was possible I should have placed an order this afternoon instead of running off to Adele's. Well, I was committed now.

A Prius drove by. It stopped suddenly, backed up and swung into a space, but the person who climbed out was not Abe. I cursed silently, longing for the anonymity of a much bigger town like Santa Barbara. Jim stood there, his hands on the open door, gazing at me. *Just my luck.* I closed my eyes for a second, but when I opened them he was still there. *Why?*

"Hi." I mustered a small smile.

"Robbie . . ."

I waited. I was not making the first move in this, whatever it was.

He shut the door and took a few steps until he stood at the bottom of the stairs. He clasped his hands in front of him and looked down at them. Finally he glanced back up at me.

"I saw you sitting there and I had to stop. I want

to say I'm sorry for springing my news on you last night like I did."

I lifted my chin. *Wonderful.* He wasn't sorry for what he decided to do, only for how he told me. I didn't trust myself to say the right thing if I opened my mouth, so I didn't.

He opened his palms. "I'm so sorry." His eyes and mouth dragged down at their outer edges. Even his posture sagged.

"You might like to know what Adele and I found out." I kept my voice level.

He frowned. "What?"

"The corrupt cop in the article, the one I sent you the link to? He's been in jail for a couple of months. And Vince told me the cop and Erica were indeed involved."

"Vince. Jon's jumpy friend from Chicago."

My cell rang in my hand. One quick look told me Abe was calling. Gazing at Jim, I connected.

"Hey, Abe," I said into the phone.

Jim narrowed his eyes.

"Robbie, I'm really sorry to be late," Abe said in a rush. "We had an emergency at work. Do you mind heading over to the restaurant and waiting for me there? Order a drink, an appetizer, whatever you want. I'll be there as soon as I can. Twenty minutes, tops."

"Not a problem. Thanks for letting me know."

"I'll hurry. We have a reservation under my name."

"Got it." I disconnected and pushed up to standing. I walked down the stairs until Jim had to back up a couple of paces to let me by. "Excuse me." I passed him and turned left on the sidewalk.

"Where are you going?" he asked, sounding bewildered.

"Dinner with a friend."

The restaurant was only ten minutes away by foot. I stayed on the main drag instead of taking the shortcut through the alley like I had in October. Getting shot at in the dark can really change your habits. I walked briskly because of the cold, and because it was a welcome relief to get some exercise. Having not only a busy schedule but also a busy brain was tough on the psyche. For me, a good workout was the best way to fix racing-thoughts syndrome, and I hadn't made time for one since Monday.

I pushed open the door to Hoosier Hollow to a welcome rush of warm air fragrant with scents both savory and sweet. A greeter about my age asked if I had a reservation.

"Yes. For two at six fifteen under the name *Abe O'Neill*. Sorry we're late."

She looked around. "Is he parking the car?"

"Um, he'll be even a little later. I hope that's okay." I glanced past her. The place was bustling, but several tables still sat empty.

"No worries. Please come with me."

I followed her to a table for two near a fireplace set in the wall facing on the street. A welcome fire crackled in it, but the back wall of the fireplace was made of glass, so passersby could see the fire, too. A pale pink tablecloth stretched over the table, which was set with dark pink cloth napkins that nearly matched my sweater.

"I'm a friend of Christina's, the chef," I told the woman. "She said to mention it when I came in."

The woman smiled. "She's great. I'll let her know you're here."

A candle in a glass sparkled in the middle of the table and bathed the pink carnations in a small Mason jar with a rosy light. Watercolor paintings of southern Indiana scenes decorated the brick walls: the Beanblossom covered bridge, a limestone building from the university, a cove with its lake water reflecting brilliant fall leaves, a snowy wooded scene with two deer bounding away. I didn't know what I'd expected—more of a country-chic decor, maybe—but this was elegant and comfortable at the same time.

I opened the menu and perused the appetizers, since my stomach was making it very clear it'd been a long time since the bread and cheese at Adele's. When a waitress appeared with a pitcher of water, I ordered a glass of Pinot Noir.

"And can I get the catfish cakes to start, please?" The description sounded fabulous.

"You bet."

I'd wait to decide on the main course until Abe got here. I idly glanced around the room. I thought the restaurant had been open only a couple of weeks, but word must have spread about Christina's talents, because it was busy. In the few minutes since

I'd been seated, diners had filled the few remaining available tables. I spied Tiffany Porter emerge from under the sign that discreetly read RESTROOMS. She wore a sleek sleeveless black dress with black four-inch heels, and strutted like a model back to her table at the far end of the restaurant. She caressed the shoulders of her dining companion, a tall, dark-haired man in a suit and tie, before she sat. I thought their table looked pretty empty from where I sat, so they must have started right when the place opened.

I had no idea of Tiffany's personal life, except she'd said she lived alone. Nice she had a handsome date on a Thursday night. Come to think of it, Max had said he often saw her out with men. As I spied Abe at the reception podium, I smiled. I had a handsome date, too.

I watched as the greeter pointed to me. Abe's eyes followed and I waved. A moment later, he sank into the chair opposite me, wearing a yellow sweater over an Oxford shirt and a neatly knotted turquoise tie.

"Welcome," I said, still smiling.

"Thanks. Sorry again for being late. Some idiot decided a utility pole in Beanblossom was his garage. We had to sister it to a new one and get the wires back up, since it knocked out power to half the town." He sipped his water. "Which, of course, isn't saying much in Beanblossom." He tilted his head as he smiled. "You look nice, Robbie. That color is stunning on you."

"Thanks." I sipped my wine to cover my sudden nerves. He must have grabbed a quick shower. He'd combed his walnut-colored hair, damp around the edges, back from his forehead. His cheeks glowed in the firelight. He smelled clean, like soap and rainwater.

"What are you drinking?" He leaned forward and touched my glass.

"An Oregon Pinot Noir. It's very nice. And I ordered an appetizer. We can share, if you want."

When the waitress approached with a basket of bread, he said, "I'll have a double Glenlivet neat."

"You got it," she said and turned away.

"After a long shift, there's nothing like a Scotch whisky."

"I like Kentucky bourbon, myself," I said. I reached into the basket and pulled out a roll with the springy feel of sourdough, both to give my hands something to do and to make my stomach act like a lady instead of a roaring, starving beast.

"How was your day, Robbie?"

"Not much happened. You know, cooking. Some more cooking. And a bit more cooking." The last thing I wanted to get into was a discussion of strangers from Chicago. Or murder.

His rolling laugh burst out as he tilted his head back. "No excitement?"

"Not really. I hung out with my aunt for a while. Not exciting, but always a pleasure."

"She's a real treasure, your Adele. I feel like I've known her my whole life. She was fire chief when I was a little boy dying to be a firefighter myself, and she must have given my mom and me a dozen tours of the station."

"She's good like that. It didn't throw you off to have a woman as chief? It's still not very common."

"Just the opposite, I think." Abe set his chin on his palm and gazed at me. "It showed me a woman could do any job she wanted to. Although I'm sure my mom might have added words to that effect every time we headed home after visiting the station."

The waitress brought Abe's drink along with a square plate holding six crispy, green-flecked patties with six small cheese-topped toasts arrayed around the edges.

"What are those?" he asked.

"Catfish cakes," the server said before leaving. "With fresh dill and capers, served with a lemon-mustard sauce and goat cheese crostini."

"Don't they look yummy?" I asked.

He held up his glass and smiled, showing his trademark dimpled grin. "Here's looking at you."

I held up my glass to his and clinked it. "And at you."

I'd just taken a sip when Buck, Wanda, and another officer in a South Lick uniform burst in through the door. Buck scanned the restaurant for only a second before striding to Tiffany's table, the two other officers following. The entire room instantly grew quiet, with only a murmur of talk and clatters coming from the swinging doors to the kitchen.

I exchanged a quick glance with Abe, then returned my gaze to Tiffany. She raised her chin, spots of color bursting onto her cheeks.

"I need you to come with me, Ms. Porter," Buck said.

"Why?" Tiffany asked. She folded her hands tight on the table.

"What's this all about?" Her companion stood.

"Are you coming, Ms. Porter?" Buck asked.

"We're here having a nice dinner," the man said. "Wasn't a crime last time I checked. Surely whatever your business is can wait until tomorrow."

Tiffany stayed seated but didn't speak.

Buck cleared his throat. "Tiffany Porter, you are under arrest for operating a sexually oriented business without a permit, operating without a business license, and other offenses."

I looked at Abe, my eyes wide, and back at the unfolding scenario.

Her companion stole a glance at Tiffany. "Now, listen here," he boomed. "This is some kind of mistake. Miss Porter isn't operating any kind of business other than her store. I'm an old college friend in town for a visit."

A white-clad Christina pushed open the doors from the kitchen, a long wooden spoon in her hand, and stared.

"Sir, she's under arrest. Ms. Porter, you're going to have to come with us," Buck said in a sorrowful tone, laying one hand on the back of her chair, the other on the handcuffs on his belt.

Tiffany very slowly pushed herself up from the table, clutching a slim bag. She shook her head at her companion and let Buck usher her out. All heads turned as she passed. The officer I didn't know took a long wool coat from the greeter and handed it to Tiffany, who draped it over her shoulders. I heard Wanda saying, "You have the right to remain silent. You have the right . . ." before the door closed.

All eyes were now on the tall man in the suit, who looked around and blinked with a scowl. "What are you looking at?" he queried no one in particular. He threw a handful of bills on the table and hurried out the door.

Chapter 26

Christina approached our table, wiping her free hand on her apron. "Robbie, I'm so glad you could make it. And so sorry if the cops spoiled your evening." Christina's hair was tucked up into a patchwork toque made of tiny squares, each in a different brilliant color.

"Of course it didn't. Christina, this is Abe O'Neill. Abe, my friend Christina James, head chef here."

Abe stood and extended his hand, which Christina shook. "Very nice to meet you, Christina."

"Likewise."

"What a surprise about Tiffany. I guess what they said means she's running a prostitution house," I said, shaking my head.

"From the looks of her date, more likely a high-end escort service," Abe said. "You know, entertaining visiting businessmen and such."

"But doing more entertaining"—Christina surrounded the last word with finger quotes—"than simply escorting them to dinner, I'd guess."

"You'd think she'd take them out to a bigger town than South Lick. Nashville, at least, or Bloomington," I said.

"Probably wanted to try out this fabulous new restaurant." Christine grinned. "Hey, sit down and relax, Abe." She glanced down at the table as Abe sat. "Looks like you ordered the best appetizer in the house. My special creation," she added. "Have you decided what to order for your main courses?"

"Haven't had a chance," I said. "Anything you recommend?"

We spent a few moments bent over the menus, with Christina pointing out this and that, until I settled on the chicken polenta puttanesca, and Abe selected the rabbit stew from the Specials menu.

"You'll enjoy those," Christina said. "Now I'd better get back to the stove. Let your server know when you're ready to leave and I'll pop out to see how you liked it, if I can."

I thanked her, and Abe nodded his agreement. I stared across the room where Tiffany had been arrested.

"I'm blown away by what happened. Did you know Tiffany at all?" I asked.

"No. I've seen her around town, of course. Often seemed to be out with one man or another. Guys who looked like they weren't hurting for money."

"*Hmm.* Same thing someone else told me, too." Almost exactly what Max had said about Tiffany. "I shopped at her store only a couple of days ago. She seemed so nice. She even goes contra dancing. What high-class prostitute goes contra dancing?"

"No idea. What I'm wondering is, is it legal to run

a sexually oriented business in Indiana *with* a permit?"

I stared at him. "I would very much doubt it, but who knows? I hope it's only a quirk of legal wording."

"Probably."

"You know, Wanda was in the restaurant at lunchtime today," I said. "She ordered a takeout lunch, but it seemed like she was really there watching Tiffany, who'd come in earlier for lunch."

"They were probably making sure Tiffany didn't go anywhere before they were ready to arrest her. Hey, we'd better eat these fish cakes before they get cold, no?"

We tucked into the cakes, which tasted as delicious as I'd thought they would. We were halfway through when the waitress brought over a plate filled with gold puffs on a bed of mesclun. The puffs were dotted with a chunky, translucent sauce. She held two fat-stemmed glasses and a bottle of red wine, too.

I swallowed hastily. "That must be someone else's order," I said.

"Courtesy of the chef. Curried potato puffs with apple chutney on mixed greens. And her specially bottled chef's red, a mix of Cabernet Sauvignon and Syrah. She contracts with Oliver Winery to produce it." She held the bottle in one palm, supporting it with the other so we both could examine the label.

"Wow. Please thank her for us," I said.

I watched as the waitress carefully uncorked it and poured a half inch in my glass. I held it forward to Abe, but he gestured for me to be the taster. After

I swirled the rich liquid in my mouth and swallowed, I nodded.

"Very, very nice."

The waitress poured for both of us and walked away.

"Wow. We're going to have to roll home." I sampled a potato puff, savoring the borderline-spicy crunchy puff, which paired perfectly with the sweet-and-sour chutney. It was exactly the right combination of flavors and textures. I kind of missed cooking gourmet dinners like I had at the Nashville Inn. But my breakfast and lunch place was worth it. Who knows, maybe I'd branch out, adding Saturday dinners after a while.

"Sure pays to know the chef, doesn't it?" Abe smiled before helping himself.

I gazed at him. Was he talking about me now?

"*Mmm*, tasty stuff," he said after downing a puff.

I glanced over to where Tiffany had been sitting. "When I was in Tiffany's shop this week, she said she didn't have an alibi for Saturday night, that she lives alone. I know the police questioned her, because of her blowup with Erica."

"Maybe when they were looking into where she was the night of the murder, they discovered she was with one of her clients. Is that what you're thinking?"

"Exactly. Or maybe they were already looking into her second business. At least they didn't arrest her for murder, too. I like Tiffany. I hoped she wasn't the one who killed Erica."

"You're pretty interested in figuring out who did, aren't you?" Abe sipped his whiskey.

"Hi, I'm Robbie, and I'm a puzzle addict." I

smiled. "But yes, I am interested. Because it's a puzzle. I'm sure the detective is doing all she can." And more. "But if I can help, well, all's good, right?"

"So you pass on information you pick up? You're not going to put yourself in danger, I hope. You really scared me, well, all of us, when you ended up with the close call last month."

"My collarbone twinges thinking about it. So, no, no danger." I crossed my fingers under the table, thinking of my late-afternoon meeting with Vince. How was I supposed to know the park would be deserted? "Girl Scout's honor. But speaking of Erica, you said you went to high school with her. Did you know a guy named Vincent who went to Brown County High at the same time?"

He gazed across the room and the years, finally shaking his head. "Can't say I did."

We ate in silence for a moment. Abe glanced up from his plate and aimed those big brown eyes straight at me. "What made you change your mind about coming to dinner with me?"

Faced with honesty or evasion, I chose a little of both. "I like you. I was hungry." I smiled. "Good enough?"

He tilted his head back and laughed again, an infectious sound that made me laugh, too. "Good enough for now."

Abe and I turned away from the kitchen door after thanking Christina and headed toward the exit. Our check had shown charges only for our initial drinks and our entrees. We'd both been way too full to order dessert, and never got to the bottom of the bottle of wine, either. Before we reached the outer door, Paula walked in from the street, followed by Max in an open-collared shirt and a sport coat. I hoped Paula wasn't still angry with me. I'd never had a chance to clear the air with her.

I greeted them. "You know Abe O'Neill?"

"Of course," Max said, shaking Abe's hand. "We play music together now and again."

"Hey, Abe, Robbie," Paula said, cradling her belly with one hand, a pink sweater stretched over it.

"What do you play, Max?" I asked. He hadn't played with the musicians at the party. Maybe he'd left before it really got going.

"Dulcimer, mostly," Max said.

"We call the group the Hoosier Hillbillies," Abe said with a grin.

"They're good. You should come hear them play next time, Robbie." Paula looked me in the eyes. "Sorry about what I said the other day. I really wasn't myself."

Whew. "Not a problem, Paula. Don't worry about it."

"How was your dinner?" Paula asked. "We've been looking forward to eating here since it opened." She started to slide an arm out of her coat, and Max immediately lent a hand, slipping it off her shoulders.

"Wonderful," I said. "Delicious. Creative. Really good. My friend Christina is the chef, and she's the best.

"Sounds perfect," Paula said. "I'm hungry all the time these days, eating for two."

Max gazed softly at her. "I cook whatever she wants. Happy mom, happy baby."

"You guys missed some excitement here tonight." Abe whistled softly.

"Yeah?" Max asked. "What happened?"

"Buck came and arrested Tiffany Porter," I said.

"For the murder," Max said with a satisfied look on his face. "Good."

"What a relief," Paula said, brushing a strand of hair behind her ear.

I shook my head and opened my mouth.

"It's been a worry to the family for the police to take this long." Max folded his arms over Paula's coat. "It's not good for Tiffany, of course. Although I've had my doubts about her from the very start."

"What kind of doubts?" Paula asked, looking up at him and wrinkling her nose. "I never heard you even talk about her except that her store is next to yours."

"No, wait." I held up a hand. "She wasn't arrested for the murder."

"For what, then?" Paula asked, her tone incredulous.

"For operating a sexually oriented business without a permit, is what Buck said." Abe pursed his lips. "Basically a prostitution ring. An escort service for rich guys is what I'm thinking."

Paula brought her hand to her mouth. "Really? Right here in South Lick?"

"Yes," I said.

"I know how those cops operate," Max said, blinking. "They haul her in for that, but then they also nail her on the murder charge."

"You think so, honey?" Paula glanced at him.

"I know so. You just wait."

Abe tilted his head. "We'll see. Have a great dinner, folks."

"Enjoy it," I added.

Abe and I walked out into a crisp, breezy night with the sky punctuated by thousands of twinkling stars. The wind must have blown the clouds away while we ate.

"Max seems pretty sure of his theory," Abe said.

"He does. Funny, I wouldn't have pegged him as a dulcimer player."

"He's quite good, actually. Our little group has fun. Haven't had a practice in a while, though. I should set one up." He gazed at me. "Did you drive over?" When I shook my head, he went on. "Give you a lift home?"

"I'd love one, thanks." I glanced up and down the street. Every curbside spot was taken. "What do you drive?"

"Come with me to the Kasbah." He offered me a crooked elbow. "I mean, the parking lot."

"Didn't realize they had one." I slid my hand through his arm. *Why not?* I savored the feeling of his muscular arm under his jacket, the warmth of his body next to mine, and how our steps matched even though he was a good seven inches taller than me.

We walked around the corner of the building to a narrow parking lot with one row of cars butted up against the restaurant and the other against the next building over.

"Now you have to guess which vehicle I drive," he

said, gesturing wide with his free arm, his voice like a game show MC's.

"I do?"

"Absolutely," he said, his eyes bright. I detached from his elbow and strolled down to the end and back. Among the high-riding SUVs, small sedans, and beefy pickups sat a vintage Mustang in one row and a sixties-era VW van in the other.

I faced him. "I would have said you were a truck type of guy. But I think I'm wrong. You're obviously delighted about this, so I'm sure it's not a regular car. I'm going to say the Mustang."

"And why is that?"

"Because you're adventurous and interesting and because among all your other talents I bet you know how to restore cars. Plus, you're a guy, and you think driving a Mustang around town will attract the ladies."

He bent over laughing, finally straightening when he was able to speak. "You were right on the money until you got to the part about attracting the ladies."

"So I'm right?"

"Nope. Guess what? Adventurous, interesting, and good at car repair also applies to . . ." He grinned.

"The VW?"

"Yup. Camper van. Come on, I'll give you the tour." He strode toward the van, which I now saw was beautifully restored. Its turquoise paint looked pristine, and the classic wide white V shape on the front bearing the intertwined VW logo didn't have a scratch. Abe unlocked the passenger door with a real key and slid open the wide door on the side. No remote beeping key fobs for this vehicle.

I joined him and peered in. The overhead light illuminated gleaming wood cabinets, benches upholstered in a very sixties-era polka-dotted fabric, a small Formica table, even a kitchen sink.

"How fun." I said. "It's like one of those tiny houses everybody's talking about. Except tinier. Do you actually take it camping?"

"Of course. It's been all over."

"What year is it, and why do you have it?" I glanced at him, loving how enchanted he was with the van.

"It's a 1965. It actually belonged to my parents, who bought it used in the seventies. Mom told me I was conceived in it, of all things. I told her that was TMI." He grinned. "And when my folks were going to get rid of it about ten years ago, I begged them to let me keep it. It needed basically everything updated, from the engine to the curtains."

"You did a great job." I muffled a yawn even the cold air couldn't keep at bay.

"Boring you?"

"Absolutely not." I laughed. "But I had a long day, and I still have prep to do for tomorrow's breakfast."

"Hop in, then. Your chariot awaits."

I climbed into the passenger seat and fastened the lap seatbelt. In a minute we were driving down Walnut to the familiar ticking sound typical of an old VW, or maybe it was simply the music of an analog engine. A friend of my mom's had driven an old VW Bug everywhere. They didn't rust out in California and many more of them remained in circulation.

I flashed back to my first date with Jim earlier in the fall, riding home from dinner in a quiet new-model Prius instead of a restored antique. I'd felt a similar attraction to what I was experiencing right now, only to a different guy. It was curious that I didn't feel uneasy about the change. If I had to guess, I'd say being dropped had a lot to do with it.

It'd only taken me ten minutes to walk over to Hoosier Hollow, so driving got us to the store in no time at all. Which was kind of a shame. Abe pulled into a parking space out front.

He laid his right arm across the back of the bench seat. "I really enjoyed myself tonight, Robbie. You're good company."

"I had a great time, too." I unclipped my seat belt and turned sideways in the seat to face him. "Thanks so much for the fabulous dinner. I'll cook for you one of these days. How does that sound?"

"Yum." He glanced at the storefront. "Hey, you want some help doing your prep work for tomorrow? I'm pretty good at following directions."

My heart went pitter-pat. I didn't want this evening to end either. "I'd love it. Come on in."

As I unlocked the front door to the store, another car pulled in next to Abe's. I turned to look but the headlights blinded me. The lights went out. I didn't hear a door open.

"Can you see who it is?" I asked Abe in a soft voice, my heart rate speeding up ever so slightly. Despite Max's idea, I doubted Tiffany was Erica's killer. Which meant the real one could be in that car right there.

"No," he said in a normal voice as he peered at the car. "Don't recognize the vehicle."

"I'm dreaming of a white Christmas," sang a deep resonant voice.

Phil's voice. *Be still my heart,* as Mom used to say when she was relieved something hadn't turned out for the worse. A car door slammed.

"Phil, what are you doing here?" I called. It had to be past eight.

Phil sang, to the same tune, "I'm dreaming of a fabulous brownie, just like the ones I made last night." He trotted up the stairs holding a stack of wide-rimmed baking sheets in his arms.

I laughed. "I totally forgot. Good for you. We would have run out of desserts tomorrow."

"Greetings, earthlings," Phil said. "I know I just brought some yesterday, but tomorrow is too busy for me to bake."

"I appreciate it," I said. "We go through them fast."

"How's it going, Phil?" Abe asked, but I thought his voice held disappointment. I felt a touch of the same. Maybe Phil wouldn't stay long.

"Most excellently. Especially now the police have stopped harassing me. I think I finally convinced the detective I did not kill Erica."

"Glad to hear it," I said. As I pushed open the door and held it for the guys, a slip of green paper fluttered to the floor.

"What's that?" Abe asked. He stooped and re-trieved the paper. The paper had been folded in

half to about the size of an index card and stapled
shut.

Phil set the pans on the stainless counter, now
whistling the tune to "White Christmas." Even his
whistle was rich and warbling. "Love note from a
secret admirer?" he asked.

Abe's gaze met mine and he watched me. I liked
that he was interested in my answer. Or maybe he
had every right to be, since until a couple of days
ago my not-so-secret admirer had been Jim.

"I doubt it." I carefully opened the paper at the
staple and read the typed message, which was not
signed. I looked up.

"What is it?" Abe asked. He moved to my side. He
didn't touch me, but his presence a few inches away
was infinitely comforting.

"I don't get it. I told you somebody stole my
Christmas tree, right?"

Abe nodded, and Phil narrowed his eyes, gazing
at me.

"This note says I'll find a Christmas tree outside
the service door. Which is right where I left the other
one on Monday."

Phil, resuming his whistling, sauntered to the service door and opened it. I followed him and flipped
on the outside light.

"Yep. Tree." Phil pointed to an even larger Fraser
fir than the one I had cut, with its trunk sitting in
the same bucket the first tree had occupied.

"What?" I stared, fists on hips. "Who would bring
back a different tree?"

"Who knew your tree was stolen?" Phil asked.

"Danna. Buck. Don. You . . ." I narrowed my eyes at Abe.

He held up both hands, palms out. "Hey, would love to take the credit. And I feel bad I didn't think about it. But it wasn't me. Is the note signed?"

I glanced at it. "In a way. It says, *From your friend.* That's it, and it's all typed."

"Dude, it's cold out here. You want us to bring it in?" Phil asked, rubbing his arms with his opposite hands.

"Yes, please. I'd hate to see a gift tree get stolen, too." I headed back into the store.

A minute later the guys stood inside with tree in hand. Needles littered the mat in front of the service door, since the tree had barely fit through. I hurried to the right of the front door where I'd planned to put the smaller tree, and slid the coat rack and umbrella stand out of the way.

"Stick it here for now, okay?"

Abe held it in place until Phil brought the bucket over. "Got a stand for it?" Abe asked.

I shook my head. "I'll pick one up tomorrow."

"I'm heading home, unless you have any more trees to rescue," Phil said, smiling.

"Sure hope not. Thanks, friend." I hugged Phil. "Hey, you want a check now?"

"No. Whenever you have time is cool. I know where to find you."

"And I'll see you tomorrow night for our log cabin assembly, right?"

"You bet." Phil pointed a finger gun at me. "Eight o'clock okay? I have an afternoon rehearsal that'll probably run long."

"Eight is fine. I picked up some candies and stuff at the store yesterday, and the cashier over at the hardware store reminded me of the icing recipe. I'll have it all ready to go."

"Perfect."

Abe shook Phil's hand and we watched him run down the stairs, whistling again. I turned back into the restaurant and sniffed. It already smelled festive in here, with the fresh sappy smell of fir that nothing else even approximated.

"Time to get to work, I'm afraid," I said as I washed my hands.

"Ready and willing, ma'am."

I cocked my head. "You've eaten here a number of times. Got any ideas for a special you'd like to see on the menu, whether for breakfast or for lunch?"

"Good question." He thought for a moment. "I often think of soup at lunchtime, but you don't offer any."

"Soup. That's a no-brainer, isn't it? I could offer soup and sandwich, except it'd have to be soup and burger. Got a favorite soup?"

"Curried chicken soup is awesome. Kind of like mulligatawny. You can use all kinds of vegetables, and throw an apple in. My dad makes it regularly."

"Sounds like you have the recipe in your head," I said, drying my hands. "You sent over soup after my accident, come to think of it."

Abe leaned one elbow on the counter and clasped his hands. "Soup is good." The dimple creased his cheek.

"Want to give it a whirl? I actually have a gallon of stock and some frozen cut-up chicken from a roasted chicken dinner I catered a couple of weeks ago. Plenty of vegetables and herbs, too."

"Deal. Show me a knife and the cutting board." He headed for the sink and began to scrub his hands.

I pulled out a good chopping knife and an acrylic cutting board, then hauled out a wire basket full of carrots, celery, onions, garlic, and apples from the walk-in. I headed back in, to the sounds of chopping, to get the biscuit makings.

As I cubed butter, I asked, "Where do your folks live?"

"They have a little farm halfway down to Story. Both are retired from teaching in the schools, where they landed after they got over doing the hippy-commune thing."

"In the VW van."

He laughed. "Exactly. They're great folks. But Don and I lucked out they didn't name us Virgo and Scorpio."

"Which one are you?" I glanced over to see him smiling to himself as he reduced stalks of celery to neat little bits.

"Scorpio all the way. An extremist in all I do, both good and bad. Better watch out." He met my gaze. "I have pretty strong feelings about issues and people. And also make colossal mistakes."

I smiled to myself. Jim wasn't the only one to have found someone passionate. As I passed the community bulletin board on my way back to the walk-in to get the milk, I noticed the poster Buck had pinned up next to the red one about the Gingerbread Log Cabin Competition, and slowed, staring at Buck's. The poster on green paper, which had come from the South Lick police station. The paper that matched what the note about the tree had been typed on. I'd bet tomorrow's breakfast profits Buck had left the new tree. Heck, I'd bet the whole day's till.

Chapter 27

As always, I wasn't quite ready to get up when the alarm went off at six. Spending the rest of the evening with Abe had been a delight. I'd put on some dance music and poured us each a little bourbon. We'd talked and laughed as we worked, with a bit of flirting thrown in for good measure. He'd gone home at ten thirty, leaving a pot of soup and a quick kiss behind.

I savored the memory in bed for a couple of minutes, then made myself get up and do my sit-ups. I took a quick shower and pulled on jeans and a clean long-sleeved store T-shirt. I fed Birdy, promising to play with him later, and headed into the store.

"You sure you can work today?" I asked Danna when she showed up at six thirty. She'd wrapped gauze around the back and palm of her burned hand.

"I'm fine. Not a problem."

"Good. I'm glad the burn wasn't more serious." For her sake, I was glad. But if it had been more serious, I'd have to investigate workers' compensation from the employer's point of view. Which I guess I should have done when I hired her. It was one more thing to add to my Responsible-Employer To-Do list.

"It hurt some last night, but I have a huge aloe plant at home, and I kept slitting leaves and spreading that jelly stuff on the burn." She showed me a plastic bag full of thick, bright green aloe spikes. "It totally makes the burn feel better, so I brought some in to use today."

"Good idea. Why don't you wear a glove over the hand, too, at least for today?"

She gingerly pulled a glove over the bandage, then we got to work readying biscuits, pancakes, and fruit salad. We were a well-oiled machine of two by now.

Danna emerged from the walk-in juggling three melons and a container of cut-up pineapple but wearing a confused expression. "What's in the big pot in there?"

"Chicken soup. Abe O'Neill made it last night."

"What was he doing here?" Danna narrowed her eyes at me. "Wait. Did you guys have a date?"

"How did you know?" I brushed a stray strand of hair with the back of my floured hand.

"You just, I don't know, had a look about you. A happy look." She set to slicing open the melons. "But what about Jim?"

"Jim has decided to get back together with Octavia Slade." I kneaded the biscuit dough with a little more vigor than strictly necessary.

"The detective? So not very nice of him. He dropped you?"

"Yep. And Abe has been bugging me to go out to dinner with him. So I went."

"Hot damn. I like it. He's cute, for an older guy," said nineteen-year-old Danna.

"He is." I cleared my throat, sensing the warmth in my cheeks. "About the soup, he offered to help do prep after our dinner, and I asked him what else he'd like to see on the menu. He not only suggested soup, he knew how to make it." I smiled. "So I let him."

"Cool." She finished cutting balls of melon flesh and added the pineapple to the bowl. "Okay if I do a spiced yogurt dressing for this today?"

I cocked my head as I cut disks of biscuit dough. "What kind of spices?"

"Cinnamon, mostly. A little nutmeg and clove. And some honey. It's really good."

"Have at it."

We worked in silence until the cowbell jangled in our first customers, who happened to be Max and Vince. Why was Vince sticking around town so long? I shook my head. That was his business. I wasn't about to ask.

"Have a seat, gentlemen. Early birds get their pick of the tables." I brought a pot of coffee over to them.

Vince kept his mug upside down. "I'd like hot tea if you have it."

"I'll bring it right over."

"Morning, Robbie," Max said.

"Hey, Max. How was your dinner last night?" I asked as I poured his coffee.

"Food was good, but the portions were pretty small." He sniffed and blinked like he'd smelled a rotten piece of meat.

I decided to ignore his reaction. Hoosier Hollow was fine dining, not an all-you-can-eat buffet of unhealthy food. I hoped he hadn't ruined the evening for Paula by complaining about the amount of food served. "What can I get you for breakfast today?"

"Orange juice and the Kitchen Sink omelet for me, with sausages." Max handed the menu back to me.

"I'll have your pancakes with a side of fruit salad, please," Vince said.

I brought over a hot water carafe with a tea bag for Vince, and Max's juice, then headed back to give Danna their order.

Samuel arrived with the full contingent of the men's Bible study group and took their usual large table. They were followed by other customers until twenty minutes later every table was full. Vince and Max had finished eating but lingered, with a map spread out on the table in front of them. I was about to clear their dishes when Octavia pushed open the door and hurried in. *Wonderful, just wonderful.* Jim might have told her about us by now. I lifted my chin and walked over to her, determined to be a cordial businesswoman.

"Good morning," I said. "Afraid we're full right now, but a table should open up soon if you'd like to wait on the bench here."

"Thanks, Robbie." Octavia's gaze focused across the room.

I followed the direction her eyes pointed. I was pretty sure she was looking at Max and Vince. She shifted her focus to me.

"Do you ever use gloves when you're working?" she asked in a voice so low I could barely hear her.

"Sure. We have latex gloves. Why?"

"I'd like to ask a confidential favor of you. When you clear the dishes from Mr. Holzhauser and Mr. Pytzynska, please use gloves and set aside a glass or a mug from each for me. Will you do me the favor, please?"

I stared at her. "Gloves so I don't get my fingerprints on them? But they'd already be on them from when I set the table, or carried the juice over."

"I know. Please help us by doing as I asked."

"All right."

"I appreciate it."

"Are you going to want breakfast, too, or is that the only reason you came in?"

"Yes, I'll eat, too. But I can wait. I'm good at waiting." She sat on the bench. She kept her back erect as she drew out her phone and began to work on it.

I shook my head a little. So Jim hadn't fed her breakfast this morning. I headed to the sink to slip on a pair of gloves.

"Hey, guys, can I get you anything else today?" I asked Max and Vince. I loaded their dishes on a tray, making sure I kept Max's juice glass separate from Vince's tea mug.

Max shook his head. "No, thanks."

Vince folded the map and glanced up at me. "Heading out to Lake Monroe for more birding today."

There had to be more interesting birds down here than in Chicago, for sure. "Have fun. And thanks for coming in." I laid their bill on the table.

At the sink, I drew out two heavy sealable plastic

bags. I checked to be sure Max and Vince didn't see, but Max was laying money on the table and Vince was shrugging into his jacket. I slid the glass into one bag and the mug into the other. I set them in the bottom cabinet and closed the door. When I straightened, Danna gave me a raised-eyebrow look.

"Don't ask. And don't touch those bags. I'll explain later." I gestured with my eyes and head in Octavia's direction.

"Got it."

I stuck the money in my apron pocket and wiped off Max and Vince's table. I made my way to Octavia.

"Table's ready for you."

She stood. I'd turned to attend to a customer who waved at me when Octavia laid her hand on my arm. I bit my lip instead of blurting out, "What now?" and turned back.

"Robbie, I'm sorry about Jim." She used the same low tone, but this one was soft where it'd been all business before.

What was I supposed to say now? "Like hell you are?" Or, "I don't give a rat's turd?" I blew out a breath, hearing Mom's voice in my head: "When in doubt, say thank you."

"Thank you." I gazed at her. "Not a problem."

To my surprise, she laughed.

"What's funny?" I asked.

"Exactly what my mindfulness teacher used to say."

I must have looked even more surprised because she continued. "Yes, even police officers can practice mindfulness. You'd be amazed at how useful it is to stay calm and present when somebody's waving a gun around, for example."

"I can imagine."

"Yes. We were taught to soften our hearts toward criminals, that they are exhibiting misplaced anger because they are in pain. Not that we don't go ahead and do our jobs, of course, not at all."

I didn't know what to say. Soften your heart toward someone trying to kill you? It was an admirable idea, but it had to be really hard to put into practice.

Octavia went on. "But Narayan, our teacher, would say, 'Not a problem' about all kinds of things, and I found it so incongruous this serious Buddhist would use that phrase. She'd even say it if someone fell asleep during meditation." She smiled as if at the memory.

We somehow ran completely out of butter, so I headed out in the van during the restaurant's usual mid-morning lull and picked up ten pounds at the market, then stopped at the South Lick Police Station. When I'd given Octavia the two sealed bags before she left the restaurant, I forgot to tell her about the feelings of disgust and anger Vince had expressed toward Erica the day before, and I thought she should know. I could call, but decided it would be just as easy to stop in in person. I pulled open the door of the station at ten thirty.

Paula was perched on the waiting room bench,

and Wanda was positioned at the reception desk behind the glass. She glanced up.

"Can I help you, Robbie?" Wanda's voice was tinny through the speaker.

"I need to tell Detective Slade something. Is she in?"

"Take a number." She gestured toward Paula and the bench.

I turned toward the bench. A pale-faced Paula sat with both hands kneading a handkerchief atop her belly.

"What's wrong, Paula?" I asked, sitting next to her.

She gazed at me, her hair limp about her face. "I lied before. I have to tell the detective something. I can't live with the lie. It's not good for the baby."

"What did you lie about?" The bench was hard under my rear end, and the room smelled like the last person in it before us had been smoking. Someone must have brought the stench in on their clothes and hair.

Paula glanced at Wanda and then back at me. "I told them I didn't hear Erica leave the night she . . . the night she was killed," she whispered. "But I did."

"Max told me you're a sound sleeper."

"What does he know?" Her mouth turned down and she let out a noisy near-whistle. "He thinks he knows all about everybody else. He doesn't even know himself." She dabbed her eye. "I am so totally not a sound sleeper. I wake up frequently. And I heard Erica leave in her car at about one o'clock. I know because I heard the car door shut and the engine start up. I like to sleep with the window cracked open as long into the fall as I can. It's healthier. So I heard the car."

"Where do you think she went?"

"I don't know. But she must have gone to see her murderer, right?" Her face contorted and her nostrils flared.

What a terrible thought. I patted her shoulder. "You're right, she must have. Did they find her car somewhere?"

"That's the thing. It was back in her driveway when I woke up."

"Really? And you didn't hear it come back?" So whoever killed her brought her car back . . . and then what? Walked home?

She shook her head. "Either whoever returned it was really quiet, or I'd finally gotten into a deep sleep."

"How did you get home that day?"

"When Erica never came home, I called Max for a ride. That was before I heard what happened to Erica."

I gazed out the window at the street and then back at her. "So you're worried that Octavia will be upset with you for not telling her earlier." The police would have wanted to investigate Erica's car for evidence if they'd known she'd gone out in it.

"That's right. I guess I shouldn't be worried. Being pregnant makes my emotions go all haywire. The smallest little thing can get me worked up." She tucked a strand of hair behind her ear.

"I wouldn't worry. I'm sure Octavia will be glad for the information." The clock on the opposite wall ticked in the silence. "Shoot." I stood.

"What?"

"I told my employee I wouldn't be gone long. I have to get back to the restaurant." I could email Octavia what I wanted to tell her. "You take care, Paula. It'll be okay."

She nodded, looking less upset and more confident.

I waved at Wanda. "Gotta run."

"Whatever," came the tinny response.

Chapter 28

"My, my, tasty soup. You did that wonderful," Adele said to Abe. They'd both arrived for lunch at the same time and took a table together.

"Didn't he?" I'd explained who made the soup when I went to take their orders. When I delivered the piping hot bowls, I waited to see how Adele liked it.

"Aw, shucks." Abe grinned. "Think I ought to quit my job as a lineman and sell soup instead?"

"You could do that." Adele savored another spoonful. "Heard y'all went out for dinner last night. Have a good meal?"

"Word travels fast," Abe said. "But then again, this is South Lick. Dinner was scrumptious." He drew out the last word as if he was tasting it.

"Totally agree. Christina does a great job," I said. "You should take Samuel sometime, Adele."

"I will consider it."

I spied Danna waving at me. "Oops. Duty calls." As I passed my desk, I realized I hadn't sent the email to Octavia I'd wanted to. And the place was too busy to stop and do it now at the noon hour, with a full house and a half-dozen people waiting. It'd been so odd to hear her talk about mindfulness training and meditation. Who knew police officers did that kind of thing? I could probably use some meditation myself. I rarely slowed down enough to simply sit and take stock of my surroundings. I sat still for puzzles, of course, but that was hardly letting my mind go blank. Quite the contrary. Puzzles, whether crosswords, Sudoku, or logic games, engaged the brain in all kinds of challenging ways. I guessed my bike rides were a kind of mindfulness. When I rode hard, my only focus was the road, my breathing, and my muscles, and it definitely cleared out the mental and psychological cobwebs. I felt better about everything when I was done. With any luck I could fit one in this afternoon if I got out right after closing up. I glanced at the front windows. It'd been sunny and cool when I'd gone over to the station, and it looked like the weather was holding.

I spent the next half hour flipping burgers, toasting buns, and dishing out soup, fries, and coleslaw while Danna covered the tables. As I worked, the image of Erica leaving in the middle of the night kept popping into my thoughts. Who had she gone to see? Tiffany? Surely not Phil. Vince at his motel? Maybe, since they'd known each other in Chicago. He could have called and asked to see her, and then killed her out of anger.

What if Erica had gone to see Max? She'd been trying to cozy up with him at the party, which he hadn't been a bit happy about. He had quite a temper, and possibly PTSD issues, according to Adele, but he wouldn't have killed his own sister-in-law. Would he? He'd have to have known how much it would upset Paula, and if I'd seen anything, I'd noticed how bonkers he was over the baby-to-be. I couldn't believe he'd do anything to imperil his future son or daughter's health. Octavia had wanted his and Vince's fingerprints, though.

I stopped, resting the edge of the flipper on the griddle. Or maybe it was their DNA she'd wanted. I shook my head. They'd have to separate out my DNA, and maybe Danna's, too. I had no idea how they did it and wasn't really interested in finding out.

Abe sauntered by on his way out as I was assembling a veggie burger. "Any time you need soup made, just give me a shout." He leaned an elbow on the counter.

"I might take you up on the offer." I smiled sideways at him, my cheeks warming.

"And I'm going to take you up on that home-cooked dinner, too. Who could turn down dinner from a chef?"

Whoa. This was moving along apace. But why not? "How about Sunday? I'm more relaxed, because we don't open on Mondays."

"It's a date. Now I'm back to work." He slid me a hip bump and headed for the door, giving a mock salute to Buck, who held the door for him.

Adele stopped by a few minutes later, after greeting a table of women she passed and stopping to chat with Buck where he sat alone waiting for his lunch.

"Abe's a fine fellow," Adele said in a soft voice.

"I like him. I'm looking forward to spending more time with him."

"I'm glad for you, honey. Talk to you soon. Come on out for lunch on Monday, why don't you? You can help me decorate my tree."

"Deal." I glanced over at my own tree, which also sat undecorated. Maybe I could decorate tonight.

After Adele left, Danna and I switched jobs, and I carried a lunch platter over to Buck. Two hamburgers, coleslaw, fries, soup, and coffee. And the guy stayed as skinny as a sapling.

"Thanks, Robbie. How you been?" he asked.

"Busy as heck. But, hey, I'm living my dream." I smiled down at him. The smile slid off when I remembered I still hadn't emailed Octavia. I glanced around. We had a brief lull, it looked like. "Can you give Octavia a message for me?"

He bobbed his chin down and back up with his mouth full.

"I talked with Vince the other day, yesterday, I guess it was. You know, the guy down from Chicago? He seemed to have really disliked Erica. I thought Octavia should know."

Buck swallowed. "Will do."

"Vince is staying at a motel in the area, the Lamp something. Sue Berry knows where. I also thought maybe he called Erica that night. What if she went over to see him and he killed her there? The motel could have cameras or somebody who might have seen her car. Or there could be evidence in his room."

He nodded slowly. "We'll check it out. Seems like

a stretch, but sometimes it's the unlikely that proves to be the reality."

"Thanks. So, some excitement last night at the restaurant," I said. "Had you guys been tracking Tiffany's, uh, business for a while?"

"Yup. Took a couple few days to hook it up with Octavia looking into her for the murder and all. But now we have good evidence Tiffany was, in fact, home that night. She just wadn't home alone."

"Maybe the gift shop wasn't bringing in the kinds of funds she wanted." I stuck my hands in my apron pockets.

"Guess not. The poor girl. She's paying a pretty penny to keep her dad in that fancy home up to Bloomington, bless her heart. Suppose she couldn't think of any other way to pay for it than selling her own body."

"I guess. And I suppose I can't ask about the murder investigation?"

"Nope, you surely can't." Buck gave a wry smile. "But I know your puzzle brain is working at it. Don't you go getting into trouble, now, hear? Octavia's good at what she does. Let her—"

"Don't worry. I'm not interested in the least in coming face to face with a killer again. I'll let her do her job."

Danna waved at me.

"My cue. Good to see you, Buck."

He delivered a mock salute, then picked up his hamburger in both hands and took an impossibly large bite, leaving ketchup dripping down his hand.

felt like I could breathe more deeply out in the open like this, part of my Californian heritage.

I stashed the water bottle in its wire holder on the frame again and started off down the road. The water was tasting kind of plasticky. Time to either scrub out the bottle or, better, find a metal one. As I rode, the usual magic of clearing my brain slipped away and thoughts came flooding back, or maybe it was because I'd cleared my brain and they had room to pop up. Thoughts about Erica and the cop, for example. Would the truth about what'd happened ever come out? Maybe the investigative reporter would dig deeper, but by rights it should be the police. They were the ones who could analyze the evidence, if any was still available. Surely the majority of the Chicago police force was honest. But why hadn't Jon's death been looked into more deeply before now?

I spied a pothole and steered around it as I pumped up another hill. A sedan passed me, giving me a wide berth, and I waved my thanks. Not all drivers were as nice, even here in easygoing Indiana. Some seemed to want to brush as closely to a cyclist as possible. Maybe they were in Max's camp, thinking people on bicycles wearing bright colors were crazy. Nothing crazy about it to my mind. We wore colorful shirts in the brightest possible hues to catch the eye of passing motorists, not as a fashion statement. Nobody wanted to be run off the road because they were wearing muted colors. And it was absolutely the best exercise around, using the big muscles in the legs to pump blood through the heart and brain. Cruising down the next hill, braking so I didn't

gain too much momentum, I considered that maybe
Jim was the reason I was even thinking about Jon's
death. Jim's guilt about not being able to keep his
twin from ending his life would be assuaged by
knowing he'd been murdered, instead. It wouldn't
bring Jon back, for sure, but it could help. So why
did I even care how Jim felt? I did care, though. Was
I jumping into a new relationship too soon? I
frowned, and barely saw a great blue heron stretch
out its pterodactyl neck on the pond to my right.

I didn't have much choice about not being with
Jim. He was the one who decided to try on a different love. And, so far, all I was doing was spending
some very enjoyable time with Abe. Isn't that what
twenty-somethings were supposed to do? I'd gotten
a little too serious after my mom died and I'd started
my own business. It was okay to have fun once in a
while.

The downslope I was on soon became the last
steep uphill on this route, and after that it would be
a descent most of the way home. Time to quit thinking and ride. I put my head down and worked the
incline. I crested the hill to a windy blast of cold air
and started down the long descent. Woods on either
side broke the natural wind, although I made my
own by virtue of my speed. I sped down, the road
vibrating through the curved-down handlebars into
my gloved hands. The air rushed by my helmet and
hummed in my ears.

Time to slow my momentum before I had an accident. I squeezed the brake handles. Nothing
happened. I did it again. No response. I pressed as
hard as I could. The brake pads weren't pressing on

the wheels. I cursed at the top of my voice. What had happened to my brakes?

I glanced up and swore again. A curve approached. My heart beat in my throat. I didn't know if I could hold on at this speed. One bump, one pebble in the road, one patch of sand or gravel, and I'd be spattered all over the pavement. I struggled to stay Zen, to do nothing but ride.

It was close, but I made it around the bend without flying off the road. The downhill continued. I'd never gone this fast. The bottom of the hill finally came into view, where the woods on the right opened up to a farm field planted with what looked like foot-high green grass. But the road I was on ended in a T, with a stop sign facing the end of my road but none for the crossing traffic. I was almost there. The turn either right or left was way too sharp to take at this velocity. Even though gravity no longer pulled me with such force, my momentum pushed me.

An SUV approached on the crossroad from the left with plenty of its own velocity. We were on a direct collision course. I'd either hit the SUV or it would hit me. I didn't think I could get my shoes out of their clips in time to drag them on the ground, which would either break my legs or send me head first over the handlebars, anyway. I had no choice. With a few yards to go before the stop sign, I wrenched the bike to the right. I bumped over the shallow berm and crashed sideways into the field. The SUV sped past on the crossroad. They'd either not seen me or thought I'd meant to go for a ride in a field.

The sudden silence roared. My left foot had clicked free from the pedal clip, but my right hadn't. My right knee was twisted and it burned. The bike lay on top of me. My recently repaired shoulder stung. The stuff that looked like grass wasn't a bit soft, whatever it was, and my calves were scratched by the rocky soil it'd been planted in. At least this time I hadn't been maliciously run off the road, unlike what'd happened in early October.

I hoisted up on my right elbow and managed to push the bike up enough to twist my right foot out of the clip. Swinging my left leg over, I let the bike fall away and collapsed on my back, hands on my chest. My heart rate slowly returned to nearly normal. I sat up and palpated my knee. It hurt, but it appeared I hadn't done more than twist it. My shoulder felt okay, too.

I'd had the bike tuned up only last month, and the brakes had always worked as designed, before then and after. I couldn't believe they went out on me accidentally. The alternative—that someone had tampered with them—was almost too scary to contemplate. I easily could have died.

Chapter 30

I swore at my phone. I'd called four people looking for a ride, but nobody picked up. Not Adele, not Phil, not Danna, not Abe. I didn't leave a message for any of them. All I could see were the field and the surrounding woods, without a single house in sight where I could have tried to ask for a ride or to borrow a wrench. It was anybody's guess where the farmer lived who'd planted the field. And this was the last time I went riding without carrying tools.

No way was I riding my brakeless bike the few remaining miles to South Lick. I was left with Jim, the police, or walking. Walking on the ungiving cleats of bike shoes worked for a few yards here and there, but it wasn't feasible for three or four miles. Neither was walking in my socks. Plus it would be dark in an hour, and I was already chilled. Biking togs were fine when the body was generating its own heat. Not so great when sweat cooled and it was windy, besides. I could call a taxi, if there were any serving South Lick. Except the only taxi companies in the area were in Bloomington fifteen miles away. They rarely ventured into Brown County except for a round-trip fare.

I would feel foolish if I called the police for a ride. And I didn't want to ask Jim for help, for so many reasons. I didn't doubt he'd offer it, if he wasn't in the sack with Octavia, that is. I kicked the gravel on the berm where I'd limped over with my bike.

A pickup truck crested the hill I'd ridden down before I crashed. I stepped back from the edge of the road as an awful thought sprang into my brain. What if my brakes had actually been tampered with? What if whoever did it had been following me to finish the job if I hadn't died in the accident? Vince. I'd been asking him about Erica only yesterday. If he'd killed her, he . . .

I let that thought go as the truck drew closer. Vince could have borrowed a truck. I had no possible way of escaping, nowhere to hide. My left hand numbed on the handlebars where I held the cycle up. My legs, still shaky from the crash, felt like they were made of tissue paper. My throat harbored a big lump of fear.

I dropped the bike and pressed Jim's number. I missed, and stabbed at it again. Was the vehicle slowing down?

Jim picked up almost instantly. "Robbie, hi."

I opened my mouth to cry for help. The truck sped past me. The driver didn't even look at me. The pickup didn't slow until it neared the corner, then it turned left and disappeared around a bend. I let out a noisy breath which ended up half sob. What I'd thought was a threat turned out to be nothing. My imagination was going to get me in trouble one of these days.

"Robbie!" Jim's alarm was obvious. "What's going on?"

I cleared my throat. "Are you alone?"

"Yes, why?"

"I hate to ask, but I need a favor from you."

"You know I'll help you if I can. What's the favor?"

"I was out riding and my brakes went out on a downhill. Can you possibly give me a lift home? It's way too dangerous to ride the bike."

"Oh, Robbie."

The care in his voice stabbed me.

"Are you all right?" he asked.

"I'm a little banged up, but I'm okay."

"Of course I can give you a ride. I'll be right there. Where are you?"

I explained my location and thanked him before I disconnected. I obviously hadn't meant what I'd said to Buck about Jim being a possible suspect in the murder or I wouldn't have called him for a ride. I knew I hadn't been serious. The urge toward revenge was a sly creature, creeping around the edges of reason, sneaking in under guise of logic.

I examined the brake cables, but they were intact. The brakes themselves sat loose and useless, though. I paced on the berm, hugging myself to keep warm, cursing the fact I hadn't strapped my small tool kit under the bike seat. I'd taken it off before the bike was serviced and never got around to putting it back.

A crow scratched out a caw from a bare-branched oak across the road as the wind picked up, hiding the sun with a gray blanket of clouds balanced on the treetops. The wind carried the damp smell of a rainstorm, or even snow.

Jim's Prius appeared on the crossroad to my right and I waved, but he didn't turn the corner. He kept driving. I pulled my phone out and jabbed his number, praying he wasn't so responsible he wouldn't pick up while at the wheel. He was almost out of sight to my left when he answered.

"You just missed me. Turn around and take a right where the road comes in."

I watched the Prius turn, and a minute later he pulled up next to me.

Climbing out, he said, "Sorry." The edges of his mouth turned up, but he looked nervous.

Good. He should be nervous about seeing me after what'd gone down between us. "I really appreciate this."

He opened the hatchback, then went around and opened the rear passenger door, too. "Let me put down the back seats. Your bike should fit easily."

When the back was flat, I slid in my cycle and closed the hatchback. I settled into the passenger seat. The air inside was blessedly warm.

"Thanks for having the heat on," I said. "It's cold out there."

He sat with his hands on the steering wheel without starting the car, then gazed at me. "I don't know what I would have done if you'd been seriously hurt. Or worse. I can't tell you how glad I am you're all right."

"Well, that makes two of us." I waited for him to start the car before going on. "But the worst thing is, I think someone must have done something to the brakes. I had the bike tuned up last month, and I've ridden since then. The brakes are not faulty."

"Are the cables cut or something?"

"No. I rode for almost an hour before they went out and they were fine. But I checked them while I waited for you. The mechanism is very loose, like they were partially unscrewed and then grew looser until they didn't grip the wheel any longer."

"Who would have done messed with your brakes?"

"No idea. And also, how? The cycle is locked in my apartment at all times." I shook my head.

"You're going to report this to Buck, of course."

"You better believe it." I stared out the side window. We were nearing South Lick proper. The landscape of occasional homes scattered amidst trees and fields turned to houses set closer and closer together, the wide porch roof of a traditional cottage looking like a visor shading the house's eyes.

"Either my brakes just went south," I said, turning to look at Jim. "Or it was Erica's killer planning to make me the next victim."

Chapter 31

After Jim dropped my cycle and me at home, I took the time to shower before calling Buck. I stood and savored the warm water streaming through my hair, down my back, over my shoulders. It had been comfortable talking with Jim as he drove. I'd been afraid I would be too angry, or he would be too uncomfortable, to spend time together. But it wasn't like that at all. Maybe we could end up friends. I'd like that. He was smart and generous, and I knew he cared for me on a certain level. Or, hey, maybe it wouldn't work out with Octavia and he'd come calling again. I'd cross that bridge when we came to it. I now realized it was still good to stay friends, no matter what.

I dressed in a thick red Indiana University hoodie and black leggings, dried my hair, and poured half a glass of red wine before dialing the police station. When Buck came on the line, I told him what had transpired.

"So you think somebody got into your house with

a wrench and fussed with the brakes, do you? Do you ever leave the place unlocked?"

He'd rhymed *wrench* with *Grinch* but I was used to that by now. "No, of course I don't leave it unlocked. And I checked the door when I came home. It didn't look like anyone had messed with the lock."

"No windows broke or nothing? Are all the windows locked tight?"

"Nothing's broken," I said. "I know I went around and secured all the windows a few weeks ago when the weather started to turn cold."

"I'll come down and fetch up the bike, then. Not sure what we'll find, but we'll give 'er a look. Give an eyeball to your locks, too."

"You'll be careful with my cycle, right?"

"Sure thing, Robbie. I know how much you like that piece of machinery. And Wanda gave me an earful last month about how expensive them things run."

After I disconnected, I examined the outer door again, then checked the one connecting my apartment to the store. My unpracticed eye couldn't see anything different. With any luck, Buck's would. Because if not, some kind of magician had slid into my house and slid out again. Under the door? Through the walls? I sipped my wine and giggled, remembering the old *Caspar the Friendly Ghost* videos Mom had rented for me when I was little. I must be punchy from the afternoon's adventure, because what had happened really wasn't funny. Not even remotely.

I glanced at the clock. I hoped Buck would show up soon. It was already five o'clock, and I was determined to decorate my Christmas tree tonight, accident or no accident. But I needed to pick up a stand at Shamrock Hardware first, and they closed at five thirty on Fridays. I paced and munched a handful of trail mix as I waited. Birdy strolled into the kitchen and nipped at the back of my left pants leg.

"Don't do that," I scolded. He had good reason, though. His bowls were empty, and it was his dinnertime. I scooped out canned food onto his little red plate with black catprints around the rim and watched him chow down as I cleaned and refilled the bowls with water and dry food. What if the person who'd sabotaged my bike had stolen Birdy, or worse? My skin tightened and the hair rose up on my arms as I leaned down to pet him. Despite being squeaky clean from the shower, I felt dirty all over again thinking of a stranger rooting around in my house. What else had they touched, examined, taken pictures of, even? I should call Max and get some new super locks installed. I'd do that first thing tomorrow.

At a rapping sound, I hurried to my back door and opened it to Buck. "Thanks for getting here so quickly."

"Not a problem. Just checked the outside lock. Don't look like nothing's out of place, like scratched or tampered with. That the bicycle in question?" He pointed behind me into the hallway.

I turned. "It is." I hadn't hung it up on the plastic-coated hooks on the wall where I usually kept it. I squatted so the front brakes were at my eye level. "See how loose this is? Even if you squeeze the lever, it doesn't apply to the wheel like it should."

He bent way over and examined the brake. "It

surely don't." He straightened. "Let me take a gander at the door leading into the store."

I led him through the apartment.

"Nice homey little place you got here, Robbie."

"Thanks. I like it." I opened the door and followed him into the store, where he closed the door and pulled out a flashlight, kneeling to inspect the lock. I made my way across the space and flipped on all the holiday lights.

"Nope, don't see nothing." Buck stood, shaking his head. "Now you haven't been poking your nose in the murder investigation, have you? I'd sure hate to think our killer-at-large is coming after you now."

"No, I haven't. Well, except for talking to Vince about what happened in Chicago. And it turns out that isn't even related to the murder."

"What all happened up there?" Buck scratched his head.

I told him what Adele and I had discovered about the investigative reporter, Jon Shermer's death, and Bart Daniel. "Your brother in uniform wasn't a fine upstanding cop at all, as it turns out."

"Shee-it. I guess not."

"Anyway, I talked to Vince about that. He didn't like Erica much at all. I told Octavia about it, though." I blinked a couple of times. "At least, I think I told her. So no, I haven't been poking around." Not too much, at any rate.

"You should be real careful now, all right?" Buck looked me straight in the eye. "Make sure all the doors are locked and secure. Keep your phone on you. I'll try to have a cruiser swing by a couple three times a day, so's to have a presence."

"Thanks, Buck. I appreciate it." I remembered the green note. "So did you happen to sort of leave me a new Christmas tree yesterday?"

"Now did you go and figure that out?" Buck's cheeks reddened.

"The note was on the same paper as the toy collection poster. It isn't rocket science, Buck. Thank you so much, though. You have to let me pay you for it. Trees aren't cheap."

"No pay. And you're welcome. Seemed like you'd had a run of bad luck, and I don't want to see nobody without a Christmas tree this time of year."

"Really, let me pay you."

He let out a slow laugh. "Nah. My cousin has a tree farm. And he owed me a favor. I didn't pay a red cent for it."

"I appreciate it. A lot. But did you ever find out who took mine?"

"Matter of fact I did. Had an idea about who it mighta been and did some asking around. There's a man lives up Gnaw Bone way. A little touched in the head, but he's got a big heart. He'd seen you unloading your tree, and he wanted one for his old mama who he lives with. So he just up and took it." He made a *tsking* sound. "What can you do? He don't make a habit of thieving. Instead of arresting him, I went on over and gave him a talking to. And then got my cousin to bring over another tree for you."

"I see. As long as you're sure the guy in Gnaw Bone won't be doing any more stealing." I glanced at the wall clock and wrinkled my nose. "Yikes."

"What, you got a date? It is Friday night, after all."

I laughed. "Yeah. A date with the hardware store." And with Phil, to make a gingerbread country store.

I hurried into Shamrock Hardware with only ten minutes to spare. The parking lot was full, though. Three guys waited in line at Barb's cash register, and several other people milled about in the aisles. A big array of Christmas stuff was for sale in a special display right up front, where a mother and a little girl browsed the array of miniature lit-up houses. Maybe I wasn't almost late, after all.

Passing Barb, I raised a hand in greeting. "Awfully busy in here. The store doesn't close at five thirty on Fridays?"

She laughed. "Holiday hours, Robbie. Open till nine every night right up through Christmas Eve."

"Perfect." I headed to Don's counter in the back, patting my pocket. I'd picked up that strange device I'd found and decided to finally ask him about it since I was coming in for a Christmas tree stand, anyway. Maybe I'd pick up a few of those little houses, too. With the lights inside, they'd look super festive in the front windows of the store. And I could use some festive after what I'd been through.

At the counter, I didn't see Don, only a skinny kid whose arms and legs looked too long for his still-growing body. His face displayed an unfortunate case of acne along with deep brown eyes. He could be eleven or sixteen, I had no idea. Old enough for someone to trust him to work here, certainly.

"Can I help you, ma'am?" he asked in a voice cracking on the last word.

"Is Don here?"

"I think he's in the office." The kid pointed to the labeled door a few yards away. "I'm Sean. I'd be happy to find something for you." When he smiled, his eyes lit up, and a dimple creased his cheek.

"Thanks. It's just that I found some kind of weird object in my restaurant a few days ago." I held out my hand. "I'm Robbie Jordan, by the way. I own Pans 'N Pancakes down the street."

Sean shook my hand. I was surprised and pleased he had a good, firm grip. Lots of teenagers didn't.

"My dad has talked about your restaurant, Ms. Jordan."

"Are you Don's son, then?" I didn't realize Don had children, but why wouldn't he?

"No, he's my uncle. And he's letting me work here part time during the holidays."

"Cool." I drew the object out of my pocket. "Anyway, I found this on the floor in my store. I have no idea what it is, or how it got there." I laid it on the counter.

Sean leaned over and studied it. He straightened. "No clue. Let me get my uncle for you."

"It's okay. I can go ask him. Thanks for giving it a look, though." I picked up the thing.

"You're welcome, ma'am."

The kid had manners, too. I'd turned toward the office when the door opened and Don ushered Max out.

"Hey Robbie," Don called. "Is our boy getting you

what you need?" He waved at me before he shook hands with Max. "Sorry I couldn't help you, Max."

Max frowned at Don before he looked at me. "Hello, Robbie."

"How's it going, Max?" I asked.

Max turned away and stepped into the nearest aisle without answering.

"Actually, Don, I need to ask you something. Here's the thing I found in my store. I asked Sean, but he didn't know what it is, either." I proffered the mystery item in my palm.

Don picked it up. He turned it all around, peering closely, and slid the two pieces apart. Bringing them back together, he bounced it in his own palm.

"I don't rightly know. We don't sell anything like it here, that's certain. Hey, Max. You still here?" he called, craning his neck toward the aisle Max had entered. "Maybe he knows," Don said to me.

Max came back around the end of the aisle. "What is it?"

"I found this little thing," I said. "Ever seen anything like it?"

Max turned it over in his big hands. He opened and closed it, and rubbed it against his pants. Peering at it, he said, "Thought maybe there'd be a manufacturer's mark on it but I can't see one." He blinked a couple of times. "Sorry." He turned away again.

"Max," I called after him. "Buck told me I should get new locks for my store and apartment. Can you help me out with that?"

He glanced back. "I can get to it next week if it isn't an emergency."

"That'll be fine, thanks."

"Can't you Google a thing?" Don asked me after Max left.

"I tried but I didn't really know how to describe it. I have no idea how it got in my store, or who dropped it there."

"Sorry I can't help you with it."

"Maybe I'll never know." And maybe it didn't matter. "Hope you still have some Christmas tree stands left."

He laughed. "Are you kidding? Got a new supply in only this afternoon. All the holiday stuff is up front there."

"Then that's my destination. Say, Sean there is a really polite kid. He's your nephew, he said."

"He's a super young man." Don lowered his voice and glanced at Sean, now helping another customer. "They've done good by him, despite the difficulties. You know, with the divorce and all."

"Is he your wife's nephew?"

Don stared at me. "You don't know?"

"Know what?"

"He's Abe's boy."

Chapter 32

I stood like a zombie in front of the racks of decorations. I glanced toward the back of the store even though I couldn't see the counter where Sean had been working. Those brown eyes and that dimple. Of course he was Abe's son. And he had the same polite manners, too.

Why wasn't I aware Abe had a son? But why should I be? I didn't know Abe that well. He'd never brought his son into the restaurant and I hadn't seen them around town together. Last night was the first time Abe and I had spent any extended time together, and his having a family had never come up in conversation other than the story of his parents and their VW. I hadn't talked about my mom or dad, either. Maybe Sean had a little sister or brother. I doubted he'd have older siblings, because Abe must have been really young, only twenty or so, when Sean was born. The news had gobsmacked me, as an Aussie friend used to say.

But I still needed to do my shopping. I spied a

tree stand I wanted. I lifted off the top one from the stack and set it in a small shopping cart. I needed lights and ornaments for the tree, too. Despite this being my fourth Christmas in Indiana, I hadn't bothered to get a tree before this year. I'd either gone back to California to celebrate with Mom, or to Adele's. I'd saved a small box full of sentimental ornaments from when I'd cleared out the Santa Barbara house after my mom's death. The collection included a tiny surfboard, a miniature yellow carpenter's drill, a starfish, and a two-inch Mexican crèche, along with a few other ornaments, plus a glass angel for the top. But since this tree was going to be in the store, I'd better pick up some more conventional glass balls, too. I added a couple of boxes to my cart, along with festive strings of red and green beads. When I saw a little muffin pan ornament, I dropped it into the cart, too.

I checked the prices on the tiny lit-up houses. A bit costly, but since they were for the store, the purchase would be a business expense. I selected a cute building with "Country Store" lettered on it, plus a brick house and a typical Hoosier cottage with the wide covered front porch. Finally I added two packages of white fluffy stuff to go under the tree and in the front window, a few rolls of bright holiday wrapping paper, spools of ribbon, and a bag of bows. I could wrap empty boxes to look like presents.

I paused with my hand on the bows. Wrapped beribboned boxes were exactly what Tiffany had put in her window display. What was going to happen to her store? This had to be her most profitable time of the year. I hoped they'd let her out on bail. But would small-town Hoosiers want to shop from her after her reputation got around, which it probably already had? We live with the choices we make, obviously. But I liked her, and I wished her well. I didn't care what she did in her spare time. Maybe I should go over there and do some shopping right now, as a show of support from one merchant to another, if the store was even open. Although with Tiffany in jail, who would be running her shop? I focused on my cart full of decorations again. One thing at a time. I'd stop by tomorrow.

"Hey, hon, you found what you needed?" Barb asked when I arrived at the cash register.

"I guess." I laughed, gesturing at the full cart. I lifted out the items, laying them on the counter one by one. I'd accumulated quite a load. I wrinkled my nose.

"What's wrong?" Barb paused, her hand on the register.

"I just remembered I walked over. I'm not going to be able to haul it all home."

"You want I should put it aside and you can come pick it with your car?"

"Thanks, but not really. Can I borrow a cart? I promise to bring it back."

"Sure you can, dear. You'll look like one of them bag ladies, though."

I laughed. "I don't care. It's only a couple of blocks." In the dark. South Lick had streetlights, though, and I would stay on the sidewalk. I paid, thanked Barb, and wheeled my way out.

The sound of my stomach growling was almost as

loud as the wheels on the pavement. I'd burned plenty of calories this afternoon without really replenishing them, and I didn't want to take the time to cook something in my apartment. A lit sign featuring a cheery red chili pepper waving a gloved hand caught my eye. Of course. A burrito to go. And it would taste like home.

I had in fact felt a bit like a bag lady with my cart full of purchases, but I made it back without incident, clattering along the sidewalk between the burrito place and Pans 'N Pancakes. After I stashed the cart around the corner, planning to return it tomorrow, I let Birdy into the store again as my Friday-night date, at least until Phil got here at eight, and after prowling all the corners, he settled onto the bench by the door and watched me with slitty eyes. I unloaded the bags, flicked on all the holiday lights, then grabbed a plate. The warm burrito, chock full of beans, seasoned meat, shredded cheese, salsa, and guacamole was almost impossible to eat without making a mess. Living alone had its advantages, I thought, as I licked my fingers. A Half Court washed it all down perfectly, with one of Phil's brownies to top off the meal.

I transferred the tree to the stand, tightened the four screws to hold it in place, and filled the big basin with water. I laid out all the decorations I'd bought on a couple of tables and retrieved the box of California ornaments from my apartment. I sang "Jingle Bell Rock" at the top of my voice as I wove the tiny colored lights through the branches. When I finished, I ran the extension cord to the same socket as the other holiday lights so I could turn them all on and off with one switch. Stepping back, I checked my skills. Not bad, and the lights glowed like home. But something was missing.

I snapped my fingers, headed to the desk, and brought up a selection of Christmas carols done in a swing style by Postmodern Jukebox. I cranked up the volume on the speakers. Now it seemed like Christmas. As I sat there, I felt the tool or whatever it was in my pocket. I laid it on the desk to study it. Maybe I could simply Google its image. I'd never tried doing that, but thought I'd read about it somewhere. I snapped a picture of the object with my phone, then plopped the image directly onto a Google Images search bar.

I swore as I stared at the result. Max had to have known what it was when I asked him. The object was a lock pick. Max lied to me. Who has lock picks besides burglars? A locksmith, that's who. Now it made sense. Each of the two prongs looked like a skinny key, with only the little bump at the end instead of all the ins and outs cut into most keys. I thought a lock pick would have looked like an ice pick. Clearly wrong.

Someone must have entered my apartment to tamper with my bike by picking the lock. Max? But I'd found this pick early in the week. A lump of ice settled in my gut and my pulse beat fast in my neck. I shook my head. If Max had left a dead Erica on my floor and dropped his lock pick, why had he broken the door in? Or maybe it wasn't Max. Maybe Vince was the killer and he stole the pick from Max. Vince definitely had had a beef with Erica.

Or the two of them could be a team. They seemed to be friendly enough. Vince might have some kind of hold over Max. Maybe he knew a scandal or a crime from Max's past that Max didn't want made public. Max was certainly a volatile, unpredictable guy with a military past, the kind of person who well might have gotten out of control at some earlier point in his life. He and Vince were both local. Vince could have forced Max to open my door to get the bike. And the broken glass in the door could have been a ruse to make it look like a locksmith couldn't be the killer. I had no idea how the pick got in my store. Either way, Max had lied to me in the hardware store. But I was going to let Octavia figure out this business.

I stood, sliding the pick back into my pocket, and pressed Octavia's number as I glanced at the wall clock. It was already almost seven. The odds weren't good she'd be at work. Much more likely to be having a romantic dinner with my now-former boyfriend. Sure enough, she didn't pick up. After the tone, I spoke.

"I found a lock pick near where Erica's body was. Someone tried to kill me by tampering with the brakes on my bike. Ask Buck, or Jim for that matter. I think maybe Max and Vince are in this together. Please call back as soon . . ." I froze. A shadow passed the side window. A shadow heading back to my apartment. I swore as the hair lifted on the nape of my neck.

"Someone's sneaking around the side of my

building! I'm calling nine-one-one." My clammy finger shook as I disconnected. Nobody, seeing all the store lights on, would go to my back door even if it was a friend dropping in. Phil was due later, but he would come in the front. This had to be Vince or Max. Whichever one of them had let himself in unasked last time. And they probably carried another lock pick.

I jabbed nine-one-one and identified myself. "19 Main Street. Someone is sneaking around to the back of my building. There might be two of them. Please send help. Quick." I heard my shrill voice as if from a distance.

"Is that the country store?" The dispatcher's voice came across scratchy and tinny.

"Yes!" My throat was almost too thick to speak.

"Are you hurt, ma'am?"

"No," I said in a hoarse whisper. "But I don't know what to do." If it was both Max and Vince, one could be waiting at the front. Or opening its lock right now. I stared at the door. If he was there, he was crouching, because I hadn't turned off the porch light and couldn't see anyone through the new door glass. At least I'd locked the door after I came in with the decorations. "Should I go out the front door?"

"I can't say," the dispatcher said. "Please don't disconnect this call. Officers are on the way."

I could barely swallow. My knees felt like rubbery overcooked sausages. As ex-military, Max surely carried a gun. I was positive he wouldn't hesitate to use it. Vince probably knew guns, too, since he grew up here.

I didn't want to die. I hadn't even met my father yet. The speakers played "I'm Dreaming of a White Christmas" in a garish counterpoint to my fear.

"I'm heading out the front," I told her.

"Afraid not," a deep voice boomed.

I whirled. Max stood inside the service door. The gun in his left hand was aimed straight at me.

Chapter 33

"Toss me the phone," Max demanded. A greasy strand of his hair hung over his face, and his jutting brow shaded narrowed eyes.

"Max," I said as loud as I could. I had to clue in the dispatcher. "Could you put your gun down, please?" My voice quavered. Under my sweatshirt I was covered in a cold sweat. The music must have masked the sound of him picking the lock on the service door.

"Throw me the phone, Robbie." The words came out slow and threatening.

I held onto it. What would he do if I kept it? He clicked something on the gun, his eyes burning into mine. I tossed him the phone. My hand wobbled so much the phone hit the door he'd shut behind him and clattered onto the floor. With barely a glance down, he slammed his heel onto my lifeline. The crunch sickened me. But I'd already called, and dispatch had to have heard what I'd said: both Max's name and the fact he held a gun.

"Who were you talking to?" He glared at me. A tic beat next to his right eye.

"The police. They're going to be here in a minute." I needed to stay alive until help arrived. "Why are you pointing that gun at me?"

"You've been snooping around all week. And you were asking about that *shlagga* pick over to Don's hardware. I knew it wouldn't be long before you figured out it was a pick. And hooked it up with me."

"What's a *shlagga*?" My heart was a jackhammer and my eyes felt fuzzy. I resisted the urge to wipe my clammy hands on my jeans.

"Women." He snorted, curling his lip. "Don't you know anything? It's the lock company. *Schlage*. Like the worthless locks on your own doors."

I glanced at the door. "If you leave right now, you can get away before the cops arrive."

He moved toward me, the gun never sagging from a straight line to my heart. Several tables stood between us. He pushed one out of his way so hard it tipped over and crashed into the kitchen counter. I backed up and scooted around another table. I had to keep obstacles between us. My fear was an icy thrumming presence that threatened to paralyze me if I didn't keep moving.

"So you found the pick," he said. "I wondered where I'd dropped it."

"I didn't think it was a lock pick." I thought for a split second. He hadn't shot me yet. What was his plan? "Want me to show you where I found it?" I took a couple of steps toward the cookware shelves. Maybe I could show him and then whack him on the head with a cast iron skillet. *Yeah, and pigs can fly.*

"We're going to go for a little ride, me and you. But sure, show me." A humorless laugh slid out of him.

I was not going for a ride with this man. He stood almost a foot taller than me and weighed a good hundred pounds heavier. Plus he had military training. And a weapon.

"So did you kill Erica here?" I sidled across the store, trying to keep at least one table between us. I took a deep breath.

In three long strides he was at my side. "I didn't mean to kill her, you know. She was relentless." He grabbed my left arm. "Forget showing me where you found the pick." His breath reeked of alcohol. He forced me to take a couple of steps back toward the side door until we were in the kitchen area. "And no. I didn't kill her here."

"I thought Vince killed Erica," I said. "Or you were in it together."

"You kidding? That wuss Pytzynska doesn't even kill spiders."

So much for that theory. When I slid my hand into my pocket, it hit the lock pick. *Maybe, just maybe.* In the pocket, I slowly separated the halves of the pick, keeping my hand as flat as I could and my eyes on Max. I curled my middle finger into the V, so the two prongs stuck out between my fingers with the hinge in my palm. The music coming from the speakers changed to "Jingle Bells," an even worse contrast to my current situation.

"Reminds me of Iraq." He glanced around at the stainless steel counters, the griddle, the deep sink. "They made me work KP after I didn't follow their idiotic rules to the letter." His mouth turned down. "I was the guy they'd trained to open up all kinds of places the military wanted to snoop in. Instead, the only thing I was unlocking was the skin on potatoes."

I swallowed. "If you didn't mean to kill Erica, why did you?"

He stared at me. "She—my own sister-in-law— came over to the house in the middle of the night after the party. I went out to talk to her and she tried to seduce me. Her sister is bearing my child, Erica's nephew! I couldn't stand it. She shouldn't have been flirting with me. It's wrong." He shook his head, his mouth turned down.

"What happened?"

"I slapped her across the face. But I've always been too big for my own good. And she was only a little speck of a thing." He glanced at the floor. "She fell down the front steps. Brick steps. Hit her head something bad." The barrel of the gun now pointed at the floor, too.

My chance. I'd started to slide my hand out of my pocket when he looked up. I froze.

"I've wanted to be a father for as long as I can remember." Anguish ripped his face for a brief moment, until it was replaced by a set jaw and flared nostrils. "I couldn't let Erica's death get in the way of that." He tightened his grip on my arm, raised the gun to my chest again, and pulled me around the corner of the counter toward the door.

"You should have told the police she fell." I tried to keep my own jaw set. This was no time to show weakness. "No crime in that, right?"

"They would have seen the mark on her face

where I hit her. I'd have been locked up for a long time." He pursed his lips. "Me, the locksmith."

"Why'd you leave her here in my store?"

"I wasn't thinking too clearly by then. Brought her back and dumped her. Dragged her in here and left her on the floor."

"Did you hit her head with my sandwich press?" I had to wait for my chance.

"Why not? That's a damn good weapon you had hanging on the wall. I broke the glass in the door after the fact, too, so they wouldn't blame the whole mess on me. Because why would a locksmith break down a door when he could slide in unannounced?" He turned his head and gazed at me like he'd just come back to the present. "And now we're going for our ride." His smile was mirthless. "I know a nice swamp outside of town where they'll never find your body. There's no way I'm missing my baby's birth. Or . . ." He looked around the room.

I clamped my teeth together so they wouldn't chatter from fear.

"Or maybe you don't want to leave your precious store," he said in a soft voice. It scared me more than the loud version. "Maybe you'd rather stay all cozy in there with your eggs and cabbages." He pointed with his chin to the walk-in.

I heard the keening of a siren over the music. *Finally.*

"Listen." I gestured with my chin to the service door. "You'd better get out of here quick. It's the police. Run out through my apartment." My heartbeat thrashed in my ears.

He glanced at the door. He swung the gun toward it and loosened his hold on my left arm.

Now. I reached up and grabbed his hair with my left hand. I swung my right fist up and jabbed the points of the pick into his eyes. I twisted and pressed, hanging on despite how terrible it felt.

I dropped the tool when Max screamed. The gun crashed to the floor and he brought both hands to his eyes. I kicked the gun as far away from him as I could, wincing, hoping it wouldn't go off. Birdy raced for the front door. I scooped him up and ran out, down the steps, onto the sidewalk.

The best thing I'd ever seen in my entire twenty-seven years were the flashing lights of a South Lick green and white screeching to a stop in front of me, siren awail.

Chapter 34

I sank to sitting on the bottom step as Buck and Wanda leapt out of the car, wearing vests and helmets, weapons extended.

"He's inside," I called, except my voice came out a squeak. I cleared my throat and tried again. "I, um, jabbed something in his eyes. He's hurt." I held Birdy on my lap with both arms, one hand in his scruff to make sure he couldn't get away.

Buck rushed around the back of the cruiser, clearing it in two giant steps. He peered at my face. "You're not hurt, Robbie?" He leaned down and laid a hand on my shoulder. More sirens approached.

I shook my head. "I'm not, but it was close. His gun is on the floor somewhere, so be careful."

"Got it."

I hugged Birdy to my chest. After the chill and adrenaline of the last few minutes, the cold of the night now pressed in.

Two state police cars and another South Lick cruiser roared up, sirens cutting out abruptly, blue and red lights continuing to strobe into the darkness.

More uniformed officers poured out. Buck directed two officers to the service door and two to the back of the building, warning them all that Max was large, armed, and possibly wounded in his eyes.

A green Prius drove up. Just what I wanted to top off my evening. Octavia, wearing a skirt, ankle boots, and a very undate-like bulletproof vest over a sweater, emerged and hurried to Buck. Jim approached me, his brow furrowed, his eyes looking pained.

"What happened?" he asked. "Are you all right?"

Buck called to us. "Jim, Robbie—get in the car and move down the block, will you? Those stairs ain't a safe place right now. And you'll be warmer."

Birdy tried to jump down, but I kept hold of his scruff and petted him all the way into Jim's car. A car that held a faint sweet smell like the one I'd detected on Jim the night of Adele's birthday party. I let Birdy go after we were inside with all the doors closed.

Jim drove a few doors down. He hung a U-turn and parked across the street so we could still see the front of the store. He twisted in his seat to look at me. I glanced back to see Birdy perched on the top of the back seat, then met Jim's gaze.

"Max killed Erica," I said. "I'm not sure, but I think he picked the locks on my apartment and jimmied with my bike brakes, too." The warm air in the car barely dented the chill that permeated me. I was so cold I felt like I'd been left to die in the walk-in after all.

"So that's how your bike went out."

"He knew I'd been asking around about the

murder. In fact, I told Max earlier in the week I was trying to figure it out. And I'd found this weird tool kind of thing earlier in the week." I told Jim about asking Don at the hardware store, and Don querying Max. "After I got home, I finally thought to Google a picture of the object and saw it was a lock pick. Then I saw a shadow go by the window and was on the phone to the police when Max picked his way in. He was about to shoot me and shut me in the walk-in." Prickles swarmed up the backs of my legs at the memory.

Jim reached out and patted my hand. I let him. An ambulance sped up and stopped in the street with its lights flashing. The front door to my store burst open. Buck walked Max down the steps. Max's hands were cuffed behind his back and Octavia grasped his other elbow. One of my blue aprons was tied around Max's eyes. The paramedics hurried a wheeled stretcher over. I looked away.

"What's up with the apron on his eyes?" Jim asked.

"It was awful, but I had to do it."

"Do what?"

I blew out a breath, terribly glad I was sitting down. "I stabbed him in the eyes with his own lock pick."

Jim hunched his shoulders. "Aah."

"I know. I was going to aim for up his nose, but I might have missed, and it could have made him angrier. Can't tell you how glad I was to have taken that self-defense class with Adele last year."

I gazed back at the store. Max now lay on the stretcher, with both of his hands handcuffed to the sides. An officer held his weapon ready even as paramedics bandaged Max's eyes. The colored lights on the Christmas tree in the front window made a bizarre backdrop to the scene. And also promised a return to normalcy.

When Buck ambled up, I opened the door and stood.

"You're clear to go back inside, Robbie. But Octavia there's bringing in the teams again, just so's you know." He leaned down and peered into the car. "Thanks for sheltering her, Jim."

After Buck stepped away, I stuck my head into the car, too. "Yes, thanks. You've helped me twice today, and I appreciate it."

He gazed at me with those green eyes. "I'd do anything for you."

Right. Everything except stay with me. "Come on, Birdy," I called. When the cat jumped out of the car, I picked him up, straightened, and turned toward home.

Chapter 35

It was nine o'clock by the time the state police teams left. They'd collected the lock pick and gun, taken pictures, and dusted the service door and other areas for prints, leaving the place a mess again. Octavia went away with them, leaving Buck sitting at a table with me. I'd put Birdy back in my apartment and given him an extra treat.

"Boy, am I glad that's all done," I said. I stood and set my bottle of Four Roses on the table. "You off duty?"

"I am, in fact." Buck grinned.

I brought two small juice glasses. "One for the road?" At his nod, I poured a little for each of us and sat. The air smelled of fresh fir, and all the holiday lights lit up my heart.

He held up his glass and clinked it with mine. "You didn't stay out of trouble again, but you're getting the South Lick medal of courage for what you did to Max."

Sucking in a breath, I hunched my shoulders, then let them down. "It wasn't easy, but I knew I needed to disable him in some way so I could escape. And when you're outweighed by a hundred pounds, you do what you can." I sipped the whiskey. "I'd really wondered if Vince was involved in Erica's murder. It just seemed weird he'd come all the way down here, and then stay, when he was the first to say how much he didn't like Erica."

"We checked him out. Turns out he had a solid alibi for Saturday night. He was still in Chicago." Buck took a tiny sip of his own bourbon.

"I guess he was simply being nice to the Berrys. And he's apparently a pretty serious birder, too, so maybe that was his motivation for staying in the area."

The cowbell jangled. Had Octavia forgotten something? As I watched, Abe pushed open the door and held it.

"I heard something went down here tonight. You okay, Robbie?" Those big brown eyes were pools of concern. "I tried to call but your phone went straight to voice mail. I was worried about you."

"I'm okay. But the phone got smashed. Totally out of commission." I smiled, then spied someone behind him.

"Come on in, Sean." Abe said to his son, who trailed him in. They walked over to our table.

"Sean just told me he met you earlier today," Abe said.

"That's right. Hey, Sean," I said.

"Hi, Ms. Jordan." Sean extended his hand.

I shook it and smiled at him. "Sit down, guys, and join us. You want a soda, Sean?"

"Yes please, ma'am." Sean pulled out the chair next to Buck's.

I stood and gestured with my head for Abe to follow me over to the glass-fronted drinks cooler. "You never told me you had a son," I said in a low voice once we got there.

"I know. I guess it never came up." He glanced sideways at me. "I really wasn't trying to hide him. I have him with me most weekends. Hope you don't mind."

"Mind? He's the nicest, most polite kid I've met in a long time. And you've taught him a firm handshake, too. Good job."

"I do my best. The manners he gets from his mother." He looked me straight in the eyes and swallowed. "We've been divorced for a long time," he said in a rush.

"No worries. Don said you were divorced. Is Sean your only child?"

"For sure. We were teenage parents. Remember what I said about making colossal mistakes?" He whistled. "Not recommended, although I adore the kid, and he's turned out great, divorced parents notwithstanding."

I pulled open the tall door. "What kind of soda does your boy like?"

"I'd prefer he has something without caffeine, since I'm choosing."

I pulled out a bottle of a locally brewed root beer. "You'll join us in a little bourbon?"

Abe laughed and shook his head. "Afraid not. I'm driving, and with a thirteen-year-old in the car? No way do I want him throwing that back at me in a few years when he gets his license. I'll take a root beer, too."

We brought the drinks back to the table.

"Young Sean here was telling me about his math team," Buck said. "Smart kid."

"I just picked him up from practice," Abe said. "They have a meet next week in Bloomington."

"I was on math team in high school, too." I smiled at Sean. "Math was simply another kind of puzzle, to me."

The boy sat up as straight as a perfectly plumb corner post. "Sweet."

"Do you like to do puzzles, too?" I asked.

"Totally." He nodded with enthusiasm. "Especially logic puzzles." He took a long swig of the root beer, and then held his hand over his mouth as the inevitable boy-belch erupted. "Excuse me."

I only smiled.

"Can you tell us what happened tonight?" Abe looked from Buck to me and back.

I'd opened my mouth to speak when Adele and Samuel burst into the store, followed by Phil. Adele rushed over and wrapped me in her arms, then pulled out a chair and plopped into it.

"Couldn't believe the news when we heard it on the scanner," she said, breathless. "Had to get right on over here and make sure you weren't hurt, didn't we, Samuel?"

Samuel arrived at the table and pulled up a chair from the next table over. "Yep. And Phil drove up right when we did."

Adele patted her chest. "Too much excitement for this old lady."

"Are you all right, Robbie?" Phil's gaze had never been so intense and full of concern. "I'm sorry I'm late. I tried to call you, but . . ."

"I'm fine, everybody." I batted away my friends' concern, even as I took it into my heart. "Adele, you and Samuel didn't have to come all the way down."

"Shoot, we were out to dinner at the roadhouse, anyway," Adele said. "We'd just left."

"And Phil—well, I'm not sure I'm up for log cabin-ing tonight," I said.

"That's about the least important thing in the universe right now," Phil said, batting away the idea.

Adele's eyes shone. "Give us the skinny first, and we'll all help put that log cabin country store to-gether afterwards."

I looked at Buck. "You want to do the honors?"

He pointed to me. "It's your story to tell, Robbie."

I inhaled deeply. "Remember the object I was asking about at the store, Sean? I'd found this funny tool near the cookware shelves earlier in the week," I told the rest of them.

Sean nodded. Adele did, too.

"I discovered when I got home that it's a lock pick. Max is a locksmith. I thought maybe he'd left it here, that maybe he killed Erica. Or that Vince had stolen it from Max and he was the murderer."

Abe's gaze shifted to Sean. *Oops.* A young person in the room. I covered my mouth, wondering if I should cut this talk of murder, but then Abe rolled his hand, gesturing for me to continue.

"As I was leaving a message for Octavia, I saw someone walk along the side of my building, so I called nine-one-one. Then Max came in the service door. With a gun." I felt again my heart pounding in my throat, smelled the liquor on Max's breath, saw the gun pointed at my heart. I squeezed my eyes shut, then blew out a breath as I opened them. I was alive, I was safe, I was with people I loved. People who loved me right back.

Sean's eyes went wide. So did Phil's.

Abe covered my hand with his. "You must have been so frightened."

"You can say that again. Terrified. He was the one who smashed my phone while I was talking to the dispatcher. But I, um"—I gazed at their faces—"I managed to disable him and get away."

"That's all that counts," Adele said. "Exactly what they taught us in that self-defense class."

"Interesting," Buck said. "You know we found your sandwich press in the alley behind Tiffany's shop, in the Dumpster. Octavia was looking at Tiffany for the murder before we figured out she'd been . . . what she'd been doing all night." He glanced at Sean, who didn't seem to notice the correction.

"But that alley is also behind Max's locksmith shop," I said.

"Exactly." Buck took a tiny sip of his drink.

"Did Max kill Erica with the press?" Phil asked.

"No. He told me she'd come by his house in the early hours after the party." I gazed at Sean. No need for lurid details. "They, um, had an argument. Erica fell down the steps and hit her head pretty badly."

"So he brought her over here to hide the fact she died at his house?" Adele asked.

"Right," I said.

"What about the press?" Buck watched me.

"He said he whacked her with the press here. You know, to make it look like she was killed here. Same thing about breaking the glass in the door. He picked the lock, but he didn't want anyone to connect the murder with him." I blew out another breath.

"Mr. Holzhauser is way bigger than you, Ms. Jordan," Sean said, his gaze intent. "How'd you get away from him?"

I glanced at Buck then back at Sean. "What I learned in the self-defense class came in handy."

"You disabled him with a self-defense move?" Abe asked. "I'm impressed."

I cleared my throat and ran my finger around the neck of my sweatshirt. I was going to do my best never again to think about how the pick had felt going into Max's eyes. I looked at each of them in turn. "Speaking of murderers, I wonder if we'll ever find out the truth about Erica and Jon Shermer."

Adele tapped the table. "We got Samuel's nephew on the case. Could be he'll uncover some tidbit the police overlooked."

"He's good, that boy," Samuel added. "If anybody can figure it out, William can."

I emptied my glass. The bourbon warmed me and stretched the evening's threat to my life to a comfortable distance. "Think we can stop talking about murder now?" I asked, setting my chin on my hand.

"You bet," Abe said.

The vintage store phone rang, the one in which

I'd installed modern innards. "Who could that be?" I hurried over to answer it, picking up the old-fashioned receiver hanging on the side of the wooden cabinet.

"Robbie?" It was the deep voice of my father. His voice was so clear it sounded like he was down the street instead of in Italy.

What a delicious surprise. "Roberto!" I hadn't been able to call him "Dad" yet. Maybe when I visited him at the end of December I'd start calling him by whatever my Italian half-sister did. "How are you?"

"I am well, *grazie a dio*. But are you? I had the strange feeling you are hurt, that I should call to you. When your mobile did not answer, I find this number."

My eyes welled up and my throat tightened. I glanced over at the table of my friends and family, lit by the soft holiday lights. My eyes took in the glowing Christmas tree, the shelves of cookware, the kitchen area.

"I am fine. I'm not hurt." I swallowed. "Yes, I'm fine."

Recipes

Apple Spice Muffins

Makes twelve. Preheat oven to 400 degrees Fahrenheit and grease a standard muffin pan.

Ingredients:
   2 eggs
   ½ cup brown sugar
   ½ cup milk
   2 cups chopped apples (about three small), any variety
   1 tsp vanilla
   2 cups whole-wheat flour
   1 Tbsp baking powder
   ½ tsp baking soda
   ½ tsp salt
   1 tsp ground cinnamon
   ½ tsp nutmeg
   ½ cup finely chopped walnuts

Directions:

Combine eggs, sugar, milk, apples, and vanilla, and mix well.

Separately combine flour, baking powder, baking soda, salt, spices, and walnuts.

Stir dry ingredients into wet with a fork until just mixed. Spoon into a muffin pan. Bake 20–25 minutes or until brown on top. Remove from pan and cool on rack.

Serve warm with butter, peanut butter, or cream cheese.

Colorful Coleslaw

Serves six. With thanks to Bill Castle.

Ingredients:
    6 cups shredded red and green cabbage
    2 carrots, peeled and shredded
    ⅔ cup mayonnaise
    2 Tbsps vinegar (cider vinegar or white vinegar)
    2 Tbsps vegetable oil
    1 Tbsp fresh prepared horseradish
    2 Tbsps sugar, or to taste
    ¼ tsp ground celery seed
    ¼ tsp salt, or to taste
    Chopped fresh dill

Directions:

Toss cabbage in a large bowl with the carrots.

In a bowl, whisk together the remaining ingredients except the dill. Pour the mixture over the cabbage and carrots and toss to coat thoroughly.

Refrigerate until serving time, then sprinkle fresh dill on top.

Santa Barbara-Style Eggs Benedict

Serves two hungry people or four lighter eaters. With a nod to Hallie Ephron and her easy from-scratch recipe for the hollandaise.

Ingredients:

2 whole wheat English muffins
1 ripe avocado
1 egg
½ cup butter
1 ½ Tbsp lime juice
¼ tsp salt
⅛ tsp ground chipotle pepper

Directions:

Warm two plates.

Peel and slice the avocado.

Make the hollandaise sauce by melting the butter slowly in a small heavy-bottomed saucepan. Whisk the egg with the lime juice and add to the melted butter along with the salt and chipotle. Whisk over low medium heat until the sauce thickens. Be careful or it turns into scrambled eggs. Keep it on a very low heat and stir occasionally until ready to serve.

Fry four eggs lightly on both sides over medium heat, fully cooking the whites but leaving the yolks slightly runny.

Split and toast the English muffins; butter if desired. Place two halves on each plate, add an egg to each, arrange avocado slices on top, and spoon the hollandaise sauce over all. Serve immediately, with salsa or hot sauce on the side.

Overnight French Toast

<u>Ingredients:</u>
1 loaf French bread (13 to 16 ounces)
½ cup Grand Marnier
8 large eggs
2 cups half-and-half
1 cup milk
1 tsp vanilla extract
1 tsp ground cinnamon
¼ tsp ground nutmeg
½ tsp salt
1 cup chopped pecans
Sour cream
Maple syrup

<u>Directions:</u>

Slice French bread into 20 slices, 1-inch thick each. (Use any extra bread for garlic toast or bread crumbs).

Arrange slices in a generously buttered 9-inch by 13-inch flat baking dish in 2 rows, overlapping the slices.

Drizzle the bread with the liqueur. In a large bowl, combine the eggs, half-and-half, milk, vanilla, cinnamon, nutmeg, and salt and beat with a rotary beater or whisk until blended but not too bubbly.

Pour mixture over the bread slices, making sure all are covered evenly with the milk-egg mixture.

Spoon some of the mixture in between the slices. Cover with foil and refrigerate overnight.

The next day, an hour before the time you want to serve, preheat oven to 350 degrees Fahrenheit.

Sprinkle pecans over the top and bake uncovered for 40 minutes, until puffed and lightly golden. Serve with maple syrup and a dollop of sour cream on each serving.

Please turn the page for an exciting sneak peek of
Maddie Day's next Country Store Mystery

WHEN THE GRITS HIT THE FAN

coming in March 2017
from Kensington Publishing!

Chapter 1

Who knew people could be so nasty to each other? While I cleared plates, I watched and listened as a mix of grad students and professors from Indiana University discuss medical sociology during their weekly dinner meeting at my restaurant, Pans 'N Pancakes. This week I'd served Chicken Ezekiel on rotini to fifteen of them, with garlic bread and a salad with winter greens from a local farmer who was harvesting even in February. From the empty plates, it sure looked like the meal had been a success.

The conversation? Not so much. Some of the terminology went right over my head. But when Charles Stilton glared at my friend Lou Perlman, the meaning was unmistakable.

"It was unethical of you to take the ideas in my paper and present them as your own," Lou went on, the silver rings on her fingers flashing as much as her eyes as she pointed at him across the wide table. "You agreed to sponsor me, but I sure didn't agree to give up my original research."

"You're a doctoral student," the diminutive

professor said, his bright green shirt a spot of color in the room. He picked up his glass of red wine and sipped. "I'm a tenured professor in the same field. I can't help it if our research is pursuing parallel ideas. I didn't steal a thing." He gazed at my shelves of vintage cookware and blinked, as if the conversation was over.

I'd met Professor Stilton in the preceding weeks. He'd been polite and friendly to me but had gotten into tiffs at a few of the gatherings. I'd have to ask Lou what was up between them.

A woman I hadn't seen before pushed back her chair. She stood and set her hands on the table. "That's enough, you two. These meetings were supposed to be a congenial intellectual gathering, not some mudslinging session."

Charles stroked his tidy black goatee. Ignoring the woman, he turned to the man on his right. "How about them Pacers?"

I watched Lou fume, nostrils flared, lips pressed together. She pushed her chair back and stalked to the restroom.

The woman who'd admonished them had come in late and I hadn't been introduced to her. Shaking her head, she picked up her plate and brought it to where I stood at the sink in the kitchen area that adjoined the rest of the space.

"Thanks," I said. I extended my hand. "I'm Robbie Jordan, proprietor here."

She set down the plate and silverware and shook hands with a firm, vigorous touch. "I'm Professor Zenobia Brown. But just call me Zen." A wiry woman, she stood a couple of inches shorter than my five foot four, and was at least a couple of decades older than my 27 years, with salt-and-pepper hair cut in a no-nonsense short do with the top a little bit spiked. She smiled. "My mom thought with a last name like Brown I needed a unique first name. Anyway, I'm a professor in the department. I live halfway between South Lick and Bloomington and I've been meaning to get over here for one of your famous breakfasts. Still want to."

"Not so sure they're famous, but you're welcome to come and sample what we serve."

"Whole-wheat banana walnut flapjacks? That's my kind of breakfast." She glanced back at the group. "Sorry about the commotion. I'm chair of the department now, and it's like wrangling cats sometimes to get these people to act civilly."

"It's okay. As long as I get paid and people don't start a food fight, I don't really care how they get along." I'd happily agreed to Lou's idea of the dinner meetings. I'd only opened my country store breakfast-and-lunch place in October and hadn't realized how slow business would be during the winter. It was cold and often snowy here in the hills of southern Indiana, but most years not snowy enough to bring a winter tourist trade. Even the locals seemed to be staying home instead of eating out. I'd reduced the days I stayed open to Thursday through Sunday to save money on my assistant Danna's pay and to keep from ordering food that spoiled because it didn't get used. So the boost of a nice flat sum every Friday night was definitely helping the bottom line. I served the same dinner to everybody and so far no one had complained.

I loaded up two platters of brownies and took them to the table, which I'd created by shoving together smaller tables into a conference table–sized surface they could all sit around. "Coffee or tea, anyone? Or decaf?"

"I'm sticking with wine," Charles said, pouring the last of his bottle of Merlot into his glass. "Which I can because I'm walking home," he added in a defensive tone.

I knew he lived half a mile away right here in South Lick. I thought most of the other students and faculty, like Lou, resided nearer the sprawling flagship Indiana University campus fifteen miles away in Bloomington.

"So great you got permission for us to do the BYOB thing, Robbie," Lou said, now back in her chair, pouring a half glass for herself from a bottle of white. "Dinner's not really civilized unless you can drink wine with it. And I'm having more because I caught a ride with teetotaler Tom over there."

Tom, a fellow grad student with Lou, ginned and waved.

"As long as I'm not a licensed alcohol establishment, which I'm not, it's apparently legal. And as long as you also pour your own." I'd laid in a supply of stemless wineglasses and a few corkscrews when I'd learned I could allow customers to bring bottles of wine. Nobody had asked yet if they could carry in beer or hard alcohol, which was good, because my research hadn't extended that far. I didn't advertise the option, and I wasn't usually open for dinner, anyway, but several times a group of ladies had brought their own wine for a special luncheon, as had an elderly local couple celebrating their sixtieth wedding anniversary with lunch out instead of dinner.

Lou tilted the bottle at Zen's glass. "More?"

I noticed Lou was carefully avoiding any inter-action with Charles, wisely so. He was still deep in conversation with the man next to him, and Lou had been talking with Zen and Tom.

Zen covered the glass with her hand. "Not for me, thanks. One glass is my limit. I'm training for a marathon. But I'd love some decaf, Robbie."

So that was why she was so wiry. I was a serious cyclist, myself. It was how I'd met Lou and Tom, in fact, who also loved riding for miles up and down the scenic hills of Brown County. But my cycling habit was offset by my love of eating. Nobody would ever call me wiry and I didn't care. I was healthy, and I did have a nicely defined waist to offset my generous hips.

I took the rest of the hot drinks orders. After I delivered the mugs, I busied myself cleaning up. It was already eight-thirty and I still had prep to do for tomorrow. We'd agreed on a finish time of nine o'clock for these gatherings. I was up every morn-ing by five-thirty to open the doors by seven, so I didn't want Friday nights to turn into an open-ended session of wine sippers sitting around talking abstractions.

The discussion had turned to the topic of public health, which apparently wasn't as controversial as the conversation between Lou and Charles had been, and didn't seem abstract at all. Snippets of talk about social change in women's paid and unpaid work and the consequences of these changes for women's health floated my way. Zen seemed to be leading the discussion, while Charles sat back with his arms folded, a little smirk on his face. I carried the remains of the rotini and the salad into the walk-in cooler. When I came out, eggs and milk in my arms for tomorrow's pancake batter, the mood had changed.

Zen stood with her hands on her hips. "How dare you say that to me?" Her eyes narrowed and nearly shot daggers at Charles.

He shrugged, then grabbed his coat. "You can take it. You're our esteemed *chair*, aren't you?" He sauntered toward the front door. "Have a nice night, fellow sociologists."

The cowbell on the door jangled his exit, but it looked like Zen's nerves were a lot more jangled.

By nine the next morning the restaurant was blessedly not in a slump. For once every table was full and a party of three women browsed the antique cookware shelves as they waited for seats to open up. Good. I'd much rather be too busy than sitting around waiting for customers.

Between hurrying from table to table, taking orders and clearing, I glanced at Danna, the best nineteen-year-old co-chef I could imagine. Her titian dreadlocks hung down her back, today tied with an orange band, as she flipped pancakes, turned sausages, and expertly ladled meat gravy on hot biscuits. The girl was tireless, nearly always cheerful, and had contributed some innovative ideas for extras to accompany our usual menu. She'd made grits with cheese last Saturday and we'd sold out. Today the Specials chalkboard read, "Warm Up Your Tootsies Omelet: roasted red peppers and pepper jack cheese, served on a warm corn tortilla and topped with fresh jalapeno salsa." It was Danna's invention, even though as a native Californian, I might have thought of it myself.

"You good?" I called to her.

She returned a thumbs up, so I continued on my trajectory to three men with the ruddy faces of those who spend a lot of time outdoors. I didn't know if they were farmers, construction workers, or even electrical linemen like my new sweetie, Abe.

"Refill, gentlemen?" I held out the coffee pot. One covered his mug with his hand, but another smiled and nodded. The third had pushed aside a plate empty except for a small pool of gravy and was engrossed in the *New York Times* crossword puzzle. He was doing it in ink. My radar went up, since crosswording, in ink, was my favorite down-time occupation, bar none, even more than cycling.

"Today's?" I asked him, sidling around to his side of the table. "I haven't gotten to it yet." I smiled when he glanced up.

"Know what the biggest Channel Island is?" He frowned at the paper. "I don't even know what channel they're talking about."

"How many letters?"

"Nine. Could be the British Channel. How do you spell brek-how?"

"You mean Brecqhou? That's only eight letters. I'll bet it's Santa Cruz. Try that."

He added those letters, nodding as he did. "That's it." He gazed up at me. "So it must be the California Channel Islands. How did you know?"

I laughed. "I grew up across from Santa Cruz Island, in Santa Barbara. It's definitely the biggest one of the archipelago, and it's gorgeous on a clear day, like seeing the top of a mountain range pushed up from the ocean. Which I suppose it is. They're all gorgeous: Anacapa, Santa Rosa, San Miguel, even tiny Santa Barbara Island."

"Sounds like you miss them. Well, thanks, Ms. Jordan. I appreciate the help." He chuckled. "Thought I was just coming in for biscuits, gravy, and bacon."

"My pleasure. Will that be all today, guys?"

When they each nodded, I slid their ticket onto the table facedown and headed for another table. The cowbell on the door jangled and I turned my head to see Maude Stilton holding the door for her tiny mother, Jo Schultz. I'd bet Jo was all of five feet when she stood up real straight, although Maude was a good five or six inches taller.

"Come on in, ladies," I called, and headed that way, instead.

Jo, the former owner of my building, handed her red wool coat to Maude and sank onto the bench. "Hi there, Robbie," she said. "How's my store?" She smiled, further creasing her deeply lined face. She always wore her white hair in a bun on top of her hair, giving her an even more old-fashioned look than her almost seventy years would suggest.

"It's good. And busy this morning, as you can

see." I gestured behind me. "I'm sorry you'll have a little wait, Jo, but I'm glad to see you." I greeted Maude, too. "There are two parties before you. Breakfast usually turns over pretty fast, though."

"Not a problem, Robbie," Maude said. "Glad you're busy." Maude, a successful local architect and Professor Stilton's wife, didn't look a bit old-fashioned. I thought she was probably over forty. Barely a line showed in her face, though, and every time I'd seen her, her streaked chestnut hair was freshly colored and cut in an elegant layered style that fell between her ears and her shoulders. She slid out of a stylish electric blue coat and hung it on the coat tree with Jo's.

"It's looking real good in here," Jo said. She might look like an older lady, but both her mind and her eyes were clear and sharp. My aunt Adele was only a few years older, and she was certainly sharp, too. "You done a good job with the renovations. And I'll bet you're glad not to be involved in any more murders."

"You can say that again." I shuddered inwardly at the memory of being face to face with a killer right here in my store at the end of November. "It's been nice and quiet for three months, and I'm planning on it staying that way."

"Say, you ever get a chance to work on the upstairs like you said you were wanting to?"

Danna dinged the little bell indicating an order was up. I swiveled my head in her direction and caught an annoyed look. Busy like we were, I had no business standing here chatting up an old lady.

"Gotta run, Jo," I told her. "I'll catch up with you later."

I ran my butt off for the next half hour, clearing, taking orders, and serving up platters of tasty, filling breakfasts. By the time I delivered an egg white omelet, with dry toast and a bowl of fruit for Maude and a half order of banana-walnut pancakes for Jo, it was almost thirty minutes later and the crush was over. Three tables were empty and four others already had their checks.

"Whew. Sorry that took so long," I said, setting down their food. "Can I top up your coffees?"

"No thanks," Jo said.

Maude nodded. "Please. And I ought to bring some to Ronnie. He's out ice fishing all day, and being nineteen, did he think to bring a thermos of something warm to drink? No, he did not."

"That's one cold way to have fun," Jo said. "But he's my grandson. I expect he has a mind of his own, and right that he should."

"I helped him bring his equipment onto the lake this morning when I dropped him off. You wouldn't catch me sitting on a bucket all day long hoping to catch a couple of perch or bluegill." Maude raised perfectly arched eyebrows and shook her head.

I didn't really want to get involved in a question of what a suitable day's entertainment for someone Danna's age was, but I was a little surprised Ron didn't have a weekend job to go to. "Jo, you were asking about the upstairs," I said. "I've been working on it this winter. So far I'm still in the demolition phase."

Jo seemed to shrink into herself a little, but she

mustered a smile. "That's nice. I know you want to make the place into an inn, like."

"I'm sorry." I cringed at my thoughtlessness. "That's not very nice of me to mention the demolition. You used to live up there. It's just that I wanted a different configuration of walls than you had." And insulation. And modern wiring. And a myriad of other improvements.

"Don't worry about it," Maude said. "We knew you were going to renovate the second floor, didn't we, Mom?"

"Of course." Jo's smile brightened. "I'm glad you're going to improve it. The place got pretty run down, I admit."

"If you need a consult on the new design, my office is just above the bank." Maude's mouth smiled, but not the rest of her face. "I'd be happy to take a look one of these days." She kept smiling as she talked.

I don't know why it was, but people who smiled while they were talking had always struck me as insincere. "I'm finding some interesting things in the walls," I said.

Maude, who had a bite of omelet halfway to her mouth, halted her fork and tilted her head and eyes toward the ceiling.

"I'll bring them by for you to look at one of these days, shall I?" I asked Jo.

"Please, dear. Please do." She glanced at her plate. "Oh, don't these flapjacks look yummy, Maude?"

Maude blinked a few times, and stared at her own plate. "Absolutely, Mom. They sure do."

* * *

Lou and I clipped our snowshoes onto our boots at the back of her little SUV in the Crooked Lake lot off Route 135. Only one pickup truck also sat in the lot, likely a late-day ice fisherman. I'd driven by in the morning on one of my days off last week and the lake had been full of guys sitting on low stools watching the flags they set up to indicate a nibble. Others were twisting giant augers to drill new holes or hauling up a wriggling fish. I ought to see if I could buy a supply of catfish or whatever they were catching for next week's dinner, or even for a lunch special.

Now we still had three hours of light before sunset at 6:30, and I needed to get out and stretch my legs in some fresh air. When I'd called Lou to propose an outing after the store closed, she was as eager as I was, and had picked me up. Winter can be a long season for cyclists when ice and snow make biking outdoors a real pain.

"You can almost taste spring," she said with a grin. "Look how much light is in the sky." She wore a cone-shaped purple and pink knitted hat with ear flaps along with a breathable pink jacket and stretchy black pants

"It's only a month until the equinox." I tugged my own striped knit cap down around my ears. My jacket was blue but my double-layer pants looked just like hers. "Funny how in late August this much light just seems sad, like summer is over. But now? It means the snow's going to be gone one of these days."

The path down to the lake had been trampled

flat by dog walkers and fishermen. We grabbed our poles and set out on the trail around the lake. Other hikers and snowshoers had broken trail, so we weren't floundering through two feet of white stuff. We both wore modern metal and plastic snowshoes instead of the traditional ones made of wood with the long point at the back. I didn't see any point in not having good gear.

"You lead the way." I pointed with a pole. "Your legs are a lot longer than mine and I don't want to hold you up." I followed her as we trudged into the woods. It was a little tricky not to step on your own shoe, especially if you had short legs. I had to adopt a wider stance than I normally walked with.

"I already had one run through here early this morning," Lou said over her shoulder. "It's a great place to exercise."

"You went running in the woods?" I asked.

"Sure. Didn't see a soul except when I did a loop on the lake."

"It's so pretty in here," I said. "We don't have snowy woods in California. At least not in my part of the state." The sun filtered through the trees and scattered sparkling light on a set of tracks that paralleled our trail for a few yards.

"Yeah, but you have the Pacific Ocean. And great wines."

"I'll say." Which I wouldn't mind a glass of when we were done here.

"Want to sprint?" Lou flipped a grin over her shoulder, then set off running, the snowshoes *fwapping* behind her.

"Are you kidding?" This was only my second time out on the contraptions. But hey, I didn't have strong cyclist's quad muscles for nothing. I gave it a try, lifting my knees and pushing off. I been at it for only a couple of minutes before I tripped. I yelled on the way down and nearly face-planted. "Yo, Perlman," I called.

Lou stopped, turned around, and *fwapped* back to me. She extended her pole. "Here, pull yourself up." She clearly tried not to laugh, but a snort slipped out.

"It's not really that funny." My own giggle made a liar out of me as I managed to get vertical again. I brushed the snow off my jacket and legs. Leaning on my poles, I shook the white stuff out of first one snowshoe then the other. "Okay if we just walk? My legs aren't as long as yours."

"Wuss." She stood there grinning.

"Show-off."

"Scaredy-cat."

"Jock." I tramped around her. "I'm going to lead now."

"Whatever you say, Shorty."

As we tramped along, I spied a pileated woodpecker through the trees and pointed out its tall black-and-white body with the distinctive red crest to Lou. She talked to me about her plans to attend an academic conference in Sweden in April. We continued in silence for a little longer, the only sounds the noise of our footwear and the crunch of the snow underneath.

"What was up with you and Charles Stilton last night?" I asked.

"He's unscrupulous and unfair. When I came to IU, I thought I could work with him. He's very charming on the surface. We collaborated on some research. That is, I researched my idea and wrote it up, but I met with him once a week to talk about it. He steered me in a particular direction, and that was fine. It was a good tip. But then I saw in the department newsletter that he's about to publish my work under his own name." Her voice was filled with disgust. "He outright stole it."

"That's terrible. Can you do anything about it?"

"Not really. I talked to Zen, but the paper has already been accepted by a major journal, and I can't really prove that he robbed me. What I can do about my studies is change them. I'm switching topics. I'm never working with that jerk again, and my coursework is finished, so I won't have to study with him, either."

"Sounds like a plan."

"It'll take me longer to get my degree now, but one good thing is that Zen is going to be my advisor."

"I liked her."

"She's very cool," Lou said.

"Did you know I bought my store from Charles's mother-in-law?"

"Really?"

"Jo Schultz. She's a very sweet, very sharp older lady, but she hadn't been keeping it up at all. The place was kind of a wreck, even upstairs where she lived."

"It isn't a wreck now. You've done a fabulous job with it."

I thanked her. "I'm working on the upstairs now, too." We kept going until we came to an opening in the trail, with a clear path leading off to the right. "Want to check that out?" I asked, pointing my pole. "It might lead down to the lake. We can watch the ice fishing."

"Sure. Lead on, O guide."

I took a right. The snow was deeper here, since it didn't look like anyone else had taken the same turn. I lifted my knees and pushed down, breaking trail for Lou until my thighs burned. After a minute the snow parted over a small stream, but a couple of wide logs had been laid over the water as a bridge. We crossed and trudged along as the path sloped downward, soon opening up to a clearing at the edge of the lake. The bank was only a foot high, so I figured out how to maneuver myself down. When Lou caught up, she just jumped onto the lake.

"Wow, what a beautiful sight." I leaned on my poles and surveyed the expanse as a cloud blew over the sun. The lake was covered with snow, of course, but the wind had carved drifts in places and swept it clean down to the ice in others. The whole scene had a bluish tint, even the trees at the far edge. A figure sat on a red stool across the way near a clearing at lake's edge. I could spy the truck we'd seen in the parking lot behind him.

"Come on. We can work up more of a sweat on the flat," Lou said.

"You're not already sweating?" I unzipped my

jacket halfway down and ran a finger around the neck of my wicking turtleneck.

"It's good for you."

"You think it's thick enough to walk on?" It had taken me, the Californian, a couple of years to trust that it was okay to walk on water. Frozen water, but still it made me very, very nervous the first time I walked on a solid lake. It just didn't seem right.

"Uh, yeah. You think ice fisherpeople would sit on it all day long if it wasn't? The paper said it's been ten inches thick all winter. Okay, wimpie?" Lou didn't wait for me to answer and set out at a fast walk. "And we can get back to my car in a straight line," she called back.

At least she wasn't running again. When a gust of wind chilled my chest, I zipped up again and followed. I wasn't a wimp. I was just a Southwesterner.

She started singing out loud, which made me smile. I caught up and walked next to her, but I couldn't quite keep up with her energetic pace. We were about halfway across when I spied a dark hole in the snow ahead. As we drew nearer, I saw that footsteps led away from the hole in the direction of the guy on the stool.

"Seems kind of far out to be drilling a fishing hole," I said.

"Avoiding the competition, I'd guess." She detoured around it and kept going.

I paused at the hole. It was a couple of feet across, and the water on top had already iced over again. I leaned over and peered in. It seemed odd that with all this cold, fish were still swimming around down there, carrying on their lives as if it was June or October. Maybe I could spot one. I saw something move and squatted to get a better look.

I stared. And grew cold, not from the wind but from dread. No fish was that brightly colored green. No fish on earth sported a tidy black goatee.